AFTERMATH

MK AHEARN

AZALA ROMANCE

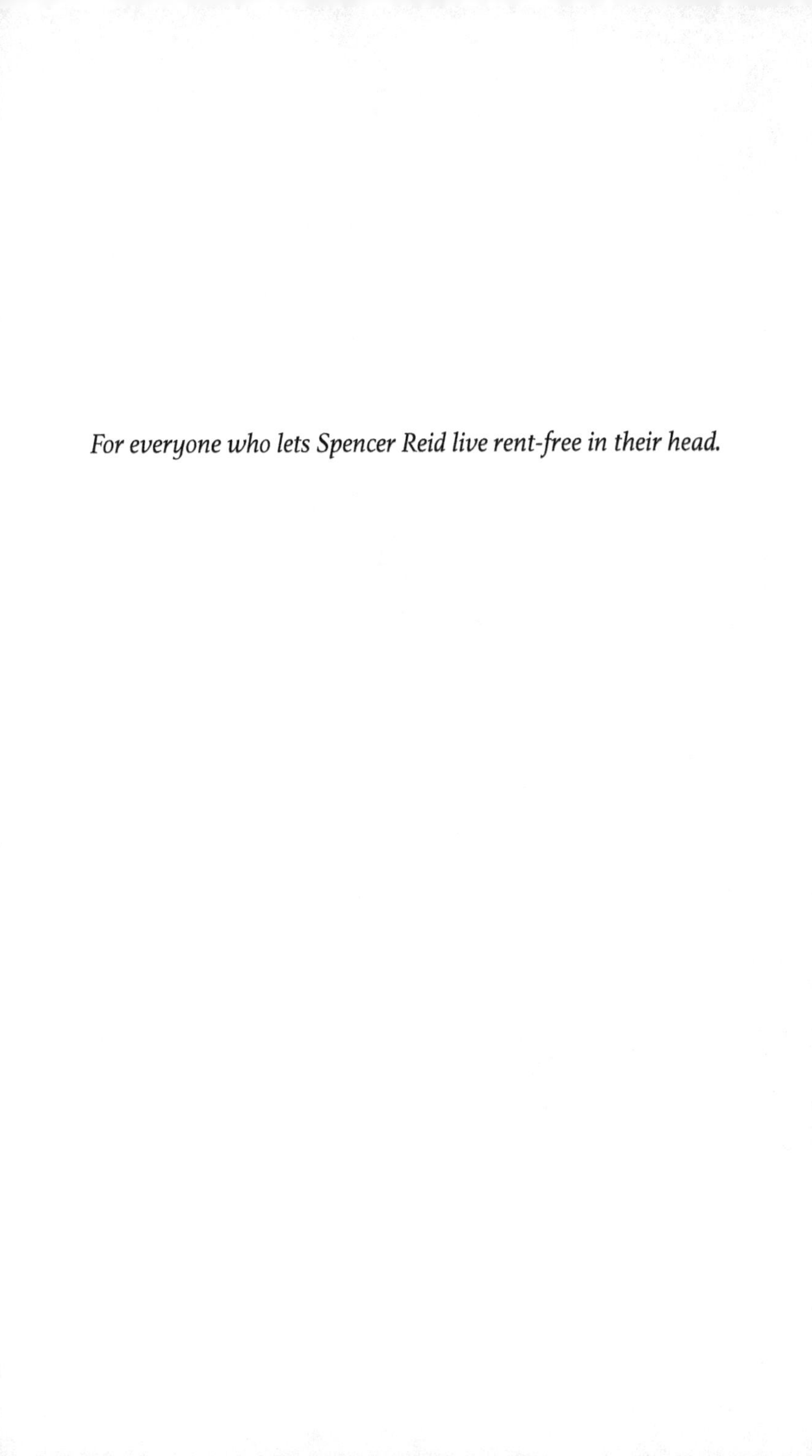

For everyone who lets Spencer Reid live rent-free in their head.

A special dedication to the person who made this book possible and shares a deep love for Criminal Minds, Allyn.

TRIGGER WARNINGS

This book contains the following potential triggers: guns (minor descriptions of FBI agents with guns and shooting), blood, violence, stalking, discussion of addiction, discussion of past miscarriage, serial killer, death

THE BRIARPORT CHRONICLE

BREAKING NEWS

The Coastal Killer Strikes Again

The Coastal Killer struck again, leaving a Jane Doe critically injured, with multiples stab wounds. The 25-year-old female was dumped on the side of Route 5. A couple traveling to the coast for the weekend found the woman and reported to police. She was taken to the hospital and treated for her injuries. She has since vanished, and police are asking anyone with information or tips to please contact them. This is the twelfth victim and police are cautioning citizens to be vigilant after dark and to travel in groups of two or more.

BREAKING NEWS

1

STONE

"Who can tell me one of the signs of ASPD?"

We were already forty-nine minutes into the lecture.

I picked up a piece of paper I'd been using for my lecture notes the entire class. I didn't need it; I had the whole lecture memorized. Actually, I had all forty lectures memorized for the entire twenty weeks at Quantico.

One of the new recruits in the front raised their hand, eager to answer the question, but that wasn't what I was looking for. That wasn't the type of trainee I was focused on.

This job had a way of weighing on you, forcing you to think quick in the field. I needed to make sure every last trainee was prepared for that.

"You," I said, pointing at one of the women, avoiding eye contact.

Her cheeks reddened, flustered at being called out. Good. If she wanted to make it through the academy, she needed to leave those doubts in the past. There were no doubts in the field.

Doubt would land you point blank staring down the

barrel of an unsub's gun. Not many agents walked away from that.

I wouldn't allow recruits under my watch to fall prey to such a situation.

"Uh, manipulation," she said softly, reservation in her tone.

"Another," I demanded, knowing it would be for her own good.

She shook her head, slightly flustered.

"It wasn't optional," I added.

"Impulsivity," she added.

Good; this time, her voice was steadier. Her shoulders relaxed, and she sat up. I saw the way her features shifted when she realized she was correct.

"Another," I encouraged.

"Lacking empathy and physical aggression," she spat back, not even a breath between answers.

There it was: the moment I'd been pushing her toward. The single second that changed her course at the academy. I demanded perfection because that's what future victims needed. They needed competent agents, ones who could think under pressure. I was hard on them because I was them once.

I knew no matter how prepared you thought you were, no matter what your IQ was, things could change in an instant. One mistake or oversight was all it took.

One of the trainee agents raised their hand a few rows back, and I nodded, noting another question would cut into my time for my final few points. I could rework it into the next lesson. I was mentally changing around the next lesson when the trainee spoke.

"Agent Beck," he started, "this is a lecture in behavioral sciences. We are at the FBI Academy. Should we not have learned this in a Psychology 101 course?"

Snickers broke out throughout the classroom, and I took a breath before answering. I knew his type—he strong armed his way to where he was, likely had lots of connections, found joy in putting down those a bit different from him.

Yeah, I'd dealt with plenty of those. It came with the territory of a higher IQ than most, and I imagined my more 'out there' style didn't help. I learned not to care as much, and a new trainee trying to look smart in front of his fellow agents certainly wouldn't get under my skin.

I walked over to the podium in the center of the amphitheater-style room. The podium ledge held my cup of coffee, and I picked it up to sip as I gathered my composure.

"And?" I asked, waving him on.

Wasting class time with these antics already subtracted— I glanced at the clock—fifty-seven seconds from my already far too short sixty minutes.

I'd surely have to cut something altogether later on now.

The longer I had to drill this all into their minds, the better off they were.

One mistake. That was all it took.

"Shouldn't we be studying actual cases and learning useful things for being field agents?" the man asked, and I saw the woman who answered my question before blush, her cheeks turning a shade of light pink.

"You arrive on scene, and the unsub is holding a gun to the head of a woman. They are on the roof of an apartment building near the edge. It is clear the unsub is reckless and has aggressive tendencies," I stated the case in layman's terms.

I met the trainee's stare, watching him devour each word.

"The unsub is a spree killer. When agents brought up the other victims, trying to talk him down, they identified a clear lack of remorse."

Other students scribbled down notes, absorbing every detail I spewed at them.

"What would be your call?"

"I-" the student started, but he hesitated.

"He's holding a gun to the woman's head, he keeps moving sporadically, there is no time to wait. You have to make the call now," I insisted, walking up the steps of the amphitheater closer to where he sat. My words came out fast, rushing.

"The unsub clearly presents signs of ASPD. It is likely he will not listen to reason and will act impulsively. If he moved the gun, I would have given the call to take the shot."

I knew that was exactly where his mind would go. It was the logical point of view...for a narrow-minded approach. He needed to think bigger.

"Wrong," I said, and pens stopped moving as everyone's stare fell to me. "That's what you would think if you solely looked at those signs and made a decision based on a narrow view. Thinking like that will have you working in a cubicle, not the field. The Los Angeles spree killer—who can tell me what the result of that case was two years ago?"

A man close to the ignorant trainee raised his hand. I spotted a tattoo snaking up his arm, a serpent wrapping the length of his forearm up to his biceps.

I nodded to him.

"The unsub had a brain tumor. He had been given the news the day prior to being caught that it was inoperable, terminal cancer. The news, combined with side effects of the tumor, sent him into a blind rage that ended with him taking the neurologist hostage on a roof the second day."

"Correct," I stated. "And do you know how we walked away from that hostage situation with not a single shot fired?"

The man shook his head.

"You all wouldn't, because that's not what you learn in Psychology 101, is it?" I muttered, glancing back at the arrogant trainee. I took a deep breath. "Because we used all the resources we had access to, our tech analysts were able to use footage from one of the shootings on the first day to identify the unsub. Mark Vizlo was only thirty-two, with no prior record, no pattern of behavior pointing to ASPD, happily engaged. We interviewed his fiancée and found out about the doctor's appointment. When we went to speak with the doctor, that's when we found him."

The class was enraptured, even the trainee I corrected staring intently at me.

"Shooting the unsub would have been premature. With the information we gathered, our better option was to give him the validation and solution he sought. We played in to his desperation and told him we'd found a second opinion on his tumor, that the doctor would be willing to operate."

"That worked?" a petite woman behind me called out.

"It planted enough doubt in his mind for him to reconsider, and it gave us a window to de-escalate the situation without further casualties."

I heard murmurs throughout the room as I walked back

down the steps toward my podium, catching a glimpse of the clock.

"If you hadn't interrupted my lecture, I would have gone on to tell you all behavioral science can only take you so far. You need to learn the ins and outs of profiling using behavioral analysis, but you also need to factor in other evidence, utilize every part of your team. Otherwise, you will make the wrong call every single time."

Less than a minute left.

If I couldn't be out there protecting innocent victims, I would be damn sure these trainees knew what they were doing before leaving Quantico.

I spun to face the class again and saw the arrogant man glaring at me, his pen gripped tightly in his hand, his knuckles white.

"That's all for today," I said, taking another sip of my lukewarm coffee. I swallowed, wishing I had a fresh cup. I'd need it for the pile of work I had left to finish for the day.

Trainees rose from their seats, gathering their belongings and hurrying from the classroom to their next lecture. The FBI packed their days with trainings for twenty weeks straight.

The sound of approaching steps echoed off the stairs, trailing down the center of the classroom.

"Agent Stone," the man with the tattoo started.

"Beck," I countered—I hadn't been Agent Stone in seven months.

"I'm sorry, another agent said-"

"It's Agent Beck," I interrupted. "And I'm late."

It wasn't entirely true. I was antsy to get out of the classroom and finish my work. Teaching trainees was uncovering old memories I wasn't ready to face from my time in the academy, and I was ready to spend my night with my books.

"I was wondering if I could shadow you," the man said. "I'd like to learn as much as I can at the academy. I'm aiming to be assigned to the Boston field office, so I'll need top recommendations."

"No," I said, stopping his ramble.

"I just thought-"

"That because you knew a single question, it would earn you my favor?" I asked, raising a brow. "Not how it works. It was a good answer, but not enough for you to earn my respect on day one," I answered, keeping my tone flat.

Was I seriously this bitter? That wasn't the Agent Stone most of the FBI knew.

He started turning away, and I saw his shoulders slouch. I tried to hold my tongue. I promised myself I wouldn't let myself get dragged down into this hole again. There was nothing for me on this path, but he reminded me of someone.

"Long sleeves next class," I called after him, unable to stop myself.

"Huh?" he asked, glancing back.

I needed top agents, not trainees with more self-doubt than when they started. I kept telling myself that was why I did it.

"Cover the tattoos. They make you too identifiable in the field. Start the habit now if you want a shot at field agent."

I saw the way he stood tall again, a slight grin on his face as he turned back toward the exit.

What was I doing?

I was smart enough to recognize the signs.

I was falling back into old habits. I groaned internally, realizing my supervisory special agent knew what he was doing. He knew how easy it would be for me to slip back into my ways, back to the days when I felt like we were truly producing a new generation of special agents who had a shot at making a difference, when my fellow trainees and I stuck together to make it to the top.

That all felt like a distant memory now. One choice had changed everything.

I had no intentions of going back into the field, not after everything I had done. My mind was of more use at Quantico, passing the knowledge on.

People had died, and it was my fault.

I shook my head, the classroom clear and the rest of my day empty.

Much to my chagrin, my supervisory special agent had hounded me to work my way back into the field. It'd been seven months already. Sticking me in the FBI Academy and giving me small tasks was never going to convince me to get back into the field. He just knew I couldn't resist at least passing on the knowledge I had. Maybe my past mistakes could prevent future ones.

It was logical, I reminded myself.

I had been the best, but even those at the top could eventually fall from grace.

I grabbed my brown leather messenger bag full of paperwork I knew needed to be finished before the end of the day and slung it over my shoulder.

It was almost 2:15 p.m., which meant I had approximately fifteen minutes to grab coffee before the café closed for the day.

I hurried out of the classroom toward where the café sat closer to the entrance of the building.

The line was long, but the moment the barista caught sight of me, she gave me the usual nod. I didn't deserve preferential treatment, but no matter what came of me, my name preceded me.

The iced vanilla latte slid across the far end of the barista bar, and the woman gave me a wave. I left the line I had just barely joined to grab my order and gave the woman a warm smile.

I slipped a ten-dollar bill across the counter and saw her grin grow further.

"How much longer do we have you until you are off on a field assignment?" she asked, her rich brown eyes filled with curiosity.

The question sent a small pang of pain through my chest.

"A while," I answered, trying to keep my smile from faltering.

"Good," she answered firmly.

I awkwardly nodded and turned for the exit.

I was grateful for the chance to still be part of the FBI. I still believed in its mission. Even if I was not the best agent for the field, there was no denying I had more knowledge to impart than most.

The warm summer air hit me the moment I exited the building, and I took a sip of my newest caffeine fix to counter it. It was late summer, and the longer I spent outside, the more I regretted the sweater vest I wore over my thin long sleeves.

I needed a vacation near the coast, where the breeze fought back the dreaded heat.

Or at least, that's what most said when I'd returned to the job. *Take a vacation, take all the time in the world.*

I'd never go back into the field, but my supervisory special agent, William Greyson, or Agent Grey, had a way of getting what he wanted, and me quitting was never one of those wishes. The second I stepped away, he was at my door to drag me right back.

It worked.

He personally oversaw my every move, and I knew those he reported to wanted him to keep a close eye, to report back on my stability.

I wasn't sure I cared. Placing my feelings never came easily to me, not as a child, and certainly not now.

"Perfect timing," a voice rang from behind me, and I turned to see Grey catching up with me. "On your way back to your office?"

"I have a bit more work to finish for the day," I stated.

"Then you won't mind me adding one more thing to those tasks."

"What?" I asked, raising a brow.

"Tips," Grey said, his voice raspy from years of smoking. "They're breathing down my neck about clearing them out again. I have plenty of agents on it, but none breeze through them like you do."

If there was a singular task I actually dreaded, it was tips.

Endless forms to review and sort, extremely mind-numbing work. It by no means pushed my mental capabilities, but it did test my patience.

Maybe that'd be good for me, to fine-tune an important skill.

"Fine," I muttered, pulling out my badge to tap into the

building as we walked up to the door. I refused to let Grey see. I didn't mind taking the tips today; I just didn't want to volunteer myself to be on them permanently.

We passed through the security measures together, Grey trailing slightly behind me.

"I want a report by the end of day," he added.

"I would expect nothing less," I said, my voice calm and steady.

It made my heart ache to see what had become of my career. I knew I missed being in the field, but I refused to go back. I was smarter than that.

There wasn't a single thing I couldn't recall, that I couldn't piece together.

Except that night.

The night that broke me.

Ruined me.

And now, I was forced back to square one.

I was a well-decorated agent, having been with the bureau for six years. No matter how much I learned, how many cases I solved, how many killers I brought to justice, this was what defined me now. I knew that.

My fist was clenched tighter than I realized, and I let go to find red marks in my palm.

"Stop beating yourself up," Grey said, lowering his voice and glaring at me. "You're clean now. You've been working your ass off at the bureau. You will be back in no time."

I didn't want it. In fact, I'd told him multiple times I would never step foot into the field again. He just wouldn't let up.

"Blythe deserved better," I barely whispered.

"Don't," Grey warned. "It never was your fault."

"Saying that won't bring her back," I pointed out, my chest heavy. I stuck to the facts.

My head swam with thoughts, flashes of memories I never wanted to relive.

Tips. I needed to focus on tips.

"Talk to someone, take time, whatever you need. Just stop putting it all on yourself," Grey said with a sigh.

"I'm fine," I agreed, trying to convince him.

He sighed again and turned off toward a set of elevators.

I made my way to the office and plugged my badge into the laptop sitting on my desk. All my work popped up immediately, and I minimized everything before opening the tip database.

It was filled with aimless tips and complaints. People used it as a means to complain about any little pestering detail in their life. Tips on loud neighbors, suggestions on how to do our jobs better, complaints about overpriced coffee.

Scrolling through and weeding out the bad ones from the worst ones, I found a tip that was my personal favorite for the day. How delusional did one have to be to believe their overpriced macchiato was a matter of national security?

The majority of the tips were useless. Some, I filtered through to send to our technology department to further investigate their integrity. There were next to none that piqued my interest.

That was, until a name caught my eye.

The Coastal Killer.

I was familiar with the nickname the press gave the serial killer whose trail went cold years prior. I hadn't worked it, but I knew the details of every major case that passed through our organization. I made it my job to know.

I paused my scrolling and clicked on the tip to expand it.

A news clipping popped up—the last victim. I checked the note submitted with the tip, but there was none.

That gave me nothing to go on. The way my heart raced a little had me sitting on the edge of my chair. I needed to quit while I was ahead, but my hand kept moving.

I combed through the other tips and quickly came across one with the same subject line.

The last four victims all visited the same bar the night they were attacked.

The note included a link to the bar's website.

I pulled up the address—the center of Briarport, Maine. It was the local bar frequented by most of the town, High Tide Pub. Hundreds of photos pulled up beside the address, and I swallowed hard, realizing anyone could have been a victim.

Still could.

It was a cold case.

There had been no new evidence for a few years. The killer had completely ceased murdering women in Briarport.

My heart pounded in my chest, my mind racing with possibilities. The endless puzzle, the abundance of evidence and leads—I knew there was more that could be done.

Why was this case grabbing my attention?

Sometimes, I hated my never-ending desire to know everything there was to know about something.

I finished flipping through the batch of tips and found four more similar notes on the same case spanning the last couple of months, all small details I was sure the FBI had already recorded, but I wasn't convinced they'd explored them thoroughly.

When we missed details, people died.

I compiled the tips and typed them into a document, adding a few of my own personal thoughts and suggestions in the margins.

I got up from the desk after emailing a copy of my briefing memorandum to Grey. The document would be in his inbox before I made it to his office a floor up. I grabbed my belongings and left the office.

The elevator was slow, and I tapped my foot impatiently on the floor.

The bar couldn't be a coincidence. It was a clear hunting ground, one that still operated to the fullest. What happened when the killer gave up his hiatus?

I knocked on Grey's door before walking in.

He sat behind his computer, typing away ,and barely looked up as I stepped in. I caught sight of the FBI seal hanging on the wall behind him, multiple awards around it, thirty years' worth of accomplishments.

'You finished the report already?" he asked, glancing up at me, never ceasing his typing.

"I sent you a write up on a few tips we received-" I started.

"Just forward anything of interest to tech," he grumbled.

"I think you should see this," I insisted.

He paused his typing and glanced at the screen as his fingers scrolled quickly, clicking here and there. I waited as he read through the memo.

"It's a cold case," he said, turning to look at me.

"One with a lot of leads," I noted.

"One with a lot of *dead ends.*"

I shook my head.

"You can't seriously think-" I started, unable to hold my tongue.

"Beck..." Grey warned. "Don't fixate on this. It's not the way to fix things."

My heart pounded in my ears. We had a chance to protect the people of that town. Someone out there was begging us for our help. Why would we pass that up?

"Send it to tech if you're concerned," Grey ordered.

"We need to look at this one," I insisted.

"Beck, I am telling you to drop it. You want to fix the past? This isn't how you do it. This won't bring her back. It won't make up for the months you lost."

"I'm not trying-"

"Just drop it," he said, turning back to his laptop. "It isn't worth it."

Not worth it? How could lives not be worth our time and resources? We had the ability to stop another potential death someday, and he refused.

I groaned, clenching my fists.

"Send a team up there," I tried one last time.

"Drop it," he snapped.

I didn't speak after that. I just turned, walking back into the hall, and shut the door behind me. I walked across to the bare wall and leaned against it, letting my head drop back. A few analysts in the hall paused but then quickly hurried along, deciding not to bother me.

I let out a sigh.

Why couldn't I just let it go? Why did I care?

I didn't know these people, but I knew there was more that could be done. Already, my mind was spinning with the little information I had, building a profile, making a list of leads to check.

I was sick of watching the world crumble around me, sick

of letting innocents be preyed on.

It was our job to protect them, to serve them. A job I had failed before.

I pushed off the wall and walked through the building, making my way to the small apartment on campus. I had a trailer in Virginia, but on days I lectured, it was more convenient to stay in town, so the academy offered me an apartment.

My place wasn't far from the offices, and I walked through the brutal heat at a brisk pace.

I should drop it.

Like Grey said, this wouldn't atone for my past.

My career was done. There was nothing here for me, and still, I'd allowed myself to be pulled back in.

The sun was already close to setting, and I could feel the breeze picking up.

I made it back in only a few minutes. I unlocked the door and slipped inside, tossing my bag to the side.

The apartment was a studio, furnished, with a kitchen and a simple, full-sized bed.

I searched through the kitchen for any remnants of food.

When was the last time I remembered to buy groceries? Eight days ago, to be precise. Had I been that caught up in lectures this week?

Books were piled high on the counters, and I brushed them to the side, looking for any viable meal option. I settled on a microwave mac and cheese I found buried in the freezer.

A bottle of scotch I had been saving sat in the corner, and my hand was outstretched for it, but I stopped myself. The microwave beeped, snatching my attention, and I left the bottle behind.

I carried the meal to my makeshift living room—a singular armchair and side table. I had no television, but again, books were piled around me. My latest read sat held open by the arm of the chair.

It only took a few bites of food before I settled back in my armchair. I tried picking up my latest read, but the words just blurred together. Every time I tried, the cold case was at the forefront of my mind.

It was eating away at me.

Why this case? It wasn't her. I couldn't bring her back.

I knew Grey was right, but still, the case nagged at me.

The more I thought about it, the harder it became to push aside. If I could just talk to the woman behind the tips, I could just confirm they were dead ends.

It would be as simple as that.

I would be doing the bureau a favor.

I stood up and searched for my phone.

It was absurd.

Every decision I ever made was based on logic.

I picked up the phone, scrolled to Grey's contact, and hit dial.

It was a minute before he picked up, and I half expected it to go to voicemail.

"Yeah, Beck?" he answered.

"I want time off," I said hesitantly into the phone.

Was I actually doing this?

"I need time and space away to clear my head, and when I come back, I will put all my efforts into becoming a field agent again."

It was a lie, but one I knew he was too desperate to see through. He'd dragged me back here from my lowest point. Grey showed up at my trailer that night and hadn't given me any other option. I knew he wanted me back in the field.

Enough to believe my words.

"I agree. Maybe some time and space is best," Grey said into the other end. "When will you be leaving?"

"Tomorrow," I answered before I could stop myself.

If I thought a minute longer about the decision, I would have talked myself out of it. I was never meant to work a case again, so why this one? What about this case could I not let go?

I finished with Grey and immediately pulled up information on Briarport. I found the first flight to Portland, only an hour from the coastal town, then a rental home with plenty of availability that I booked for a few weeks. I had no intentions of returning, not until I chased away whatever haunted me about this case. I needed to put my demons to rest, to move on with my life, once and for all.

2

———

LENNY

THE GLASS DOORS to the museum slammed shut behind me, closing out the brutal summer heat. I walked past the small desk that housed will-call and the service desk. No one was sitting there, but I didn't expect them to be. It was only 7:00 a.m., and I was always one of the first to the museum. We didn't open until nine, and I liked having the extra time for personal research.

A clash rang through the small museum, and I startled, realizing on this particular morning, I wasn't alone.

"Shit!" someone shouted from the back right corner of the space.

I hurried through our set up of exhibits: portraits from local artists, facts about our town, and in the back corner, an exhibit showing off the one famous actor who grew up in Briarport, although I could never recall his name.

Mickey L.

Michael L.

Unimportant. Potential murderer breaking into the museum should be my focus.

Boxes were toppled, and a random assortment of documents were spread across the carpeted floor.

"Barren?" I called, seeing the older gentleman gathering papers from the floor.

He jumped at my voice and dropped the papers he had just picked up. "Lenore," he said, the surprise on his face fading.

"What are you doing here so early?" I asked. "Your shift doesn't usually start for another few hours."

He scrambled to pick up the documents, and I knelt beside him, gathering as many as I could hold.

"Francis will have my head if I don't finish organizing these boxes today," the older man said. His blue eyes darted around, like the museum director might materialize in the middle of the exhibit.

The older woman ran a tight ship; she was punctual, a perfectionist.

When tourists flocked to New England for summer on the coast and beautiful fall foliage, Francis became even more uptight and meticulous.

The exhibits needed to be pristine, and museum-goers needed to be kept happy. I'd seen the consequences of a sloppy exhibit only once before. Multiple employees ended up on a watch she called *probation,* or what I liked to call *torture.* Longer shifts, cleaning duties, and every last action inspected with a fine tooth comb, like we were incapable of making up for our mistakes.

I shuddered at the thought of ever ending up on her bad side. I floated along and kept my head down. The research I was conducting was far too important to risk.

The museum had its perks, and I planned to continue utilizing them as long as I could.

"I won't tell Francis about this if you won't," I joked, and Barren let out a deep chuckle.

We finished picking up the documents, and I helped him move the boxes out of the exhibit area to the back offices, the area off limits to the public. It was where I did most of my work as assistant curator.

I pulled my long, dark curls out of my face, realizing the work was more extensive than I originally calculated.

We walked back and forth together, picking up the twenty or so boxes one at a time.

"Three years, and you still won't tell me the secret to getting on her good side," Barren teased as we stacked the boxes in a corner of the office space.

Filing cabinets sat beside them, some of the drawers partially open, brand new and empty. I knew Barren would soon fill them with most of our records. I ordered the new organization system myself only a week prior. Before, all the documents had been stored in the basement in cardboard boxes, which Barren and I now hefted across the museum.

"There is no secret." I shrugged.

"Oh, come on," he pushed. "You can't tell me you became her favorite by coincidence?"

"I'm not her favorite," I muttered under my breath, already regretting my choice to help.

It was the same old thing every day. I'd worked my ass off to get the position, and most of the long-time employees despised me for it. They whispered constantly about the ways I must have flattered Francis to get the position.

I rolled my eyes.

Every shift, I came in early and stayed late. I put in extra hours at the museum to document records and sort through them. I helped research new exhibits and planned events. Each time I went the extra mile, Francis trusted me a bit more, enough to stop looking over my shoulder at my every move.

Freedom to conduct my personal research—it was the only reason I took the job in the first place.

"I gave some thought to the exhibit idea you pitched," Barren said.

At last month's team meeting, Francis invited new ideas. I couldn't waste the opportunity to make my true goal more obtainable.

"I don't think it's a great idea," he said warily.

Neither had Francis at the meeting; she'd shot it down immediately. I'd presented a bit of my personal research, but as soon as I started, she cut me off, turning down the idea. Instead, she tasked me with a new project: updating a few of our existing exhibits to give them new appeal.

"But it's a piece of this town's history," I pointed out, not willing to give up hope just yet.

"A fresh piece of history," he argued. "A little too fresh. Give it more time, and maybe she will reconsider, but for now, I think everyone feels the same way. The Coastal Killer is not someone we are ready to welcome. That bastard shoved rings down victims' throats. I can barely think about that without getting nauseous."

The killer's modus operandi.

I sighed, adding another box to the pile we created.

"But people deserve to know the victims," I pointed out.

"Do you really think tourists will want to visit an exhibit

focused solely on the victims?" he asked, hesitation in his eyes.

"They're assholes if they don't," I mumbled.

"I agree," he noted. "But that's unfortunately the depressing truth of it. Tourists are only interest in the infamous Coastal Killer. It was all the headlines were four years ago. That type of gore and tragedy is just not something any of us are ready to remember."

"I just think the victims should have some sort of memorial," I said.

Selfishly, it would give me an excuse to share the project I'd been working on the past few years, a way to avoid hiding from Francis' control over everything, to continue the research without the added stress of concealing it all.

"Besides, they never caught the damn bastard. If he's still out there, we don't need that attention turned to us," Barren said with a nervous laugh.

It wasn't fair. The Coastal Killer disappeared a little over three years ago. Without a trace, he just vanished into thin air. The FBI gave up, local police gave up, and eventually, our little coastal town went back to the peace it had known before the killings started.

Every time I thought about it, my blood boiled. The killer deserved to rot in prison, and instead, he was enjoying life comfortably elsewhere.

Everyone had giving up hope.

This shouldn't be the normal. There was still so much evidence left to look at, but no one cared.

"Imagine the podcasters and true crime junkies," Barren pointed out, seeing the disappointment on my face. "They'd flock here if they heard we had the inside scoop on one of the most notorious killers in a decade."

I gave him a weak smile. All I wanted was justice for the victims, and if no one could provide that, then the least I could do was preserve their memory.

One of my first weeks on the job, I had stumbled across all of the old newspaper clippings while processing records, and the idea started to form there. It became my passion project.

There was so much good we could do with our position.

"At least it'd give tourists someone other than Milo L.," I teased, forcing myself to stop harping on the topic.

"You mean *Micah* L.?" Barren asked, raising a brow.

"Yeah, that guy," I said, waving him off.

"That guy has been in like every movie known to man," he said, the starstruck effect glazing over his eyes.

"Not you too," I groaned.

"Francis forces us to know everything about that exhibit. How have you gotten away with not even knowing his name?"

I placed the very last box on top of the stack and shrugged. I didn't interact with the tourists or exhibits as much as everyone else. I remained behind the scenes, finding new exhibits and documenting old town records. It was the way I preferred it, out of the spotlight of the busy attraction.

"That's what happens when you're the favorite, I suppose. A promotion, more leeway," he huffed. "I've been here thirteen years, and it's always the same for me."

The old man scowled, adding his last box to the pile.

Probably because of that attitude.

I worked hard to prove I could handle the responsibility of assistant curator when our prior one retired. They were one of Francis' closest friends, so I had huge shoes to fill. If I had to put in the extra time and effort, I would do everything I could to keep working my way up.

"I thought I heard you two chattering," Francis said, and I turned to find her hands on her hips, lips pursed.

"The boxes are all here," Barren said quickly.

"Perfect," Francis said, her face lighting with delight. "Now, there are a few exhibits that look a bit drab. I need you to go work on those before we open for the day."

"But-" Barren started, his shift technically not starting for an hour. He shut his mouth and thought better of the comment.

"I'll start on organizing the new filing system," I offered before she had a chance to assign me to a new task.

"Always on top of everything," she chirped.

I just knew exactly how to remain on her good side. It wasn't rocket science, but it did require a bit of trial and error.

I turned and got to work, burying myself in the work of sorting through all the old records, arranging them in a more organized fashion in the large metal cabinets.

My shift was over before I knew it, and I gathered my belongings from the small desk I claimed as my own in the back room. My work computer was still on, and I sent myself an email before shutting it down, my usual routine on days I was able to contribute to my personal research.

It was a busier than usual day at the museum, tourists

flocking inside for a reprieve from the brutal heat or a break from the overcrowded beaches.

Visitors all gravitated toward the same three beaches, unaware of the hidden gems our town had to offer.

Some days, when I went home early—a rare occasion—I liked to take a dip in the water of the hidden stretches of beach close to my apartment.

The walk home was only a ten minute stroll. I walked along the sidewalk out front of a stretch of shops. The further I walked, the more I caught sight of the ocean, heading straight for it. The summer breeze carried the smell of the salty waves through the air, putting me at ease.

Shop owners cleaned their hanging racks and signs outside their little stores and brought them inside. Most of the tourists had fled to the most popular restaurants in town for dinner, leaving the streets open to the locals who knew better.

Three years ago, I never would've walked home when the sun was already dipping and I was alone. The police had made it all but mandatory to travel in groups and avoid being out after dark.

Many credited strict curfews and regulations as what drove the killer away. Maybe they moved on to a new town, or maybe they were already rotting in a prison cell for another crime.

Something in my gut, though, told me they were lying in wait for the right time to return. I never thought the Coastal Killer was done.

A hand on my shoulder had me tripping over my steps and my heart completely stopping in my chest.

"I thought that was you," a deep voice said, wrapping an arm around my shoulder to steady me.

I was so deep in my thoughts, I hadn't even heard the footsteps behind me. My heart raced, and I took a deep breath, recognizing the voice and turning to find my brother next to me.

"Off early?" he asked.

"Hey, Calvin," I said with a sigh of relief. "Francis forced us all out because she had some fancy cleaning service coming. I think her exact words were *these exhibits better shine.*"

I laughed remembering her frantically shoving us out the door promptly at closing.

"So, the workaholic had no choice but to go home and relax for once?" he asked, raising a brow, a grin spreading across his lips.

"I'm not a workaholic," I said, pushing his arm off my shoulder and scowling.

"Perfect. So, you'll stop by for dinner next Friday, right?"

Shit.

He had been trying to get me to come over for dinner with him and his wife for months. I'd only seen their new house once.

"I-" I tried.

"No excuses, Len," he scolded. "Mom and Dad barely hear from you. We live in the same town, and I barely get to see you. You can do one dinner."

My mouth hung open, searching for a reason. I appreciated my older brother looking after me and caring enough to keep inviting me over, but I had just received my promotion at work, and with Francis getting older, my only goal was to become the museum director when she retired someday.

I could never achieve that without putting the extra hours in and proving myself with my research.

My career was all I had left.

I loved my family, but my parents lived hours away, and we only saw them at the holidays. Ever since my brother had gotten married, I saw him less and less. It didn't bother me; I loved Eloise. They were perfect together, but he had his own family to look out for now.

"Please, Len," he said. "For me?"

I hated when he pulled the sad puppy dog eyes. He'd been doing it since we were children, and our parents always fell for it. I knew better, but how could I deny him when he was pleading so hard and laying on the guilt so thick?

"Fine," I huffed out.

"Perfect. I'll see you at six," he said before turning off down a side street I knew led to his house.

We only lived minutes apart, and somehow, I managed to avoid seeing him more often.

I liked it that way, keeping my solitude. I used to enjoy the noise of it all—the busy town during tourist season, the social gatherings, my overbearing, but lovable, brother—but recently, I'd grown to seek the silence.

Three years ago, I found my purpose, and I poured everything I had into that.

A few more blocks, and I found myself outside a little boutique, a narrow alley beside it. I turned down it, making my way to a door at the back.

I typed in a four digit code on the pin pad outside and heard the little click of the door before I pulled it open. Not even two steps in, a set of stairs rose to the second floor above the shop. I hurried up them and passed by two doors of the top landing marked one and two. I kept going up a second flight to the third floor and found the door marked three.

My purse was cluttered, but I found my key quickly and unlocked the door, letting myself into the apartment.

Instantly, I was greeted by a fur ball making its way between my legs. I heard the soft meow from the living room, letting me know the other was on its way.

"Let me in, Birdie," I said, trying to move forward without stepping on her.

I dropped my purse on a little side table next to the door and hung my jacket on a hook next to it. I caught a glance of myself in the mirror hanging above the table and saw my curls had started to turn frizzy from the humidity. My hands found the clasp on the necklace I wore and unclipped it. It was a present from my mother I reserved solely for work. The large statement gems on it were inconvenient for anything else. My mother had said it complemented the golden undertones of my light brown skin.

I didn't see it, but I'd never had an eye for such things.

I walked down the short hall to the open space that made up the living room and kitchen. The food bowl on the floor of the kitchen was completely empty, and I quickly realized why the two cats were making such a holler.

"Okay, okay, I'll feed you guys," I assured them.

I pulled open the small pantry in the corner of the kitchen and found the bag of food. Both Birdie and Alonzo already sat beside the bowl, watching to ensure I didn't go somewhere else with the delicious bag of kibble I had just pulled out.

"I wouldn't dare," I promised them, holding up a hand in innocence.

I was truly becoming the crazy, lonely cat lady. I groaned to myself.

"Don't look at me like that," I said as I poured the food, and Alonzo gave me a sympathetic look, like he knew exactly what I'd become.

Bitter and alone.

The perfect mixture for me to grow old and die alone with my fifty rescued cats.

It was like I was a magnet. I acquired Birdie and Alonzo both within the last three years when I moved to the apartment. Both had made their appearance in the alleyway below at different times.

I had no reason to turn them down.

They needed a home and food. At first, I ignored them, hoping they'd go home to wherever their owners were. But the more frequently I saw them and the rattier their fur became; I assumed they were strays.

I think I saw a lot of myself in them.

That was when I realized I truly was losing my mind.

I related most to a pair of cats.

I figured there was some sort of distribution system, a higher being that knew exactly what I needed. It was like the world knew when you needed a cat and then dropped it one day on your doorstep. Stubborn little things, unwilling to go away until you accepted you were now their owner.

The more the little creatures grew on me, the more I thanked God every day for putting them in my path.

Again, I realized I was spending far too long obsessing

over the two little fur balls eating chicken kibble in my kitchen.

I sighed and walked to the only other room of the one bedroom apartment. My room had just enough space for a queen size bed and a dresser across from it. The walls and dresser top were bare of decor. I hadn't found anything fitting for the new life I had built myself.

I'd been living in the apartment for three years since I found my new job and ran from my old life. The ghosts still haunted me.

I wasn't ready to put down roots and accept that this was my life, not until I finally secured the position of museum director. Only then would I allow myself to believe I made something of myself.

I walked over to one of the two windows in the room and cracked it open. Again, the salty air hit me as I inhaled deeply. The silence outside let the beating of waves reach me.

The sound was a comfort, allowing me to sleep at night and blocking out all the noise of the world.

I left the window open, knowing I would leave it that way all night.

I could see just over the few shops between the ocean and me.

A pounding on my door pulled my attention away, and I hurried through the apartment. I checked through the peep hole and recognized the face instantly, although I'd already recognized the frantic knock.

I pulled open the door, and before I could even get it open, Mallory slipped in.

"You are never going to believe the shit I dealt with today," she said, throwing her hands up and walking past me straight to the living room.

By the time I caught up, she'd already thrown herself onto my couch, laying back with her hands behind her head, as if she arrived for some twisted form of therapy.

I took the bait.

"What'd you deal with today?" I asked, a small grin growing across my face, knowing I was in for a long rant.

"Tourists," she said, horrified.

"Tourists?" I repeated, as if I'd never heard the word in my life. As if they didn't frequent Briarport every year, every day of the summer.

"Yes, tourists," she scoffed, sitting up on the couch and glaring at me.

"What about tourists?" I asked her, raising a brow and sitting in the armchair set in the corner of the room.

Mallory ran the shop beneath the apartments; she was the entire reason I had a place to live. I'd met her right around the time I secured a position at the museum. I'd been practically homeless at the time, living with my brother and his then fiancée in their tiny one bedroom apartment. He let me crash on the couch for a few weeks, which then turned into three months, leading to my desperation to find my own place.

I think Mallory saw that and decided I needed a friend. She was some of the only noise I could stand. Plus, she didn't make me talk about myself or why I constantly threw myself into work. She really just liked to talk about herself, and I was more than happy to listen—or at least pretend to listen.

There was nothing wrong with that, right? Not when it was mutually beneficial.

At least I kept telling myself that as she droned on about the tourists of the day.

"Can I try this? Is that on sale? Do you have more sizes? Do you have suggestions on where to visit in town? Like, obviously, I do, but still." She groaned. "It never ends! Everything is all about them. They touch everything and leave the store a mess. And you know who has to deal with it?"

She looked at me expectantly.

"You," I guessed.

"Yes, exactly," she said, throwing her hands up. "Anyway, I came here to see if you wanted to enjoy a wine night together? We could crack open a bottle of Merlot and watch shitty reality shows together."

She tucked her long, black hair behind her ear, waiting for my answer.

"I have a few work things to finish up tonight, can we take a rain check?" I asked.

Alonzo jumped onto the couch, and she shooed him off, sending him running to my comfort. The plump orange cat jumped up into my lap, and I let him tuck himself close to me.

Mallory glared at the feline before her gaze flicked up to mine. The scowl on her face sent a twinge of guilt rushing through me. I hated bailing on her, but I couldn't let what I'd found wait.

"Fine," she sighed dramatically. "But I'm coming back tomorrow, and you aren't bailing on me then."

I forced a smile to my face.

"Deal," I said, knowing there was no way to avoid it.

She lived a floor below me, so even if I wanted to avoid her, it was impossible. Besides, a wine night could be good for me. Maybe my brother was right. Maybe I was turning into a workaholic.

Mallory got up to leave the apartment, and I hurried from my chair back to my bedroom, where I knew I left my laptop. The screen lit up the moment I opened it, and I swiftly pulled up a tab with my email. I spotted the museum email address with my name attached to it at the top of my inbox.

Inside was the newest piece of information on the Coastal Killer I'd found while helping Barren sort through the documents for the filing system.

It was an article; one I hadn't seen before. *The Briarport Chronicle*, a small news outlet in the area, had published a story on the final stabbing the Coastal Killer ever committed. I had to send it to the tip line.

No one ever answered the tips I sent, but I continued anyway. I wasn't sure what pushed me to do it. The idea had come to me one night when I was watching the news far too late and a story about a kidnapping came on. The news anchor had plead with the audience to submit any tips to the FBI hotline. I'd pulled it up out of curiosity and found a simple form I could submit.

It didn't specify cold cases as excluded.

I dragged the pdf file from my email over to the upload box on the form. Again, I filled out the form with all the usual information—I'd done this a million times now.

My hand hovered over the mouse pad as the cursor remained on top of the submit button. Every time, I second guessed myself. Was I doing the right thing?

The victims deserved justice, and their families deserved closure.

That thought alone guided my hand to click the button.

3

———

STONE

I HAD my suitcase packed within hours. I wasn't planning to stay long, just enough to confirm there was a case and leads and bring back enough evidence so the FBI couldn't possibly turn down re-focusing on the case.

I owed it to the victims.

I couldn't bring her back, but I could at least try to protect the people of Briarport.

My suitcase was stuffed with records I'd printed from the FBI database, alongside a bit of clothing. I eyed the bottle of scotch sitting on the counter, and, before I could stop myself, I stuck it in with everything else.

I'd been reviewing all the papers I printed and taking notes, neglecting sleep.

A buzzing sound pulled my attention away from rummaging through my belongings to pack. I found my phone sitting on my bed and read the name on the screen.

"Hey, Mom," I answered. "What're you doing up in the middle of the night?"

"It's 5:00 a.m. here," she answered. "And I know you

usually wake early to get a little extra work done before lecturing."

I looked out the window and found the sun already up. That meant it was already 8:00 a.m., and more time had passed than I originally thought.

How had it already been all night?

It'd been months since I lost chunks of time, and never like this. The hyper-fixation on this case had to be to blame. There was no other reasonable explanation. It was either that, or some form of neuropsychiatric disorder, but I had no other signs pointing to one.

At least none I noticed.

"You've been working far too much again," my mother scolded. 'Were you up all night? I can hear it in your voice. You got no sleep."

This was a battle I would never win. It didn't matter if I had every academic tool at my disposal or a PhD in Forensic Psychology framed on my wall. There was no handbook on how win an argument with your mother.

"I haven't been working too much," I tried countering. "I've just had a lot on my mind."

My mother knew the bare minimum of everything that happened. She knew I took leave and that I was back working at the FBI Academy, but I refused to worry her with unnecessary details. It would only result in her jumping on a plane from California to Virginia, and I refused to burden her with that.

"Mhm. I will have to speak with Ash-"

"Grey-" I interrupted.

"Same thing," my mother scolded. "He's putting far too much on you."

He was putting far too *little* on me. Academy work was time consuming, but it was nothing compared to my time in the field. Long hours and stake outs, pulling all-nighters to build a profile and prepare to brief local law enforcement, being called at any hour to pursue a lead.

"You should come home," my mother added. "Take a vacation, come spend some time with me and your sister."

Lyla was only ten, making her eighteen years younger than me. My mother had her with her second husband after my own father passed away.

"Is Lyla up?" I asked.

"She is," my mother confirmed. "Just like you, I swear."

"Can you put her on?" I asked.

"Fine, but that doesn't mean I'm forgetting about all this."

"I wouldn't dare think that," I laughed.

I heard shuffling on the other end of the line and imagined my mother making her way to the small kitchen in our family home. The home I grew up in.

"Hey, Winston," Lyla's voice came through the phone.

"Hey, Lyla," I said gently. "How have you been?"

A twinge of guilt coursed through me. I hadn't been home to visit in over a year. Sure, there were plenty of phone calls and even the occasional video call, but I knew I'd put off seeing them for too long. Especially Lyla—she deserved more than that. I just couldn't bring myself to face them yet, not with knowing what I'd caused and become. The months I'd spent at rock bottom were far too much for even myself to face just yet.

"I got an A on that project you helped with," she said proudly. I could feel the giant grin through the phone.

I had sent her one of my FBI challenger coins, something

to do with a presentation on what each student wanted to be when they grew up. No matter how many times I insisted it wasn't the job she wanted, Lyla's only dream was to follow in my footsteps.

I never wanted her to experience the pain I went through, but I was still proud of her.

"That's fantastic. Although, I never for a second doubted you'd get anything less," I said, smiling.

She was never the sister I expected, but my heart couldn't help but swell every time I spoke to her.

"Are you working a new case?" she asked, and I noted the hopeful tone.

It'd been awhile since I was away on assignment. Lyla loved hearing about the new places I traveled. I couldn't help but give her a little of what she hoped for.

"I am," I lied.

Was it really a lie? Technically, I was working a case...a cold case.

I wasn't so sure the FBI or Lyla, for that matter, would accept my technicalities if they all knew exactly what I was doing.

"I'll be heading to Maine soon," I continued.

"To Augusta?" she asked.

"I'm flying to Portland and staying on the coast, in Briarport," I answered.

There was a pause of silence.

"Time to go, Lyla," my mother's faint voice came from the background.

"I have to go," Lyla said sadly.

"School this early?" I was an early riser to get work done, but there was no way schools were making children go in as early as 5:00 a.m., were they? It'd be counterproductive to the amount of sleep children needed combined with the average bedtime.

"No, silly," Lyla laughed. "Mom and I woke early today to get the best bagels from Don's for the week."

Don's Bakery, the staple of our small California town. I checked the calendar on my wall beside me, realizing it was Tuesday. That one day of the week, the bakery had half price bagels and a giant selection of flavors.

I envied them.

"Send me one," I joked.

"Pretty sure it will get stale in the mail," Lyla laughed.

"You're right. I'll just have to get my own soon."

A promise I planned to keep the moment I finished this case. I missed my family, but I had to work through everything haunting me before I could see them, for their sake and my own sanity.

Briarport had to have the answers I sought, to put to rest the feeling I couldn't shake of failing more people.

"I have to go, but Winston, listen to me," my mother said, taking the phone back. "You deserve a break from so much work. You're so young. Don't let life slip you by."

It was always something similar. She meant well, but I couldn't help but feel this was it for me. I ruined my one chance in the field, and now all I was left with was my knowledge. It was the sentence I deserved. I could never escape the burdening awareness of the mistake I made. All I could do was make sure no one else made the same ones. It was why I was so hard on the trainees I took on.

"I love you, Mom," I said, avoiding her plea.

"I love you too," she said before hanging up.

I checked the clock and realized I had only two hours to make it to the airport before boarding. Sleep would have to wait.

I pushed back my sleeves as my plane descended into Portland.

"Does that mean something?" the curious woman beside me asked.

I'd managed to avoid her prying questions most of the flight, finally getting in a nap, but at boarding and now descending, I wasn't as lucky.

She was staring straight at the sage worked into my sleeve of tattoos wrapping up my right arm.

"Wisdom," I answered.

I'd carefully selected every single detail of the tattoos.

She tilted her head, studying the rest, and I pushed down my sleeves, growing self-conscious. There were some I preferred she didn't ask about.

"It's kind of feminine, isn't it?" she prodded.

The woman didn't know when enough was enough. My distant gaze out the window wasn't enough to stop her intrusive comments.

"I don't think so at all," I commented. "In fact, multiple cultures considered sage to be a symbol of wisdom and wellness. The ancient Greeks referred to their philosophers as sages. In Medieval European cultures, sage was linked to longevity and wisdom-"

The woman pulled out earbuds and stuck them in her

ears, cutting me off. I sighed. At least I'd earned my peace back.

The flight attendant made her final round, collecting trash, and I passed across an empty plastic cup I'd acquired early in the flight. The woman beside me ignored the voice that came over the speaker asking everyone to put their trays and seats up. I tried tapping her shoulder, and she rolled her eyes before turning to me.

Oh, now I'm the nuisance.

"That needs to go up," I tried to say politely.

"Why?" she scoffed.

"Because they just made the announcement," I answered.

I already knew where things were heading. It was a matter of if it was worth my time to pursue the argument. I sighed and gave in.

"I don't see the point," she went on. "I'm still using it. Where am I going to put all of this?"

She waved to all the clutter she'd managed to compile on the flight. I saw one of two routes: let the flight attendant deal with it or save her the hassle and explain myself.

"An emergency is most likely to occur during take-off or landing," I started.

The woman's brows shot up. Her mouth started to open, but I continued.

"If your tray remains down, it obstructs your path to make an emergency evacuation. Time could be crucial if we were to make an emergency water landing. Do you truly want to be stuck on this plane with me because we couldn't get by your tray?" I asked.

She started to answer but closed her lips, pulling them tight.

She brushed all her belongings off the tray and locked it up in place.

I tried to hide the growing smirk on my face. I couldn't help myself. Her face had turned a shade paler at the mentioning of an ocean landing, and I failed to mention the statistics of it happening were likely far from ever being a concern for her.

Maybe it will save the flight attendant the hassle on her next flight.

I watched out the window, spotting the Atlantic Ocean beneath us.

The waves lapped against the shore, and the boats looked like small bugs floating on water, yet it felt like any moment, the plane would connect with the ground. Even my own logic couldn't comprehend the feeling.

Within five minutes, we landed in Portland, and I found myself pushed back against the seat as the plane braked. I held tight to the arm rests and watched the woman beside me squeeze the neck pillow she held in her lap, wide eyed.

The plane slowed, and the pilot came over the loud-speaker to announce our welcome to Maine. I couldn't see much beyond the airport outside the plane window, but I was eager to catch a glimpse at the New England coast. I'd seen Boston and even other smaller portions of the area, but this was the first my time at the FBI had brought me to Maine.

The largest producer of lobster, a popular vacation spot in the summer, and a perfect winter resort for skiers. The facts raced through my mind from the research I'd conducted on my taxi ride to the airport.

I sat close to the front of the plane, and the moment the seatbelt sign turned off, I unbuckled myself and grabbed the leather satchel beneath the seat in front of me. Our portion of the plane was the first to make our way into the aisle.

I deboarded the plan and hurried my way to baggage claim to find my suitcase and the firearm case I'd checked.

I pulled the rental car down a narrow road surrounded by thick pine trees, the pavement covered in dirt and rarely traveled. The house I rented was on the outskirts of Briarport, and the map had shown little surrounding the place. I read each and every one of the reviews, and most said the same thing.

Clean space, great views, and private.

Privacy was my main concern.

If I was going to be working on an active cold case, I needed a space quiet enough to concentrate and secluded enough so I wouldn't be bothered by outside distractions.

The road went on for a few miles before it turned into a long, curved bend and the pavement slowly shifted to solely dirt. The trees became sparse, and I could see the single building on a hill at the end of the road.

The light grey house with a white porch was surrounded by a bright, colorful garden, the flowers all in full bloom for summer. The closer I approached, I could see the ocean just beyond the hill the house was perched on. I knew from the listing the back side of the house was solely a rocky cliff with the water as a neighbor.

I parked the car in the single spot driveway close to the house. My suitcase and other belongings were in the backseat, and as I pulled them out, I could hear the crash of waves.

I couldn't help myself and left the items at the start of the front walkway, abandoning them to venture into the backyard. A short, white fence lined the edge where the plush grass turned to rigid stone.

The breeze from the ocean below brushed against my skin the closer I moved. I inhaled deeply, taking in the salty smell and letting it remind me of the pacific coast I grew up near. With my eyes closed, I could almost picture home while I leaned against the fence.

"Hey, neighbor," a deep voice called.

I startled and let go of the fence, pulling myself away from the edge.

The three miles exact I'd calculated between myself and the nearest house by road was apparently not enough.

An older gentleman walked up a path I hadn't noticed before at the edge of the yard. It trailed down the cliff edge, and from what I could see from where I stood, led off into the town below.

I had a great vantage point over town, where I could see all the houses and shops but still keep my distance. Or so I thought.

"You must be Nelson," I said, noting the man looked exactly like his profile picture on the house rental listing, even wearing the same newsboy hat.

"I sure am," he said with a cheery smile. "Welcome to Briarport."

He added the last part like he was a salesman straight out of a commercial, baiting tourists to town, and his pronunciation seemed to drop the final 'r'.

"Boston?" I asked.

"How'd you know?" he asked, tilting his head.

His pale skin and freckled cheeks, in addition to his blue eyes, had me guessing he was Irish. He likely moved from South Boston, and recently, judging by the remaining thickness of his accent.

"The accent," I pointed out.

"You've visited, then," he said.

"For work." I shrugged.

It'd been two years prior when I'd worked on a case in Boston. A triple homicide with a threat left behind promising massive lives lost had the FBI visiting the New England city.

He nodded and ran a hand along his grey stubble peppering his chin.

"Anyway, I just wanted to make sure you were settling in, was all," he said. "I saw the car parked in the driveway while I was walking the path and thought I would stop by."

"Thanks," I forced out, even though it was breaking clause seven of the terms and agreement both of us checked we would comply with when renting the place. Technically, the agreement outlined that Nelson needed to give reasonable notice if coming to the property for anything. Showing up on the lawn, unannounced and two seconds into my stay, felt a little unreasonable. I supposed that was just what friendly, small town neighbors did, though.

I'd have to get used to the idea and account for it while working if I were to call minimal attention to myself. Poor relations with those who lived in Briarport year round could hinder my progress.

I wasn't used to working these cases alone.

My last active case with the FBI, I had my partner beside

me. She'd always known what to say, the type of person everyone loved.

I tried to channel a bit of her into myself.

"I just arrived, but I already love the place," I assured Nelson with a small smile.

He nodded.

"Anything you need, feel free to call. You have my number on the fridge inside the place, and I am only a short walk away. I live in the small house at the beginning of this path," he said, pointing back to where he'd emerged from. "Seriously, anything at all. This town is more than happy to provide. It isn't often I have someone rent this place longer than a week. Most of the seasonal renters own their own places along the beaches."

I wasn't sure how to answer. It wasn't often I grappled for answers, but the truth wasn't something I wished to share with Nelson. I needed my work to be kept quiet and away from the FBI realizing where I had taken my break.

"I am just testing out the area before committing to anything," I answered quickly.

"Well, I hope you find it all to your liking. I can tell already you'd fit right in."

People were odd, the way they completely pulled things out of thin air sometimes. I'd just met Nelson, and nothing in my behavior or words exchanged could have possibly given the impression I would be a good addition to the town.

He turned and walked back to the path.

"I am sure I will see you around town soon," he called back as he waved over his shoulder.

I gave a short wave and turned back to the driveway to retrieve my suitcase.

The handle extended up, and I pulled my belongings along the pathway to the porch, lugging them up the steps.

Inside felt exactly as I expected from the few photos shown on the listing: simply coastal decor and minimal furniture.

To my surprise, a small bookshelf sat in the corner of the living room to the right of the door, and I spotted a few familiar spines amongst the books.

Maybe Nelson was right after all. Maybe I *would* like him.

I made my way up the stairs directly across from the door to the second floor and found the single bedroom. A makeshift office space and bathroom were the only other rooms to share the floor.

I left the suitcase in my room and ventured back down to evaluate the kitchen and dining spaces. The kitchen was long and took up the back side of the house. A sunroom was built off the kitchen and overlooked the backyard and ocean.

I opened the door for the cool breeze rolling in with the lowering sun. The house was hot and stuffy without any A/C running.

That would be my next task: to find the source of keeping the house cool.

First, I needed to set up what I had packed with me on the case.

I picked one of the emptier walls of the dining room and started hanging up pieces of information I had. I cursed myself for being a complete stereotype out of a crime show, but it was the most efficient way for me to review the details and make connections.

I hung a map I had printed, which I marked the dump

sites for each of the killer's victims and the bar where many had last been seen.

Everything fell within the boundaries of Briarport, making me believe I was looking for a local. The times of killings varied throughout the year, and as Nelson had noted, there were seasonal visitors, but this made me doubt they were the unsub.

This had to be someone living in town year round.

I kept hanging bits of the case and tips on the wall, adding sticky notes with my own thoughts next to everything.

With everything hung up, it was easier for my mind to map out the next most logical step. There were multiple tips hung, all from the same source. She'd laid out many pieces of the story for the FBI, and I planned to look into every detail. I found the name of the submitter next to one of the tips I'd placed on the wall.

My next step needed to be Lenore Calder.

4

———

LENNY

"Lenore," Francis called out into the back room. "Someone is here for you."

Her tone sounded impatient. I knew she hated visitors during working hours, and I didn't blame her. They were a distraction.

"I'll be there in a moment," I called, hurrying to save my work I was typing up, but she'd already walked away before my words reached her.

I stood from my desk chair and smoothed out the linen pants I wore. The museum was kept much colder than the scorching weather outside, and finding a balance between not melting on my walks home and not freezing at work was the current biggest debacle in my life.

I walked out into the exhibits, glancing around for Francis.

She stood nearby with a tourist, who held up a brochure, pointing to parts. She caught my eyes and nodded over to a nearby exhibit. I saw a single person standing in the area she motioned to.

A tall man dressed in slacks and a vintage style, short sleeve button down stood admiring the exhibit on our town's annual clambake. We were approaching the thirty year anniversary. It was only a few weeks away, so Francis had us set up an exhibit on it, hoping it'd lure more tourists back into town.

"Francis said you were looking for me," I said, interrupting the man and watching his rich brown eyes settle on me.

He pulled out a wallet and opened it to flash a badge at me.

FBI.

I crossed my arms, the intensity of his stare making me shrink back into myself. He was handsome—definitely not what I pictured for an FBI agent.

"Are you done?" he asked.

"Done with work?" I asked, thrown off.

"Done deciding whether I fit the criteria you've predetermined makes an agent," he said, frowning.

"I-" I started but shut my mouth. I tried to hide the blush darkening my cheeks, but it was no use. "I've just never met an agent," I muttered, my eyes lowered.

"Everyone does it," he said. "If that helps."

Was he trying to cheer me up after he'd so quickly flustered me?

"Where can we go to discuss?" he asked, his tone straight to the point.

"To discuss?" My cheeks darkened a shade, and I felt warmth filling my face.

"The tips you sent," he said, raising a brow. "You were the one who submitted the tips on the Coastal Killer, right?"

I glanced around, hoping Francis hadn't overheard. My new promotion would be taken away just as quickly as it was given if she knew I was using museum resources to send tips to the FBI.

It was part of my due diligence as the one in charge of organizing and preserving our town records, right? I had an obligation to pass along any information that helped solve the case.

Somehow, I knew Francis would never see it that way, especially not after she'd turned down my idea for a tribute to the victims. She'd think I was working on the project against her instructions, and that was cause enough for her to strip me of my new position.

In all fairness, I *was* working on the project without her knowing, but I planned to keep it that way.

If my work and records I kept could help catch the Coastal Killer, then I would continue. For the town I was growing to love, the people in it, and the victims who would never know what Briarport came to be.

"Um, back here," I said in a mere whisper, hoping Francis wouldn't notice.

"What?" he asked, leaning in.

"Just follow me," I huffed.

I wanted the FBI to look into the Coastal Killer—part of me couldn't shake the feeling the person responsible for so many deaths was still out there—but I'd finally worked my way up in my job. Maybe digging into it all had been mistake?

I shook my head. No, this was the entire reason I worked my way up in this job, the one goal I had, my purpose after I lost everything years ago. I'd get justice for the victims.

I led the agent into the back room, where'd I'd spent the majority of the day cooped up working.

"I'm Lenore," I said, feeling obligated to introduce myself to the complete stranger I was now stuck sharing my work with.

"I know," he said nonchalantly.

Duh. He had read over the tips I sent and asked for me by name. My heartrate picked up, my body feeling warmer again.

"Are you going to tell me your name?" I huffed, trying to hide my embarrassment. I barely knew the man, and, already, he was getting under my skin.

"Agent Winston Beck," he answered. "But you can just call me Beck."

He smiled, his hands shoved into his pockets. I realized he had to be at least a foot taller than me. Not that it was hard. I was only five feet, one inch tall. That one extra inch was very important to me.

He followed me to the desk, where my computer sat with a dark screen. I sat down, booted up the computer, and typed my log in quickly.

"What do you want to know?" I asked, my heart pounding, feeling him hovering behind me.

He leaned over the chair, placing his right hand directly beside me. I watched the muscles in his arm tense and spotted the tattoos snaking up his arm. He was more muscular than I expected at first glance. A new heat rose in my stomach, and I shoved it aside.

"I'd like to see everything else you've been collecting on this case that wasn't in the tips you sent," he answered, his voice low, breath brushing against my ear.

"That's not all here," I admitted, keeping my voice low and glancing up into Beck's deep brown eyes.

He raised a brow.

"Some of it's just on my laptop, which I don't keep here," I explained.

"What do you have here?" he pushed.

I opened my files and found the one I'd labeled for records on the Coastal Killer. It was mainly scanned-in news clippings, police reports, and the non-gory crime scene photos that had been made public. I scrolled through, letting him glance over what the museum kept on record. It was only about 200 files, and some were entirely useless, with even a few duplicates.

"This is everything we keep here," I said, reaching the end of the file.

"And what do you keep on your laptop?" he inquired, taking a step back.

I turned in the chair, my hands in my lap, feeling his scrutiny on my face. "Um-" I stuttered.

He crossed his arms, and my hands turned clammy. Any second, Francis could come in, and I would be completely out of luck. I was already brainstorming the excuse I would use when he left.

"If it's anything illegal, I'm going to find out eventually. Better to admit it now," he pushed.

"No, it's not like that. It's just-" I started, then paused to watch the doorway. "It's a personal project."

I chose the words carefully, realizing Beck was analyzing every word out of my mouth, like I was a suspect in interrogation.

Was I a suspect to him?

Panic took hold of my chest. I tried to keep my face neutral, but I failed miserably as I saw understanding cross his face,

"Your boss has no idea, does she?" he asked.

I shook my head slowly. "She turned down my idea for an exhibit using the research."

"So, she doesn't approve of you working on this research?" Beck guessed.

"You could say that," I huffed.

My heart was pounding at my ears at this point, praying to God Beck wouldn't reveal what I'd been working on to Francis. If she knew, I was a goner.

"And you kept working on it?"

Was that curiosity in his eyes, or was I imagining things?

I realized a second too late I was staring, and he was still waiting for his answer. I nodded. There was no point in hiding it. I had a feeling if Beck wanted information, he'd get it, no matter what.

"You wanted to make an exhibit on the Coastal Killer?" he asked, frowning.

"No," I said hurriedly. "I wanted to make an exhibit on the victims. A memorial, a way to remember who they were."

I let out a breath of frustration. Why did everyone always fixate on the killer? "No one else seemed to think it was a good idea, so Francis tasked me with a different project and expects I've ceased work on this."

"Sometimes, people aren't ready to face hard truths," Beck murmured.

"Hard truths?" I asked.

"Like for one, that your boss is likely never going to take

on this exhibit, yet you are still working on the project she tasked you with stopping," he said.

I scowled.

What was his issue?

Everything out of his mouth was so calculated and logical. Even if Francis told me to stop, it didn't mean all hope for my research and memorial was gone. If I could just find more on the killer, or if the FBI finally caught them, the town would be more open to the idea. I knew it.

"And two, some people aren't ready to face the reality of these people being gone. They were friends, family, colleagues; that isn't an easy truth to face," Beck added.

"I guess," I muttered, turning back and closing out of the files.

"Email me the rest," Agent Beck stated, walking over to an empty desk and finding a pen and sticky note. He jotted down something and held the paper out to me.

"What is this?" I asked, taking it.

"My email." He adjusted the strap of the bag he carried.

I read over the generic government email he'd handed me in disbelief. That was it? He just expected me to hand over everything to him and be done?

I'd worked long hours to collect all of this.

"No," I answered, handing it back.

My arm remained extended, but he didn't move. His eyes narrowed on me.

If he was going to continue my research, I wasn't going to just hand it over. I wanted to help, to ensure the Coast Killer finally answered for their crimes. It was my entire motivation, the reason I started the project in the first place. I couldn't just hand it all over and let it go, the same way I couldn't let it go when Francis turned down the exhibit.

"No?"

"This is all of my research. I'm not just going to hand it all over. I want to help you."

"I'm a federal agent," he noted. "You're a civilian. This is an investigation, not a project."

"I know that," I grumbled. The longer his eyes remained on me, the more flustered I became. It was like he could peel back every layer of the walls I kept up and slowly pick them apart. I felt disarmed.

"I could get a warrant for your laptop. You'd be hindering an investigation," he pointed out.

Fuck.

I hadn't thought that far when I opened my mouth. I needed a new angle, a way to convince him he needed me.

"There's more to track down, documents I can pull easily through our systems. Documents you wouldn't have to go through entire processes for if you allow me to help," I tried, standing from my chair.

I crossed my arms, my white blouse clinging to me, making me feel warmer than I was. My eyes wandered to the clock, realizing there was only an hour left in my shift.

"I can take you to my apartment in an hour," I offered. "I'll show you everything I've gathered, and I promise to give you access to the resources I have if you let me continue to help."

It was a deal I hoped he couldn't refuse. He was a single agent working on a cold case. I didn't know much of the bureaucratic workings of the FBI, but I knew enough to know this was not their priority.

Genuis, if I did say so myself.

I tried to keep the satisfied grin from my face, my foot tapping, waiting for Beck's answer.

His face remained firm, and I saw his muscles in his arms tense up. The tattoos running down his right arm held my attention, and I followed the vines that climbed up his forearm to his bicep.

"That's my offer, or come back with a warrant," I said, turning my chin up.

He continued to stare at me, and I worried he may just walk. His eyes gave nothing away. I could see his mind racing but couldn't piece together a hint at what he was thinking.

I heard footsteps approaching the door and glanced toward it. Francis's voice carried into the room, and I knew I had little time to get him out of there before more questions arose.

"I will meet you at the café across the street after your shift," he said, nodding to me as he walked toward the door, hands slipping into his pockets.

My heart pounded.

Had that seriously worked? Damn, I was a better negotiator than I thought.

Years growing up with an older brother, and I was glad I at least had something to show for it. I never would have survived as the pesky little sister if I wasn't able to bargain my way into holding his favor.

I hurried to the employee bathroom in the back office space. I beelined to the sink, catching a glance in the old mirror above it. The faucet took a moment before cold water rushed out of it. I splashed it onto my face, the cold chasing away the heat overwhelming me.

Deep breaths, in and out.

That had been far too close. Everything I'd worked for the past three years almost came to an end, and then I would've been back where I started three years ago when I lost everything.

I push strands of hair out of my face and grabbed a paper towel, blotting my face dry and hoping no one would notice the beads of water left clinging to my curls.

I shut the faucet off and took a step back to look in the mirror once more.

Inhaling in and out, I got my heart to steady.

I didn't care if Agent Beck refused to warm up to me or allow me to help. This was my research, and I would see it through until Briarport had the justice it deserved.

5

STONE

I sᴀᴛ in the cafe for approximately sixty five minutes before I spotted her dark curls swaying as she crossed the street, a small blue bag slung over her shoulder that couldn't have held more than a wallet and keys.

Her work must've truly all been on her home laptop if she was leaving with so little.

The aroma of the brewing coffee was soothing to me and allowed me to clear my mind.

Surely, I was finally losing all my sense, allowing Lenore to help any further with this case.

I didn't want her to help, but I didn't see many other options. There was no way I would be able to request a warrant to seize her laptop, and she wasn't handing it over willingly.

Stubborn.

And clever.

I had to hand it to her, I knew when I was being played. She knew I needed her and her resources, and I could tell she was already piecing together the little support I had from the FBI.

Better to keep her close.

I took a sip of the cold brew I'd been nursing as she entered the café. Her deep brown eyes immediately found mine and stalked across to where I sat.

"Coming?" she asked impatiently.

I stood, gathering my leather bag and drink. "How far do you live from here?"

I'd worn my old tennis sneakers, but I wasn't prepared to walk much further than a few blocks. I hadn't been expecting needing to walk anywhere. It was becoming a poor habit, letting the unexpected creep up on me.

I was losing my touch.

At least I still had my mind, everything I'd learned tucked away in it. A small hope that I would be able to contribute something further to the FBI and our nation's security—the only way I knew how to make up for my mistakes.

"Only a few minutes' walk from here," she said and motioned for me to follow her.

Our walk was silent, and I kept a few paces behind Lenore, watching the way her curls swayed as she walked.

Could I rid myself of her?

She was far too observant. The last thing I needed was Grey showing up in Briarport and dragging me back to Quantico. I'd really lose my badge then. He'd put his reputation on the line for me once, but that was all I got.

One more chance.

And honestly, I didn't even deserve that.

I wasn't going to squander the only chance I had to make

up for everything. Blythe never would've let something like this pass.

I shuddered to think what she would've thought if she'd seen what I'd become after her death. A complete pit of nothing. I didn't feel. I never wanted to feel again. I let myself slip away into the bottom of bottles, and when that started not to work, I found something new.

A wall slammed up in my mind, blocking out the memories of those few months.

Grey pulled me out of the darkness I was succumbing to, a place I never would have been able to crawl back from if I kept going.

I tossed my empty cup into a trash bin we passed as I finished the last sip of my drink.

Lenore paused at an alley, and I tried my best to forget about it all, to leave the past in the past, even though I knew every study, therapist, and bit of logic said that would never work. I wasn't ready to face that reality.

Instead, I was focusing on Briarport.

Lenore backed up a few feet from the alley and opened the door to the storefront beside us. I turned around to follow.

Inside, I found a small boutique filled with clothing, jewelry, and other miscellaneous tourist items.

I brushed past a rack filled with stickers, a display water bottle atop it, showing off the multitude of stickers the shopkeeper was able to cram over the surface. I spotted one that read 'Sea You In Briarport!' and cringed.

"Len!" a voice shouted from the register. "You never visit me down here!" The high pitched, shrill voice pierced my ears as the woman ran from behind the counter. "Today has been horrific."

No one was even there. How could it have been so terrible?

"You say that every day, Mallory," Lenore noted.

"And every day is as bad as the last. The tourists are completely endless," she said indignantly.

"Mhm," Lenore hummed. "I need to use the apartment entry."

"The pin pad broken?" Mallory asked.

"No, it's just-" Lenore glanced back to me.

I wasn't a criminal.

I couldn't blame her for not wanting to take me through the direct entrance, or risk me seeing the code to get in. The statistics of women living alone and violent incidents supported her caution. I couldn't deny facts.

"You've brought a man home? In broad daylight?" Mallory started yelling.

"No," Lenore said quickly. "He-"

Her mouth opened and shut, looking for an answer, but she failed to grasp for anything other than the truth.

"I'm just here to fix something," I offered.

Relief washed over Lenore's face, her hands going slack.

"If something broke, I would've fixed it," Mallory said to her friend, ignoring my presence.

It was like I didn't even exist in the conversation.

Textbook narcissist.

The need for Lenore's full attention and acting superior— I wasn't sure how Lenore put up with this woman on a daily basis. A friendship so one sided would be exhausting.

Maybe that was just the excuse I told myself for keeping most people at arm's length, unable to fully throw my emotions into any sort of relationship. Facts and research were what I placed my trust in; emotions were far more complicated, unpredictable.

"My laptop," Lenore added. "He's here to fix a bug on my laptop."

Clever.

She'd beat me to coming up with a new excuse for my presence. I doubted this woman knew anything of Lenore's research, and it seemed Lenore was just as keen to keep it that way.

"I didn't know tech freaks made house calls," she scoffed, finally glancing my direction.

Ouch.

Can't say that I wasn't used to the comments. My unusually high IQ made me a target even at the FBI Academy. My brain was my weapon; I was never built to be the strongest or most agile. Knowledge was power.

"Mallory," Lenore hissed.

"Not the first I've heard it and won't be the last." I shrugged. "And I don't have, what did you call them? Endless tourists? Just me and my tech all day long."

The frown on her face was worth every second of the ruse.

I couldn't help but let myself feel a bit of satisfaction.

"Best we get going," Lenore interrupted, grabbing my arm and tugging me past Mallory, whose eyes were wide.

"Key, please, Mallory," Lenore demanded, her tone serious.

Mallory made her way back behind the counter and tracked down her key ring. She tossed it over to Lenore.

We walked toward a door behind the counter, unlabeled.

The key ring jingled as she sorted through the multiple keys and found the one she wanted, placing it into the keyhole and unlocking the door.

Turning back to Mallory, she shook the keys to get her friend's attention. Mallory reapplied her lip gloss, leaning on the counter to get a look in a compact mirror she held in her other hand.

Lenore pulled the door open and tossed the keys back to her friend. Mallory barely had time to catch them, putting the mirror down.

"You owe me," she muttered, tucking the keys into a purse behind the counter.

"Wine night soon, I promise," Lenore called back.

We passed through a narrow, empty hall. My eyes adjusted to the dimness, leaving the brightly lit store for the space without any lighting at all. Mailboxes hung on the wall at the end of the hallway.

It opened into an entry with a single staircase. She led me up the stairs to the third level. There were only two apartments, and Lenore unlocked the door to hers, letting us in.

"It'd be easier if you just emailed it all to me," I tried, hoping she'd change her mind. I didn't want a partner. I hadn't worked alongside anyone since I'd gotten my partner killed.

Brutally murdered, and it was my fault.

I coughed to clear my throat of the feeling of bile rising in it. The images of that final case were relentless.

"Water?" Lenore asked.

"Thanks." I nodded.

I followed her down the short hall into the combined living room and kitchen. A soft brush against my legs startled me, and I almost tripped over the feline beneath me. Its black fur brushed against my light colored slacks.

"Alonzo, leave him alone," Lenore scolded. "Sorry," she added. "He likes attention."

Odd creature.

Most cats weren't fans of socializing. In fact, cats were what I believed most referred to as small assholes—knocking things off counters, pestering for food, and refusing to cuddle when their owner wanted. I'd never owned one, but my observations all suggested the same.

"I fed him once and never got rid of him," Lenore muttered.

Another cat trotted across the room, orange with a white belly. I did my best to avoid the two felines as I pushed further into the apartment.

"Birdie, not you too," Lenore hissed.

I stood awkwardly in the center of the living room, unsure what to do with myself. I felt all too aware that I was now in a stranger's apartment.

"You can sit," Lenore offered. "Or keep hovering there. I promise, I'm not going to run with the research."

I dropped my bag onto the couch and sat down, looking around the tiny apartment. It was a comfortable space, but I noticed little of Lenore's personality in the decor. The walls were mostly bare, aside from a few frames bearing family and friends photos. I spotted one of Mallory and Lenore, her smile barely reaching her eyes.

My breath hitched thinking about the draining friendship.

Why did I even care? I didn't know her.

I moved on to a small bookshelf tucked into the corner of

the room. I didn't immediately recognize any of the spines, but I made note of many of the titles written on them to search later. Almost every classic sat on my own personal bookshelf, but these were different. Pinks and pastels made up most of the color scheme, and it didn't take much deducing to realize they were romance books.

Not my typical choice, though I could give it a chance. There was always room for more reading.

Lenore startled me from my focus, placing a cup of water on the side table next to the couch. The noise jolted my attention, and I found her carefully studying me, skepticism in her gaze.

"Thank you," I said, grabbing the cup and taking a sip. The ice cold water woke me from the endless thoughts that raced through my mind. It was ludicrous that I was even sitting in Lenore's apartment. Never in my career would I have involved a civilian in a case, not like this.

Why didn't I say no? What about her made it impossible? The probability that the FBI would find out and force me home was what I kept telling myself, but deep down, I wasn't convinced.

She grabbed her laptop from a nearby armchair and sat down in it. "Most of the research I have is on the victims. I don't know much about the case beyond what was made public record that the museum has," she started, her eyes scanning the screen.

"Do you have it printed?" I asked, eager to get a look at everything she had.

She paused and glanced up, frowning. "No," she said slowly.

"Do you have a printer?"

I knew the moment I asked, it was a self-evident answer. Everything Lenore had was mainly in the space we sat, aside from her bedroom. I supposed she could've kept one in there, but I spotted other office supplies and her laptop accessories throughout the living room.

It was a reasonable guess.

"No," she answered quietly.

"Thats alright. You can just show me what you have then," I noted.

She glanced to the empty space on the couch beside me and hesitated.

"It was your decision not to email me the work," I noted, her continued hesitance slowing my efficiency.

"I barely know you," she pointed out. "And I'm not just going to hand over three years of work to a stranger." Her laptop slid closer to her in her lap as she sank further into the chair.

"Again, you have no choice," I explained.

"Then get your warrant, and I'll be waiting here," Lenore countered.

"I'd prefer your cooperation."

"And I'd prefer to work alone, but we can't all get what we want," she muttered back.

"Touché," I answered.

She stood suddenly and walked over to the couch, sitting beside me and adjusting the laptop so I could view the screen. "This is everything I have so far."

Her screen filled with multiple sub-folders, all labeled with the victims' names and different key parts of the case. I spotted at least fifteen names and even the *High Tide Pub*. Lenore opened a few and started scrolling, but it was hard to track what each document was with her own naming conventions and organization.

"May I?" I asked, motioning to the computer.

She handed it over hesitantly, and I clicked quickly through many of the documents, reading over all of the information she'd compiled.

Ages of the victims, the areas they lived in, their occupations, just about every detail of their life that could have made them a target. She'd started a diagram to link similarities, but there were none that connected all of them.

"Impressive," I admitted. I knew recruits who wouldn't have gone as far as she had.

"Thanks," she breathed.

I found a stray folder with a single article inside. It filled the entire screen with a familiar news article. I'd seen it before: the final article published on the Coastal Killer's last victim, the Jane Doe who had never been identified. She left the hospital before anyone had a chance to make a positive identification.

The article was short, discussing the curfew police implemented and the missing Jane Doe. I knew how the story ended. No one ever came forward with more information on her.

I didn't blame whoever they were. Their luck was spent on surviving that attack, the one that ended the Coastal Killer's rampage. For all we knew, the killing stopped because Jane Doe vanished. Their anonymity and disappearance could be the one thing holding the unsub back from surfacing again.

Their one failure.

It was also the one lead the FBI failed to follow. The

woman left the hospital without a trace. It was the closest large hospital in the area, about thirty minutes away. As the article detailed, she'd been stabbed and taken there for critical care. When Jane Doe woke after being unconscious and being stitched up, she vanished before nurses could gather her information. Without prescriptions and proper wound care, I would be shocked to learn they'd survived, or with minimal health issues after all of that.

"You don't have any more leads on Jane Doe," I noted.

Beyond the article, there was nothing else in the folder, no information known about the Jane Doe or leads on where she may have gone.

"The police never identified her." She shrugged. "There wasn't much to go on."

That was where she was wrong. There was plenty to start with, to build a profile of the woman. My mind raced with the endless possibilities. I could start at the hospital, but I doubted I'd get far, not without a warrant, and even then, it would be minimal. The hospital never figured out who the woman was, and the police already had all their information on what she looked like and her injuries.

Multiple stabs, including a substantial wound to the lower abdomen.

"I have folders on every other victim," Lenore noted.

"Those are a great start," I said.

I watched as she flinched at the comment. It'd been a compliment, not a way to downplay the work she'd done, but I could already tell my words had discouraged her.

She glanced to her clasped hands, watching her fingers fidget with a ring she wore, the anxious tick a way to soothe her growing discomfort.

"Is this news source still in business?" I asked.

"*The Briarport Chronicle*?"

I nodded, turning the article I had opened toward her.

"They are, but I don't see the point?"

For someone as naturally brilliant as her, I was shocked she didn't see the missing piece.

"She's the key," I answered.

"No one has information on her besides what is in the article. It's a dead end. I've tried," she answered. "No one wants to see this case closed more than I do, but you won't find anything looking into her. The FBI already tried."

She was deflecting. Why?

"Yes, but they weren't me, and I know far more tricks than they do for finding the information I want," I pushed.

She tensed and curled her fingers into fists. *Maybe it was too hard.*

"I think I have a printer at my rental," I added, changing the subject. It wasn't worth pushing her to close off when I'd just met her. "Would you mind bringing this laptop by this week for me to print the documents?"

She could email it to me, but I didn't add that. I should've just asked her to do so, to cut her clean out of the case and continue alone.

Why was I making an excuse to see her again?

She was holding back.

Instinct told me she knew more than she said. Was she protecting someone? Was she withholding pieces of research from me to put herself ahead at work?

She opened and her mouth and shut it. "Fine," she answered. "But it will have to be a time when I'm not working."

She crossed her arms, her lips pulled thin. I could tell she was growing sick of my prying.

The plump orange cat, Birdie, jumped up onto the couch and crawled her way beside lap. She purred, rubbing against the side of the laptop and glancing up to me. I furrowed my brows. I always thought I most related to cats, creatures of habit who wanted to be mainly alone, but this one feline was an anomaly to me.

Lenore made a sound that sounded like her tongue clicking, and the cat stretched its neck to look over at her. It moved faster than I expected, standing and walking directly across the keyboard to her.

"Stop being such a menace," Lenore scolded as the cat settled beside her.

"When are you off work next?" I asked with a soft laugh.

"Friday."

"Then it's a date," I joked.

"It's certainly not," Lenore said quickly.

"Is that not what people say?" I asked, frowning. *Was I seriously that out of touch with society?*

"I mean it is-" she started, flustered.

"I'll see you Friday," I said, standing and heading for her door without another word.

I felt the sudden urge to hurry out of the apartment. I'd just met Lenore, and already, she'd found a way to fluster me and leave my mind reeling. Usually, I was the one in the room with all the answers, and, somehow, I was at a loss of words today.

I never expected her to be this far into the case.

Her work was impressive, and the quick glimpse I caught at the museum told me she threw herself into everything she did with such attention to detail. The director, Francis, had many glowing words about Lenore when I first arrived looking for her. I'd admittedly also done research on her before coming as part of my all-nighter.

"Wait," she said, following me and grabbing my arm.

I turned my head to glance back at her, those rich brown eyes gazing up at me. My heart pounded.

"Are you actually going to let me help?" she asked.

I didn't want to necessarily call it helping. She would bring me the documents to print, and then we would go our separate ways. Was that truly helping with the case?

It would end after that, nothing more and nothing less.

"I'll see you Friday," I answered instead. "The house on the outskirt cliff to the west of town."

Her hand let go of my arm, but my heart continued to race. It was the first real touch I'd felt in months. I'd barely let anyone close enough to feel the warmth of the brush of skin against my own. I hurried out of the apartment and let the door slam shut behind me.

6

LENNY

"Who was he?" Mallory demanded later that night after Agent Beck left.

She sipped on the glass of wine I'd poured her as our movie played in the background. Every wine night took place in my apartment. I'd pushed to hold one in Mallory's, but she was far too embarrassed about what she claimed was a mess.

I doubted it. Mallory was the most particular perfectionist I'd ever known, but it was useless to push.

"No one," I answered for the thousandth time. She wouldn't drop it.

I took a sip of my wine, letting the crisp taste wash over my tongue. A car engine revved outside, and I startled before I could set the wine glass down, spilling a drop on the couch.

"Shit," I muttered.

"That's why you never should have bought a cream-colored couch," Mallory said, her eyes never once leaving the rom-com she picked out.

"It'll come out," I said, more as a prayer than an answer.

I hurried to the kitchen to dig through my cabinets to find

anything I could use to clean it. Random cleaning supplies rattled in my lower cabinets, and I found one that looked similar to fabric cleaner. I grabbed a paper towel from my counter and made my way back to the couch.

Mallory paid me no attention.

The stain was small, barely bigger than a quarter. I sprayed the fabric cleaner on the couch and blotted at it. Never scrub—that was the only trick I'd learned from my father growing up.

Scrubbing will only guarantee you're stuck with the stain. His voice echoed through my head. I kept blotting until I could barely see the red anymore.

"That stuff smells like chemicals," Mallory complained.

I couldn't smell a thing. "It's odorless," I countered.

She shrugged and returned to the television. "So who is he?" she pushed again without looking at me.

"I told you, he was here to fix my computer," I answered.

She scoffed. 'You expect me to believe that?" she asked. "Seriously, Len, give it up."

Was there harm to telling her? If it was an active FBI case, others in town would find out too. I didn't see the use in hiding it from Mallory.

"He's an FBI agent," I admitted, sitting back down on the couch.

Mallory spit out her wine, choking on the liquid.

"Mal, I just cleaned up," I groaned.

"Back up," she demanded. "An FBI agent!"

"He just needed some records from the museum," I quick defended, like a suspect put on the stand.

"About what?" Mallory pushed, her full focus on me for the first time.

"The Coastal Killer," I admitted.

"You mean the case you're obsessed with," she said.

"I'm not obsessed," I defended. She tilted her head and narrowed her eyes on me. "Not obsessed," I repeated. "It's a case I'm working on for the museum to build an exhibit. It's for work, Mal."

It wasn't lie; it was just a stretch of the truth. More than a fraction of the things out of Mallory's mouth were an exaggeration, but I loved her for it. The world seemed brighter, livelier, the way she saw it. Her stories gave me hope that one day, I'd see the world a bit brighter, forget the past and move on.

"Your work seems to always follow you home," she scolded. "You need a break."

"Have you been seeing Calvin?" I prodded.

"Your brother hates me. But if he's saying the same, then you know I'm right."

"He does not hate you," I countered.

"The beach mistake," she reminded me.

It was a hot summer day, and Calvin had invited me to join him for a midday swim in the ocean.

"That wasn't your fault," I shrugged.

Mallory had joined at my invite, which Calvin didn't mind at all. It wasn't until Calvin invited Mallory to hit the volleyball he brought back and forth that the day took a turn.

"I broke his nose," she said.

"It wasn't broken, just slightly bruised and bloody," I laughed. His nose bruised with a lump for days following. His fiancée? She had thought he'd been in a fight.

"He's been weird to me ever since," she pouted.

"He's not weird to you," I sighed. "I'm sure he's forgotten all about it."

He hadn't, but I wouldn't admit that. Although, the beach incident wasn't the reason he avoided Mallory. Their personalities just weren't meant to mesh.

"So, this FBI agent," she pushed. "How long is he here?"

"I don't know," I answered as I realized the credits were rolling on the television. I'd missed a third of the movie entirely.

"You didn't ask?" She raised a brow. "I saw you looking at him like you were ready to take him to bed, and you didn't bother asking when he was going back?"

"I was not-"

"He'll just break your heart. It's for the best," she added.

"What?" I pulled my legs in close, knowing what Mallory meant. She had her quirks, but I owed everything to her.

Without her, I'd still be living in my brother's home or possibly without a home, and I'd never have thought life was worth pulling myself out of the depression I'd fallen into.

My life had taken a turn three years ago, and soon after, I'd met Mallory.

"You don't remember what you were like right after *him*," she hissed the last word. Mallory refused to say his name, like it was a poison. Honestly, it was. The toxicity I had to purge from my life, my mentality, was pure poison fed to me by the person who destroyed my life.

I didn't want to think about him.

"I'm not in that place anymore," I promised.

"And I never want you to be again," she said with a sympathetic smile.

Mallory may have been a pain at times, but I knew she

was always looking after me. I didn't care how much she bothered others with her confident attitude and never ending sass. She'd been there for me when I most needed a friend. That was what counted.

"Mal, I promise. Never again."

She stood from the chair and walked over to the couch, sitting down next to me. Her arms wrapped around me, and I could smell her vanilla chai perfume. She pulled me close and squeezed me tightly.

"You're going to suffocate me," I giggled.

"I just needed to remind you how much I love you," she teased.

"I love you too, Mal," I answered as she let me go from the hug.

I leaned my head onto her shoulder and pulled the remote out of the crack of the couch cushions. A list of movies popped up on the streaming service as I clicked through and found one that looked interesting. I turned it on and let myself become completely lost to it.

At some point, I started to doze off from the combination of wine and the time growing late. Mal carefully slid out from under me and lowered me onto the couch. I could barely keep my eyes open as I let her tuck me in. A blanket was tossed over me and a pillow slid under my head. I pulled my legs in and cuddled up with the warm blanket.

The television still played, and I heard Mal tiptoeing her way out of the apartment.

"Goodnight," she whispered before opening the door and slipping out.

My hand hung off the couch, and I'd completely lost the blanket at some point in the night. I almost rolled off before catching myself and realizing where I was. I'd crashed hard after Mallory left.

I stood and made my way to the kitchen to get the coffee brewing and breakfast started. My fridge was bordering on empty for groceries, but I managed to find some strawberries and yogurt. The smell of brewing coffee filled my apartment, and I inhaled deeply.

The second best scent next to the salty air by the ocean.

My hand held a mug steady as I poured the coffee into it. I found oat milk in my fridge and added a splash to the cup. Steam rose from it, and I placed it aside on the small island that made up the center of my kitchen while I ate most of my breakfast.

A meow from beneath me pulled my attention away before I could take that first blissful sip of caffeine.

Alonzo sat at my feet, his green eyes bearing into me.

"What?" I asked, and he meowed again. "You have food," I assured him, pointing to the full bowl only feet away from him.

Birdie came trotting out of my bedroom.

"You slept on my bed, didn't you?"

She plopped down next to Alonzo and stared up at me. I picked up my coffee and finally took a sip. The warmth brushed against my throat as I swallowed.

"Not you too," I groaned. "I have work. I don't have time for this."

I probably should never have the time for full conversations with my two cats.

Maybe I was losing my mind. I was talking to my cats and

about to meet an FBI agent, one who drove me crazy in the single hour I spent with him, who made me feel like my senses were all jumbled.

No, I promised to never do this to myself again.

I'd had enough of men for a single lifetime. My last relationship had been three years ago, and the years following, I spent every second working on myself and rebuilding the shattered pieces. I couldn't do that again.

Mallory was right. I was a mess the last time, and I would be damned if I allowed that to happen again. My heart was off limits. The only thing I was committing to was finishing the now-lukewarm cup of coffee and spending every hour of the day working harder to become museum director.

I hurried to my room and threw on a maroon sun dress. My work flats sat next to my bedroom door, and I slipped them on. Within five minutes, I was clothed and completed my speed morning routine I reserved for days I was late.

And checking the stove clock as I walked out, I was most definitely late.

I was ten minutes behind schedule. Thankfully, I was always the first to work and likely still would be.

"I will see you both later," I said to the two felines still watching me with their judging, knowing stares.

My phone vibrated in my purse on my walk to work. I hesitated to pull it out, afraid I would see Francis' name flash across the screen to yell at me for being late. Guilt got the better of me, and I fished through my bag for it.

My mom's contact popped up on the screen.

"Hey, Mom," I said, answering the call.

"Oh, Lenore! Wonderful," she cooed into the phone.

I was in for it.

"I was so delighted when Calvin told us you would be joining us for dinner next week," she went on.

Shit.

He'd failed to mention the part where my parents were also coming. Did I forget a holiday or birthday? I racked my brain for anything significant this month, but nothing came to mind.

"What's the occasion?" I asked, trying to keep the surprise from my voice.

"Does there always have to be an occasion for us to visit our children?" she answered, and I could hear the scolding in her tone.

"No," I answered quickly.

I paused outside the museum as I arrived at work, hoping to hurry and wrap up the call before going inside.

"If you must know, Calvin invited us for the weekend," she replied.

So, he knew.

I was going to murder him the next time I saw him. Not really, but he was definitely high on my list of frustrations. He knew exactly what type of conundrum he walked me straight into, the probing questions and the backhanded compliments.

I loved my parents, but they weren't the most sensitive of people.

"Will we be seeing you before Friday?" my mother added.

"When do you arrive?" I asked.

"Late next Wednesday."

At least I had plenty of time to prepare for their arrival. I let out a breath of relief. I just needed to avoid them for a little over a day to make it to dinner.

"Eloise and I will be doing brunch on Thursday. You should join us," she added.

"I work on Thursdays," I noted.

"Perfect. Then we will just drop by the museum after."

"That's not-" I started.

"I will see you then," she said cheerily before hanging up.

"See you then," I muttered.

What did I do to piss of the universe so badly?

I had my quiet little life and routine, and I'd managed to keep that intact until now. My parents never pushed over the past three years, but I couldn't hold them off any longer. I was running out of time to keep asking for space or making excuses for distancing myself.

The door to the museum shut behind me, the cold air inside slamming into me and pulling me from my thoughts.

"Late," Barren teased, spotting me.

I scoffed under my breath. It was the first time in my life I was even being close to late, and I still had fifteen minutes before I technically clocked in for the day.

"You're just unprecedentedly early," I countered.

"Someday, you will be just like the rest of us," Barren teased.

Never willing to put in the work needed to get ahead.

"How so?" I entertained.

"Normal," he laughed. "Not hours early every day and not here after hours. Don't you have other things to do, hobbies or friends?"

The question stung, and I tried to hide the hurt from my

face. Mallory was my friend, and I tried plenty of hobbies. My most recent fixation, crocheting, had ended in lots of spare supplies and at least three half started and abandoned blankets.

"This job is my passion. I don't need more than that," I settled on.

He shrugged. "What was that guy yesterday looking for?" Barren asked, changing the subject.

"Who?" I asked, hoping I could avoid sharing more than necessary.

"The one asking Francis about you? Is he your boyfriend?" the old man asked, tilting his head.

"No," I quickly answered.

"I heard he's staying at Nelson's place."

How did information already make its way around Briarport on Agent Beck? He'd been here barely a day, and it was peak tourist season, yet somehow, the locals still managed to flag the newest stranger in town.

"Interesting," I said, pretending to care.

I didn't care.

I repeated that over and over in my head, yet somehow, a lump formed in my throat every time I thought about seeing him again the following day. I could've just emailed him the files, but he'd insisted I come to his place.

A door slammed out back, and Barren hurried off, terrified into starting work by our director's arrival.

I swallowed hard to clear the feeling in my throat. One more day, and I'd see him again.

7

STONE

I BARELY SLEPT, I couldn't turn my mind off. There was no set time for Lenore coming over, but that didn't stop me from spending most of the night preparing. I went over every single fact of the case, the documents I brought, and made sure I had food.

Guests expected snacks, right?

I never hosted. Working alone was always preferable, and my mind worked better when left to peace and quiet. What was I doing?

This went against every standard and routine I set for myself.

It was the early morning hours, and I caught a glimpse at the sun rising over the ocean from the back sunroom. The pinks and red were beautiful on most days, but I found them hard to admire anymore. Ever since that day, the color red just reminded me of blood.

So much blood.

Her body lying helplessly on the floor of that room. The

same room I didn't make it to in time. One miscalculation, and I'd failed her.

I turned away, focusing on making myself breakfast and coffee. I'd spent Thursday locating a grocery store and stocking my fridge with the essentials. My work was cut out for me, and I knew I'd need at least a week or two minimum in Briarport.

I grabbed a copy of *The Briarport Chronicle* at the store. I tried to crosscheck the articles in the latest edition with the journalist who wrote the final article on the Coastal Killer to confirm if they still worked at the paper, but I found myself at another dead end, not one worth pursuing.

There were other leads to follow.

If the FBI were opening the case, they'd first speak to the police. I needed to tread lightly with local law enforcement. I was uninvited and not acting on official FBI direction, so I needed to keep my contact limited.

The local sheriff's office was where I'd go next after compiling Lenore's document, once I perfected my ruse. A single FBI agent in Briarport, wrapping up some unfinished documentation for a cold case. It wasn't perfect, but with refining, it would do.

My chest tightened at the thought of a less than perfect plan. Mistakes caused casualties; I needed to be nothing short of impeccable.

I walked into the dining room where I'd assembled my working evidence board and brought my coffee with me. The sticky notes and a stray pen sat on the table from my last batch of notes I hung. I found the picture I'd printed of the High Tide Pub and grabbed the sticky notes.

Hunting ground.

I scribbled down the two words and hung it directly beneath the photo. That would be another stop along my venture through town.

I added numbers beneath the names of the twelve total victims, including the final one, Jane Doe. I made sure each victim was placed in order; every small detail could matter in the end. The first victim to a crime always told me a lot, and the way the victims progressed helped fill in gaps.

My eyes felt heavy to where I had trouble reading the small print on some of the documents on the wall. I moved to the other side of the table behind me and pulled out a chair.

My hand rubbed my forehead, a distant headache forming. The caffeine from the coffee wasn't kicking in fast enough.

I leaned my elbows on the table, my head falling into my hands. My eyes hung heavy, and I tried to keep them open, but each blink got slower and slower.

I knew the signs.

Riddled with anxiety over Lenore coming by and my cognitive functionality barely intact, sleep deprivation crept in before I even realized.

I blinked again, forcing my eyes back open.

My eyes closed shut slowly once more, but this time, they didn't open again.

BANG.BANG.BANG.

The rapping of a fist against the front door jolted me awake. I picked my head up off the table, seeing the wall of leads I'd carefully hung, and then turned toward the entry.

Another round of pounding came, and I stood quickly.

The door was only a few paces away, and my hand hesitated over the doorknob. I pulled it open before I could come to my senses and stop myself.

Lenore stood outside in her blue sundress, clutching her laptop. Her gaze met mine, and I watched her avert her eyes. I froze, unsure what to say first.

"Are you going to let me in?" she muttered as she pushed by me.

I suppose I have to now.

"The dining room," I said and pointed toward the left, but she ignored me and found it anyway. She placed her laptop on the table and turned to me, placing her hands on her hips.

This was a mistake.

Her brows furrowed, and I had that feeling wash over me that I'd missed something. Had I left her this angry? Maybe I never should have asked her to come; it was far too expectant. What kind of person just invited a complete stranger to their place without even knowing them?

"I think I saw a printer upstairs. Let me grab it," I said.

"You don't even know if you have a printer?" she said, her eyes widening.

"I do. There is definitely one upstairs, just-" I paused, watching her nostrils flare. "Let me just get it."

My voice trailed off before I turned and hurried up to the office space. I found the printer I knew sat on the wooden desk in the corner and grabbed it. Only a few seconds passed before I was once again downstairs. I rounded the corner, but Lenore was gone.

"Len?" I called out and set the printer on the table.

She already left?

I heard shuffling in the kitchen and followed it. Lenore stood at the counter, making another pot of coffee. The smell of the morning's pot had faded, but already, the new batch filled the room. I inhaled deeply, letting the scent ground me.

Deep breaths. You can get through this and then be free of her.

I caused the problem myself, impulsively inviting her here. Already, I could see what a mistake it had been.

"The printer's ready," I offered.

She nodded without turning to face me.

"I'll just-"

"Want some?" she asked, finally turning toward me.

I could see in her eyes something was bothering her. It was easy to spot the quiet heaviness within them. I could place the signs but not the cause.

Maybe I was the cause.

I barely knew her, so why did everything in me hurt to see that darkness?

"I already-" I started, but I stopped myself. "Yes, thank you."

I couldn't deny her this small thing. Before I could say anything else, I returned to the dining room and found an outlet for the printer. Its little screen lit up, and I let out a sigh of relief that it was functional.

Lenore came back into the room and set the mug down on the table for me.

"Thanks," I said.

She opened her laptop and pulled up the files she'd shown me earlier in the week. "All of them?" she asked curtly.

"Yes," I confirmed.

The process was more torturous than I expected, and guilt increasingly built inside me as we spent over an hour watching each of the documents print slowly. It took minutes just for a single page to make it through the printer.

Len sat opposite of me at the table, closest to the wall, but her back was turned to me. For the entire hour, she'd just stared at the documents on the wall.

"Are you hungry?" I asked while the printer chugged along.

She shrugged, not saying a word.

I stood and moved to the kitchen, searching for the snacks I'd prepared. I had an entire spread of fruits and vegetables with dips, waiting to be consumed. The moment I opened the fridge to grab them, I realized I was hungrier than I'd thought. The fruit looked refreshing, a mix of berries and grapes. I carried the snacks into the dining room.

"My favorite," Len said with a weak smile.

"Hm," I murmured, glancing up from the tray I set down.

"Strawberries," she said. "They are my favorite."

"Mine too," I said, feeling self-conscious.

"My mother used to buy them as a treat every summer for us," I told her.

"A treat? It's a fruit," she pointed out.

I let out a soft laugh. "Even my knowledge has its limits, and at five years old, I didn't know the difference between strawberries and a true dessert."

I saw her lip pull up ever so slightly. Progress.

"Did you grow up near Quantico?" she asked, and I found her full attention on me.

"California," I answered.

"Do you miss it?" she asked.

"Sometimes, but I'm happy with where I ended up." I shrugged. "Have you always lived in Briarport?"

I knew the answer was no, but I didn't mention that. I felt like a stalker. Light stalking for a good reason wasn't exactly stalking, was it?

I couldn't even begin to reason with or defend that thought. Instead, I brushed it from my mind. I'd taken all necessary precautions before coming, and I couldn't take those back.

"No," she answered. "I used to live closer to my parents until three years ago. My brother lived here already, so I thought I'd give it a try."

I worked to organize all the printed papers while Lenore snacked on the tray. She tried to help where she could, but it was impossible to explain my organization conventions to her. We spent another hour working to hang everything up. Lenore helped under my guidance.

"We still don't have much on Jane Doe," I said, glancing over the wall.

"There isn't much out there on her." Lenore shrugged. "I doubt we need it."

She couldn't truly believe that? Not with all this work she'd done.

"She's the key to everything. She's the only person who may know more about the unsub than anyone. I think if we can find her, we just might be able to track down this killer once and for all," I pushed.

Lenore's reluctance had my mind reeling. Could she genuinely not see how this played into everything?

She crossed her arms and ignored the comment. Every passing moment, I felt like Lenore pushed herself further and further away. I wanted her help on this. It was unexplainable; I worked alone and preferred it that way, but not with her. The second I'd seen how much research and work she'd put into this case, it was like I couldn't bear the thought of removing her from it.

I would hate if someone took all my research and cut me out.

I kept repeating the thought, assuring myself there was a logical explanation. Something kept nagging at me, though. There was a reason I needed her, beyond just respecting someone's work.

"You didn't have to stay," I noted as we finished up.

"I wanted to," she shrugged, keeping any emotion from her face.

I hated feeling like I'd done something to contribute to her on and off displeasure with the day.

"I'm sorry for making you come all this way," I tried, hoping it may help alleviate some of the growing tension.

She shrugged, adding extra tape to some of the hanging documents.

"I didn't mind," she said.

"Excuse me for being blunt, but it seems as though you did," I noted.

I didn't know how to be anything other than straightforward. I couldn't tiptoe around emotions like some could. It was never a skill I honed.

"It's not you," she sighed.

She took a step back to admire our work. With everything hung, it really was beginning to look like something out of a cliché crime show.

"It feels a bit like me," I said.

"Oh, you're one of those men," she said, raising her brows.

"What men? "

"The ones who think the world revolves around them."

"I am not one of them," I hurried to deny.

"Seems like it," Len teased with a weak smile. "If you must know, my parents are coming to town."

"And that's bad?" I asked.

"Very," she said quickly. "I'm unprepared is all. They are good people, but I'm not ready for them."

"Impromptu visits aren't really my favorite either, so I get it," I said sincerely.

A look of relief washed over her face, like she'd been expecting judgement and was surprised to find none. A bit of her apprehension faded away, but I still saw that look in her eyes, the one telling me that something still ate at her.

I cleaned scraps off the table of papers we'd cut to hang and the practically empty food tray, carrying it all to the kitchen to clean and dispose of. When I returned, I found Len standing in front of our work, staring at the question mark representing the Jane Doe. She didn't hear me.

I moved closer, observing the way she seemed lost in thought. I caught a glimpse of her face, and something clicked. Her brows were pulled together, and her lips pressed into a thin line. Concern shadowed her gaze.

I expected to find confusion or curiosity, not this.

My mind immediately fell into its usual pattern of pulling every piece of information I had together. Every conversation, bit of evidence, and emotion I'd seen from Lenore about the Jane Doe—it all started to fall into place. There was only one explanation, even though I had been blind to it initially. I cursed under my breath at not getting there faster.

I've lost my touch.

"It's you, isn't it?" I asked, and she startled.

"What?" She turned, a new panicked look in her eyes.

"Jane Doe," I said gently.

"No," she whispered and shook her head. "You're mistaken."

I took a step closer and reached out to place a hand on her shoulder.

She tensed at my touch. Her head turned to meet me half way as I moved beside her. That look of panic melted into sadness. "Don't-" she started.

I hated to push. I knew what it was like when everyone expected you to share. "When I joined the FBI, I had never once been on a team. I preferred solitude in my projects. I didn't see a need to rope others in," I started.

Her brows pulled in, but she absorbed every word I said.

"When I was placed on a team, I was forced to find a way to make it work. If I wanted to see becoming an agent through, teamwork wasn't optional. So, I did the only thing my brain knew how," I explained.

I wanted to slow my story, make it last forever as I saw the way Lenore's gaze settled on me. Her dark eyes glanced over me, and I watched her guard slowly falling. She listened, truly listened.

Each word I spoke, I watched her mind race. I knew I was right about her, and the way her mind spun right in front of me confirmed it.

"What?" she pushed.

"I analyzed my own team. I made files for each person and filled them with strengths and weaknesses, ways I thought I could compliment working with agents and ones I needed to problem solve."

Her eyes darted back to the wall at my pause.

"Blythe told me it was something a stalker may do," I laughed softly. "She was right, as always, but it's how my mind works. I analyze things until I make sense of them."

She tensed, turning back and shying away from me, like I may just crack open every secret she ever held.

"And you know what doesn't make sense to me?" I asked. "Your research."

"My research is thorough," she argued, scowling. Her eyes crinkled, and I held back a smile at the look of pure confidence that washed over her while challenging me.

She was everything I wished for in the agents who went through Quantico. I'd waited months to find someone who could replace me, someone who could challenge me, who could think just as analytically.

Len had a ways to go if she were to ever chose that path, but I'd found my match in this woman.

Not that Len would ever wish to become an agent, but maybe she could be more help than I had planned after all.

"I don't doubt that," I said. "But you are omitting one key piece."

"I gave you everything I have," she said and crossed her arms. She was putting that guard right back up.

"Do you know who the only person on my team without a file was?" I asked.

She shook her head.

"Myself," I answered and watched the realization wash over her. The ruse was up, and now, it was her move.

"I didn't need a file on someone I knew better than anyone."

"I-" she started.

She took a step back. I reached up and pulled the question mark off the wall. I didn't need it.

I had her.

"You are the Jane Doe. You don't need a file on yourself. You already know everything you need to."

She shook her head.

"No," she insisted, but I pushed and held firm.

"I don't believe for a second that you've done such thorough work, but this key piece, you've left blank."

"It's a dead end," she argued.

"Because you've made it one," I countered. "You're smart, Len. You're clever, more so than most initial recruits I meet in week one at Quantico. You can't expect me to believe you cast aside this one key piece of the story as useless."

"I-" She stopped, her words failing her. "I have to go," she said quietly and grabbed her laptop quickly off the table.

She made for the door as fast as she could. I tried follow, but the second she was out the door, she jogged off.

I couldn't force her to admit it. Chasing her was no use. I was observant enough to know when to stop. If I continued to push, she'd bury herself behind endless walls I would never break through.

I sighed.

Maybe I had pushed too hard. We needed this piece of the story more than anything. This couldn't be the last I saw of Lenore.

"Mags," I said, a smile already growing on my face.

"Stone, to what do I owe the pleasure?" Mags chimed through the phone.

The nickname stung like a bullet lodging itself into my chest. Memories were surfacing, ones I preferred to keep buried.

"I need a favor," I said.

"What type of favor?" she asked, and I imagined her leaning closer to the phone I knew sat on her desk.

"The type where you don't report it to Grey."

"Oh, is the Agent Beck finally abandoning doing everything by the books?" she gasped dramatically into the phone.

"Mags..." I warned.

"I'm teasing," she assured me. "Anything for you, Stone. Lay it on me."

"I need you to look into a bar and find me information on it."

"A bar? What's the name?" she asked, and I heard her long fingernails tapping against her keyboard.

"High Tide Pub in Briarport, Maine," I answered quietly, like if I spoke any louder, Grey would somehow learn what I was doing.

"Briarport? As in, the Coastal Killer?"

My heart raced, and I could feel my cellphone slipping in my hands, slick with sweat.

"Yes, the same one," I answered. "I'm looking into the cold case."

"If you're on assignment, why am I keeping this from Grey?"

"It's not for assignment."

Silence hung between us, and I thought for a moment the line may have disconnected.

"I'll keep this discreet," she said, her tone turning serious. "Give me a few days, and I'll have everything you could possibly need."

"I appreciate it. I owe you," I said, but my heart didn't stop pounding.

It was a risk, but I didn't want to go in blind, not if I was bringing Lenore with me. I needed all the information I could gather.

"I'm just glad you're back," she said.

She was one of the few who knew everything. Blythe and Mags had become close during their time working together. My heart pained for the loss I knew she experienced too.

"Thank you, Mags."

I clicked the phone off and set it down on the empty nightstand next to my bed. I climbed in, ready to shut my mind off for the night. Sleep was the only escape I had from it sometimes. As useful as it was to think how I did, sometimes, it was a curse, never being able to turn off seeing everything from an analytical point of view.

I pulled the covers up and shut my eyes, praying I could escape just for a little. My chances were completely split. Some nights, sleep was the remedy I craved, and during the other half, the PTSD slipped through the cracks, and the nightmares came crawling right back, placing me right back into that moment.

Blood pooled on the floor.

I knelt in the puddle of it, the warm, sticky liquid clinging to my clothing. Another body lay only feet away, but I didn't bother to check its pulse. I ignored every protocol I'd been taught. My mind was blank, nothing but red filling my vision.

"No, no, please," I begged.

I grabbed her lifeless body, cradling it in my arms.

I was too late, far too late.

Blood coated my hands. I couldn't tell exactly where it was coming from, but there was too much of it. I searched for the wound, my hands scrambling across her torso to find it.

She wore a bulletproof vest that left her lower abdomen exposed. I felt gently around and found the tear in her skin. It was too wide, something from a blade.

I covered it with my hand, trying to minimize the blood.

She wasn't moving, wasn't responsive to my touch at all. Her skin was cold to the touch.

"Help!" I yelled at the top of my lungs.

I knew back up was too far. We should've waited, should have followed protocol the way we were taught.

A hand on my shoulder startled me.

I glanced up to find a young girl staring down at me, her eyes filled with terror.

"Go find help," I ordered sternly.

I needed to get her away from the scene, away from the blood soaking the ground.

I used my hand cradling Blythe's head to feel for her neck and pulse.

There was nothing, not even a weak beating.

She was gone.

I woke, sitting up straight, and grabbed for my phone.

My heart was racing, and my skin had a cold sweat coating it. The phone trembled in my hands as I swiped a finger over the screen to turn it on. The time flashed on the screen: 3:00 in the morning.

I put it down and laid back in the bed.

If I couldn't get a grasp on these nightmares, I was going to slowly drive myself back toward that dark place.

It was the reason I'd drowned myself in alcohol and drugs those three months after her death. Only the haze they left me in drove away the memories, and now, they were all coming back again.

I sighed as I pulled the covers tight and tried to close my eyes. I knew it was useless; my mind would never settle now.

I stayed that way the rest of the night, eyes closed but refusing to allow myself fully back to sleep.

8

LENNY

He knew.

He knew, and I ran.

I ran until my legs ached, and I found myself miles down the stretch of beach I frequented when I could. This time, the sand and waves were a blur. My mind raced, every horrible thing I feared plaguing me, and I couldn't stop it.

He knew, and now everyone would know.

I was the coward who ran. The Jane Doe who snuck out of the hospital before they could even identify her. I'd been mutilated and left to die, and by some stroke of luck, I'd survived.

I'd been unconscious for weeks, my body recovering. When I woke, the wounds were healed, but the scars remained.

Weeks, and no one had come for me.

The nurses said the FBI had taken extreme cautions. No one knew who I was, and they kept my appearance away from the press. There wasn't any trace of my identity for them to contact my family. They kept the hospital I'd been taken to completely secret, afraid the killer might seek me out.

I was practically a ghost.

I feigned not remembering anything. What happened, my name, who attacked me, all gone like distant memories, but that was never true. I knew, but I couldn't stand the idea of reliving it all. I didn't want to become the whole focus of the investigation.

I knew he would never forgive me if I did.

So, I pretended I couldn't remember when I woke, just long enough to heal a little more and leave. They never found my wallet or anything about my identity, the killer taking those things.

The nurses were patient and understanding.

Shock.

That was what they said it was, assured me it would come back. I just needed rest. I didn't want it to come back. It was already there, and I would've done anything to forget.

All but one nurse, one who was the entire reason I was able to make it out before anyone knew who I was. She showed me a kindness I could never repay. I'd lost everything and was about to be thrust into the middle of an investigation and the spotlight.

She saw that and took mercy on me.

I bent down and picked up a pebble from the rocky shore, throwing it as far as I could into the ocean. Amidst the waves, it barely made a splash. That was exactly how I felt—in an ocean of people and cases, my story barely mattered.

Right?

I'd seen Agent Beck's face. He'd been adamant I was the key to solving this. If he knew what I knew, he wouldn't think so. I was a coward, and I hid from the truth. Even though I remembered, I never let myself fully remember.

I knew I was attacked, that I'd survived the Coastal Killer. I knew who I was and what I did, but I didn't have any idea who had done this to me. They'd hit me from behind, it was dark, and I wasn't feeling well.

What use was I?

Just another drunk woman who didn't listen to her fiancé. No one knew the truth or what I lost that day.

That's what Jake had said, that no one would believe me. Until one day, he finally just left. He never came looking for me in the hospital, never told anyone I was missing at all. I wasn't allowed to have a job, no friends, nothing that would risk ruining the perfect life he built us.

His perfect life.

I'd wanted to go to the police so many times those first few days, but he refused to let me. I was an embarrassment to him. If anyone found out who he was marrying, and the consequences I'd caused, he'd be ruined.

Consequences that devastated me. Loss that was incomprehensible.

He left me because of it.

I'd been helicoptered to a large hospital over half an hour from Briarport. We lived in between the two. The possibility of ever running into one of those nurses again and being recognized was impossible. I kept far from the local sheriffs and kept out of trouble. No one ever had to know.

Except now, Beck knew.

Before I knew it, my knees buckled, and I knelt in the damp sand. The water barely reached me each time it drifted in across the sand.

My head fell into my hands, and I felt hot tears stream down my face. Beck was right, and now I'd run yet again from the past. I couldn't escape it, yet I kept trying. What did that make me?

I picked my head up, gazing out into the water again through streaky vision. Birds flew close to its surface, and I felt my heart slow the longer I watched.

A seagull landed close by, a few others joining behind it. I could feel its beady black eyes on me.

"I don't have food," I muttered and it hopped closer, cocking its head at me.

"I don't want company," I grumbled, but it just stared blankly.

"I'm a coward," I whispered, afraid if I said it too loud, the world would topple around me.

I'd built the perfect life in Briarport, one that kept my past buried.

And now, that was slipping away.

9

———

LENNY

I WALKED HOME AS QUICKLY as I could after sitting on the beach for hours. The memories of walking in the dark still haunted me, and I tried my best to make it back each day before the sun set.

The sky was already turning a shade of orange that let me know my time was up.

I'd wiped my tears and brushed the sand off my knees before beginning the walk home.

It was further than I realized. My blind panic had driven me miles down the beach, and I knew, at this rate, I wouldn't make it back with the sun still up.

I found one of the outlet paths that led to the main road, running along the beach. My phone only had ten percent of its battery left, and I used it to call a ride. I wasn't willing to risk the long walk alone. At least I knew my sanity was partially intact.

A red SUV pulled up to where I stood on the sidewalk, and I checked the license plate with what I'd been provided when I called the ride at least five times before I got in. I made sure the driver knew the name of the person they were picking up.

You could never be too careful.

I used to think I was untouchable, that nothing could possibly happen to me.

I was wrong.

I sat in the back seat and watched out the window as the sun set on the ride home. By car, it only took twelve minutes to get to my apartment, a walk that would have taken me at least forty minutes.

"Thank you," I said when the man pulled up, and I hopped out the car.

I hurried down the alley and inside, anxiety washing over me. What if they'd waited and watched what door I went in? Could they guess I lived alone?

Every horrible thought crossed my mind, motivating my steps to quicken.

I typed in the pin on the keypad, but a red light flashed, locking me out. I tried again, and it failed.

Not now. Please, not now.

I glanced over my shoulder, realizing the car was still sitting at the end of the alley. A lump formed in my stomach, and I tried again.

Still nothing.

I heard the sound of a car door and swallowed hard. Sweat beaded on my forehead, and I pushed on the door, hoping it might budge. My hands found the door handle and turned it over and over, but nothing happened.

Please, please, let this work.

I risked a glance back and saw the man approaching from his car.

Maybe I deserved this. Maybe it was karma for what I had done.

My fist pounded on the door, and I tugged at the handle again. The door was firmly locked in place.

I pounded once more, and a hand on my shoulder startled me, causing me to jump back. I raised my hands instinctively, not ready to go down without a fight.

"Woah there," the driver said with a smile. "You forgot this."

He held up a purse.

I instantly glanced down and around myself and saw my own was missing.

"Thank you," I said softly, taking the bag from him. My heart was still pounding in my ears as he walked back to his car. The door flung open, and Mallory stood wide eyed in the entry.

"What on Earth are you doing out here?" she asked. "And why are you trying to break our door?"

"The pin didn't work," I said.

"Because I had it changed today. The lock company called and said their system had been tampered with, so I opted to change to a new code. You would know that if you'd checked your texts," she muttered.

I looked down at my phone and realized I had multiple missed ones. At least ten were from Mallory wondering why I wasn't home and to tell me about the pin change.

"I'm sorry," I sighed. "Long day."

"Where were you?" she asked. "I thought it was your day off." She moved back to let me in and followed me up the stairs.

"It was," I answered. I unlocked my apartment and pushed inside, hearing greetings from Alonzo and Birdie.

"You know your lease said no pets," Mallory grumbled at the animals.

"If you throw them out, I go with them," I reminded her.

"You're still avoiding the question," she pushed.

I set down my bag and phone and made my way to the kitchen to scour for any form of leftovers I could find for dinner. "I'm not avoiding," I answered.

"Then where were you?" she pushed.

"I was with Beck," I admitted.

"Lenore, seriously?" she said. "When will you learn to take my advice?"

"I do take your advice," I promised.

She groaned, joining my hunt for food. We settled on leftover cheese pizza I added some leftover pieces of bacon to. I diced up the meat and added a bit to each of our slices.

"You don't even have time for groceries, so how do you have time for a man?" she asked.

I shook my head. "I don't need time for a man. I was just helping him."

Mallory made her way to the couch and kicked her feet up. Her pizza was gone before I even made it over. I settled next to her and pulled my legs in close, savoring each bite.

Comfort food was the best solution to such a long day.

"What's wrong?" Mallory asked, tilting her head.

"Nothing. What are we watching tonight?" I asked, deflecting.

"Len," Mallory warned. "Don't do that."

I finished the last bite of pizza and searched the side table for the remote. The television clicked on as I picked it up and hit the power button. Alonzo and Birdie both made their way up onto my lap.

"Even they know something is up," Mallory said as she nodded to the cats.

Damn cats, giving me away. They always knew when something was bothering me, but it didn't mean I needed them to reveal it to everyone else around. *At least wait until guests were gone to give me pity cuddles.*

"Hello?" Mallory said, waving a hand in front of my face.

"What?" I asked, shaking my head and glancing to her.

"You went vacant," she sighed.

"I just had a long day, that's all," I said.

When I met Mallory, I was in a low place, but there were still secrets I kept from even her. She knew Jake left me, and she knew I'd been completely ruined by it. I had zero self-esteem, no job, and no place to live when he kicked me out. She'd been there and picked me up off the ground.

"You're thinking about him, aren't you?" she asked.

"Who?"

"You know who," she said and narrowed her eyes.

"I'm not." Why did the room feel a thousand degrees hotter? I glanced to the thermostat on the wall and saw it was still the same exact temperature.

"You always have the same look when you think about him," she pointed out. "Is this because of that FBI agent? Did he try to push you into doing something? You clearly aren't ready to go back to relationships anytime soon."

"No, no, it wasn't like that at all," I assured her.

"Len-"

Thud, thud, thud.

I nearly jumped out of my seat as a knock on the door

startled me. I was on edge. The case, the driver grabbing my purse, and now this?

I heard a piece of paper slide under the door and stood from the couch. Mallory strained her neck to see, and I walked down the short hallway to find a single piece of paper on the floor. I spotted the pitch black writing before I was close enough to read it.

I picked it up, and my breath caught in my throat.

Stop looking.

Those were the only two words scrawled across the sheet. My heart felt like it was exploding through my chest, and I could barely manage a deep breath.

"Len, what is that?" Mal asked.

"Nothing," I said weakly, trying to crumple up the piece of paper.

Mallory stood from the couch and made her was across the room faster than I could dispose of the threat. She held out her hand, but I clung to the ball of paper. She stepped forward and reached for it, but instinctively, I back away.

"Seriously, Len?" she asked, raising a brow. "Let me see it."

"I-" I tried to come up with an excuse, but my mind went blank. "Fine," I sighed and handed it over.

She worked to flatten it out, bringing it into my kitchen and smoothing it out on the island countertop. "Len..." Mallory warned. "What is this?"

"Probably just some dumb prank."

She pushed past me and opened the apartment door, but no one was out on the landing. The door slammed shut as she moved to the windows, looking out all of them frantically.

"They're probably long gone by now," I said.

I leaned against my kitchen counter for support. My head was spinning, and my stomach felt nauseous. How did these things keep happening to me?

"We'll check the cameras," she assured me.

I wasn't sure who was more spooked, me or Mallory. Her face was a new shade of pale, her eyes filled with concern for me.

"I'll be right back," she said and hurried out of the apartment.

I didn't have the capacity to move from where I held myself up. One of my hands slid across my chest, over my heart. Its consistent pounding was the only thing I could focus on. The steady beat thrashed against my hand. I could hear it ringing in my ears.

My apartment door opened again, but I barely registered it.

The laptop was opened and pulled up to the security system Mal used before I could even wrap my mind around everything. She scrolled through footage for a few minutes while I continued to stand in the corner, growing more nauseated by the second.

"Here it is!" she said triumphantly.

I snapped my head in her direction, finally pulling myself together. I couldn't let someone hold so much power over me, not after all these years spent rebuilding who I was. I was different now, better.

I moved closer to Mallory to get a better view of her laptop screen. She tilted it toward me, and I hovered over her shoulder, watching as she clicked play on the camera feed.

At first, there was nothing, just the empty sidewalk and

the view outside her shop. It was closed now, most people having gone back to their rentals and homes for the day, so there was no foot traffic on the camera.

I almost thought Mallory could be mistaken until I spotted a shadowy movement on the pavement. It took a second before the person came into view. They were dressed fully in black, and from the angle of the camera, it was hard to tell their height and build looking down on them.

They kept their head down and avoided the camera, like they knew it was there. It wasn't hidden; that wasn't the purpose of it. Mallory had it installed for general security on the front door of the shop. It was meant to be seen and deter.

The person rounded the corner into the alley, and we watched, waiting for them to return. It took five minutes before they came back around, this time walking directly toward the camera. Their head was still down, and I couldn't see any of their face.

It was barely anything, but it was a start. I took a deep breath, my heart finally no longer pounding.

"Can you email me this?" I asked.

"What're you going to do with it, Len?" Mallory asked slowly.

"Give it to Agent Beck. It could help him," I started.

"Isn't this proof enough you should stay far away from him? The note literally said stop looking," Mallory exclaimed. "I think you should listen, Len. That man has brought nothing good with him to this town."

"You barely know him," I muttered.

"I don't need to. I've known you three years, and never once have you received a threat at your door like this," she pushed. "Then suddenly, he comes to town, and now you're wrapped up in whatever he's doing, and threats are being slid under your door. Does that not worry you?"

"I'll be more careful," I assured her.

"You shouldn't have to. You should be able to enjoy your life without looking over your shoulder all the time. You did enough of that with Jake," she said.

Pain radiated across my chest. I saw it in her eyes, Mallory knew exactly what she was doing, bringing him into the conversation. It was a sore spot for me, but not one I was going to let keep me from this case.

Not when this was the newest piece of evidence. Not when the killer may have resurfaced. All I could think of was the other victims who were not as lucky as I was. I was given another chance. I had to use it to do good for them.

"Mal, please, just email me it," I sighed, too tired to argue more with her.

She rolled her eyes. "You never listen to me," she grumbled. "Promise me you will consider staying far away from him and the trouble he brought."

"I can't-"

"Len, just promise," she pleaded. "I don't want to see you hurt, by him or some creepy stalker."

"Fine, I promise," I said, knowing she wouldn't let it go.

She quickly downloaded the video and pulled up her email. I heard a ping from my email app on my phone within seconds.

"Sent," she sighed. She closed the laptop and started for the apartment door. "I'll see you soon," she promised, leaving me with a pit of guilt in my stomach.

I tossed and turned in my bed, unable to shake the feeling. The note and the two words on it haunted my thoughts.

My cats slept on either side of my legs, and I carefully slid myself to sit up in bed. I turned on the small lamp on my bedside table and opened the drawer, pulling out the paper.

I couldn't bring myself to throw it out. What if it could help in some way? What if I was wrong about it all, over-reacting?

My mind went back and forth.

I took a sip from the water glass I filled and left sitting on the nightstand before trying to will myself to sleep, turning back and forth under my sheets.

It was a useless task. It wasn't like I actually thought sleep was possible; I wasn't that delusional. I just thought maybe, my body would force my mind to at least rest, to take a break from everything that happened during the day.

Not even that seemed possible now.

My phone was sitting on the nightstand, and I rolled over and grabbed it, opening it to my emails. I found the one Mallory sent and played the clip over and over again. There had to be something, anything, I could use.

I kept watching until my eyes stung. I rubbed at them lazily, trying to clear the hazy vision. The answer had to be there.

On my tenth watch through, my eyes started to hurt, and I felt a headache inching its way in. I was about to close out the video when a small pop of red caught my eye.

I'd seen it in every play through. I thought it was just a zipper or design on the stalker's black jacket, but this time, I saw it, the way it dangled and moved, like it was hanging out of the pocket, not attached to it.

It was so subtle. I rewound the video to make sure I hadn't imagine it.

Again, I watched the small red speck dangle. There was no denying it: a keychain hung, barely visible, out of his pocket.

I shot out of the bed, finding slippers and a bathrobe and tying it around myself. This couldn't wait; my mind would never let me rest until I let him know. I'd raced out of there less than a day before, and it was eating at me.

Alonzo and Birdie shifted to settle in the center of my bed without me in the way to stop them.

"I'll be back," I assured them before leaving the room and finding the keys to the car I kept parked nearby for rare occasions.

10

STONE

THE LOUDEST THUD woke me from my sleep.

I jolted upright and hopped out of bed. I quietly pulled open the nightstand drawer and pulled out the gun I kept stashed inside.

I held it in front of me, slowly walking through the room, careful not to make more noise than necessary. No noise followed the thud, but it was loud enough and close enough for me to know it came from inside.

I kept close to the wall, exiting the bedroom and making my way down the short hall to the stairs.

My footsteps felt deadly loud in the quiet of the night, and I sucked in a breath as a floorboard beneath me let out the deepest creak. My body tensed, every single hair on my arm standing.

Rustling sounds carried up the stairs, and I paused to listen. It was too far away; I couldn't make out anything distinct beyond movement in what sounded like the dining room.

Was I being robbed?

I took each step one at a time, moving painfully slow downstairs. I could hear the shuffling getting louder. The closer I got, I poked my head around the corner, but it was completely dark, and the only thing I spotted was light from some screen on the table. The wall between the entry and the dining room partially blocked my view.

I got to the last step and started my careful approach. My gun was still raised, and I refused to take my eyes off the person moving around the dining room.

They were small in stature from the silhouette I could see and wore some type of robe. It was hard to make out details in the dark.

"Raise your hands slowly," I demanded.

The person jumped back from the table, startled, and quickly threw up their hands, ignoring my instructions.

"Turn around," I breathed. My eyes widened as they adjusted to the dark and realized who stood in the middle of the dining room.

"Lenore? What are you doing here?" I demanded.

"I had to show you this," she said a bit frantically.

She moved aside to show me the screen of her laptop she'd opened on the table. I lowered my gun still pointed at her, which did not seem to faze her in her frantic rambling. She started going on about a stalker and note, but none of her words made much sense, and she was speaking too fast for me to process.

Had I pushed her too far earlier, making her admit she was Jane Doe? Was this her final break?

"Len, slow down," I instructed. "Start from the beginning. Are you all right?"

"I'm fine," she said, quickly brushing me off. "Like I was

trying to explain, I think I found footage of the Coastal Killer."

"No one's ever found footage from any of the attacks. How could you possibly have some?" I asked.

Her words still didn't make sense. The FBI thoroughly searched every surveillance option, checking all cameras within a certain radius of every attack site. There's no way she could've obtained it from the local bar without some form of law enforcement to back her, so I doubted she'd already explored that option.

"New footage," she said

"There hasn't been an attack in years," I muttered. I still felt like Lenore could be having a psychotic break, having to face past events. Most peoples' minds found a way to protect them from hard truths, blurred reality.

"They came to my apartment," she said, and I froze.

"What do you mean, they came back for you? Did they try to hurt you?" A new panic washed over me as I realized the gravity of her words. I dragged her into this mess, put her straight in harm's way.

"Someone slipped a note under my door that said *stop looking*. I can't imagine what else it would mean. I had Mallory send me the footage that showed someone coming and leaving at that time. You can't make out much, and they clearly knew what they were doing, but I did see one thing."

I took a step closer to see her laptop screen as she pressed play. I watched the footage as someone dressed in all black avoided the camera's sight best they could and entered the alley to her apartment.

So they knew what they were doing. The FBI always assumed that much in its profile.

There was a few minutes before the person returned, still avoiding the camera, their head down. My stomach sunk, realizing how close the killer could have been to Lenore, and it was my fault. I'd been careless and wrapped her up in the case for completely selfish reasons.

"There," she said and paused the screen, pointing to a small red fleck on the page.

"I can't make out what it says, but it looks like some sort of keychain tag. What if it's something that can help us identify them?" Her eyes looked up wildly to me, and I saw the heavy bags under them, like this kept her up most of the night.

"So you walked here in the night and broke into the house to show me this?"

It was dark, but I could tell by the way her body shifted that her face had warmed at the question. "It didn't feel like it could wait," she muttered.

"You're right. I'm glad you brought it right to me, and I'm glad you're safe," I admitted. "But maybe next time, you should knock first so I don't hold you at gunpoint."

"I did knock," she grumbled. "And I didn't walk, I drove," she added, crossing her arms for good measure.

I turned and flicked on the light switch. Lenore stood in front of me in a fuzzy, pink bathrobe and slippers. I held back a chuckle of surprise. She frowned deeply and hugged her arms around herself tighter.

"It didn't feel like it should wait, and my laptop can't zoom in on it without it turning blurrier," she reiterated. "I can email you the video, and I'll let you get back to sleep."

She closed the laptop and started to head for the door.

"You shouldn't stay there," I' blurted out.

I got her into this mess; it was my responsibility to protect her. I thanked every entity out there for the fact that all the Coastal Killer left was a warning. It reaffirmed what I initially believed: Lenore was the key to this all.

"Stay here tonight, and we can figure out something else tomorrow," I insisted.

She hesitated but turned away from the door eventually. She nodded and looked toward the living room.

"You can take the room upstairs. I'll take the couch," I said quickly.

"It's your place," she started.

"Actually, it's Nelson's place," I answered, and she gave in without a fight.

The next morning, I made a call back to Quantico.

Len was still upstairs, sleeping from what I could tell. I hadn't heard a sound come from the second floor since I woke. It wasn't surprising; I'd been up before the sun was completely risen.

"Mags," I spoke into my phone.

"Stone, I don't have all the information you asked for on that bar yet. I've had to do what I can between cases."

"That's not why I'm calling," I said, starting to second-guess my ask.

Mags was already doing enough for me, and risking her own job to find this information, could I really ask her for more?

"I have a video, footage from outside of a shop," I started slowly. "It's hard to make out, but the person I'm trying to identify looks to have a keychain hanging out of their pocket.

When I zoom in on a laptop, it distorts the picture, but I'm wondering if it's something you might be able to make out."

"Send it my way, and I'll get to it as soon as I get to the rest of the information you asked for," she said.

I heard footsteps walking across the second floor, hurrying down the stairs.

"Thanks, Mags," I said, hanging up before Len could hear me.

"How did you sleep?" I asked as she rounded the corner into the living room.

She still wore her fuzzy pink robe, and her hair was a slight mess, but in a way I found to be adorable. Had I really become so analytical that I was noticing these things?

"Better than I expected," she muttered, rubbing sleep from her eyes. "I think it helped knowing you were down here."

"You can stay here for the foreseeable future," I promised her.

She shook her head quickly, her eyes narrowing. "I can't stay here," she started. "I have work and the cats to take care of, and Mallory would lose her shit if she found out I was staying here and not my apartment."

"Mallory can get over it," I retorted. "You have a *stalker*."

That sentence alone should be enough to scare anyone, but Len barely flinched.

"And I'm really grateful you let me stay here last night, because I was far too tired to be driving home, but I'm fine. I've survived three years without them coming for me. I'll be fine."

"They've been emboldened. It's been three years with nothing, and now they've come out of their safety just to threaten *you*. They're playing with you, letting you know they know exactly where you are and what you're doing. I cannot let that go. I dragged you into this. I'm going to make sure I get you out of it alive."

"I can't stay here", she insisted.

I run my hand along my chin, trying to think of a better solution or way to convince Len this was the best option. When it came to her, my mind felt blank. Suddenly, every answer that always came so easily was barely within my grasp.

"I'll stay at your place," I decided.

"Absolutely not," she argued. "Mallory will never allow that."

"Again, I really don't care what Mallory thinks," I noted, stepping closer. "And Mallory won't know. I'll make sure of it." I was only inches from her now. I could see the rapid rising and falling of her chest, even with her arms crossed to hide it.

Her hands slowly slid down to the belt holding her robe together. She looked hesitant, and her hands fidgeted with the tie around her robe, trying to tighten it. She let out a small grumble.

"I need to go home and change," she said. "And I need to feed myself and my cats before my shift at work."

I forgot it was the weekend, the busiest time for the museum. It'd be hard to keep an eye on Lenore while she was working all day.

"Can you take personal leave?" I asked. "Just until this all passes over."

"Absolutely not," she exclaimed. "Francis would have my

head for that. I just got this promotion; I can't take time off now."

Her eyes were narrowed on me, her nose wrinkled a little bit.

Lenore Calder was the biggest challenge I had faced, but there had never been a challenge I couldn't overcome.

My hand ran through my hair, pushing it back. A deep sigh escaped my lips.

"I'll figure something out," I muttered to myself. I didn't have time to argue with her before she needed to be at work. I had far too much to get done, and I could tell she was growing impatient to leave and head to work.

"I'll come with you," I offered. "I can make your breakfast while you get dressed and ready for work. It'll save you time."

Practical excuse to keep a close eye on her.

"Let's go," she said and turned toward the front door, leaving the house and letting the door close right in my face.

I followed her out to the car, a small blue two door convertible. I had to duck and contort myself to fit into the car, my height a hindrance.

Len drove through town like she hadn't been in a car in years. I held tight to the handle of the door as she took a corner quickly. I'd participated in car chases, following criminals, that felt less dangerous.

"Next time, I drive," I said, swallowing hard.

"It's not that bad," she insisted.

"You almost just hit that curb," I pointed out.

"Well, I don't drive often. I can walk everywhere in Briarport. And Jake never-" She stopped herself. "I'm just rusty, that's it."

"Rusty," I agreed, my stomach turning with both nausea and guilt.

We made it back to her apartment in minutes and I followed her inside and upstairs. She kept glancing around, like someone might be following us.

It wasn't a possibility I dismissed. I hadn't seen anyone tailing us, and nothing outside told me anyone was watching the building, but I kept my guard up.

We made it inside her apartment without running into Mallory. I wished Len would stop worrying so much about what her friend wanted and more about her safety.

She hurried to the bedroom, and I heard meows of morning greetings. I found my way to her fridge and opened it, trying to find something I could put together for her.

There were no eggs, eliminating my first idea on what to make. Between her freezer and fridge, I found some berries, which I washed and put into a bowl, and some frozen waffles, which I toasted and added butter to. It was nothing gourmet, but it would do.

She came back out to find the small array of food and nodded a thanks to me. "Is there caffeine?" she asked.

Shit, I'd forgotten the coffee.

"I can make some now," I offered.

"Don't bother. It would just make me late," she said, her voice sounding a bit panicked.

I really messed up.

I had to fix this. "I'll grab your coffee from the café across the street from the museum. You just focus on getting there on time," I assured her.

What was I doing? I had things I needed to do for the case.

I was operating on borrowed time; the FBI could end things in seconds.

"Fine," she said.

I walked with her in silence. She barely acknowledged me as we parted ways, and I headed for the café across the street while she made her way inside the museum.

I ordered two lattes, hoping she had similar taste when it came to caffeine.

Why did the idea of Lenore enjoying the same drink make my heart speed up a little?

The drinks were ready in no time, and I found straws, which I grabbed for both of us. I carried them across the street and watched as tourists meandered into the museum. It had only been open minutes, and it was already busy.

My phone buzzed in my pocket.

"Hello?" I answered, forgetting to check the caller ID before I picked up.

"Winston!" Lyla squealed through the phone.

"Hey, Lyla," I said, a smile spreading on my face.

It'd been only days since I spoke with her last, but I was enjoying finding my way back to what felt like normal after so long.

"You will never believe it," she said, and I could hear the pride in her voice through the phone.

"What?" I asked, my heart swelling with happiness.

"I looked into Briarport, since I knew you would be staying there for your case for a bit," she said. "And they have bagel shop just like Don's!" She practically screamed the last part into my ear.

"I will have to check it out. What's it called?" I asked.

"Seaside Café," she answered. "A very obvious name, if

you ask me, but it looks like it is right in the center of town. Have you seen it?"

"I have not, but I promise I will report back the second I try it," I said and meant it.

There was little I wouldn't do for my sister. Every piece of me was dedicated to protecting her innocence, encouraging her curious mind. If she kept on the path she was on, she'd surpass me in no time.

An idea started to form in my head as I walked toward the museum. "I unfortunately have to go, but tell Mom I said hi," I said.

"I will," she said and hung up.

I spotted Len's boss standing nearby as I entered.

I gave a friendly smile toward Francis, who hurried over.

"You're the one from the other day looking for Lenore," she said, quickly remembering who I was.

"I was," I admitted.

"Are you back again to distract her?" she asked, raising a brow. Her tone told me she didn't approve of me disrupting her best employee more than once.

"I'm actually in town working on a project for the FBI," I said to Francis.

I saw the interest peak in her eyes, but she kept her face stoic. "And how can we help you with that?" she asked. "You are welcome to request any of our records."

"The project is a little more extensive than that. I was hoping you might be able to lend me someone who is familiar with the town and its recordkeeping, someone who could help me with research outside the museum."

"I'm not sure about that. We're very busy," she started.

"I completely understand. The FBI would never ask if it weren't important."

Her arms folded, and she bit the inside of her cheek.

"Once this project is finished, it'll be national news," I went on. "And I couldn't think of a more worthy establishment to share credit with."

I knew from the little Len had told me about Francis exactly what words to say to play into her self-interest. Francis valued the museum above all else, and the more prestige it found, the more satisfied she was.

"National news?" she asked.

"Certainly," I said and shrugged. "Any research or project the FBI is doing is going to catch the attention of national news." I relaxed my shoulders and let my arms settle by my sides. I kept my features trained to be uninterested, like it was no big deal.

"And you would just need someone from the museum's help? And we would receive part of the credit?" she asked, and I could tell her full attention was now on me.

Too easy.

"Yes, I was hoping I could work with whoever your best is. That is, aside from you, of course. I know the museum can't function without you here," I said, giving her a large smile.

I watched the older woman's cheeks turn a slight pink. "Well, then Lenore, who you spoke to the other day, would be our next best," she said.

"Perfect. It's settled," I said. "I'll let Len know myself."

I left Francis standing with a smug grin on her face. The temptation of the museum making national headlines was far too great for her to resist.

I made my way through the museum, looking for the

familiar golden brown skin and long curls. The place wasn't big, but it did take me a few minutes to find her. She was tucked into the back corner of the museum, dusting off a plaque.

One of the best researchers, and these were the things Francis had her doing. I found my fist clenched and relaxed my hands, not realizing I'd let the thought take over for a moment. Len had a beautiful mind, and it was a waste to have her cleaning up the exhibits all day.

"Here is your caffeine," I said, holding out the iced latte to her.

"Thanks," she murmured. She turned back to what she was doing, dusting with one hand and holding the latte with the other.

After a moment, she turned and noted me still there. "Why are you still here?" she asked.

"Francis said I could borrow you for the case," I said.

She let out a slight chuckle. "There is no way you convinced Francis to let me out of this place," she said.

I shrugged, and her eyes widened when I didn't turn and leave.

"You didn't seriously convince her?" she asked, raising a brow.

"Thanks to you, I knew exactly how," I answered. "Now, let's go. We have a lot of work to do." I turned to leave and hoped she'd follow. I continued walking without checking behind me and made it outside before I paused to make sure she had.

Len hurried after me, leaving the museum, her blue skirt blowing as the wind picked up. She gathered her loose curls and pulled them back into a loose bun. Without them blowing into her face, I noticed the way her deep brown eyes had a golden tone to them. The bright sun highlighted it, and it was hard to look away.

"Francis seriously allowed you to borrow me to work on this case?" she asked hesitantly.

"She doesn't know what case you're working on, just that the FBI has research that'll be national news."

Len almost choked on her latte. "She's probably going to kill you," Len pointed out.

"Then she better hope the Coastal Killer doesn't first," I answered.

I turned to lead her to where we were heading next. I'd memorized all the streets and locations in town off a map I printed before coming. I had a perfect memory, so there wasn't any detail I couldn't recall after studying it.

The local sheriff was my first planned stop, to get it out of the way and hope no one there contacted anyone else at the FBI.

My stomach sank, thinking about the lies I had to spin.

Lenore trailed behind me, finishing the rest of her latte before we made it to the sheriff's office.

The building was an old brick establishment, the small sign out front marking it. It didn't surprise me that the town didn't have the resources to handle a serial killer on their own. I headed for the door but realized Len had stopped walking, instead staring at the building.

"Are you coming?" I asked.

"I-" she hesitated. The last time she dealt with the same deputies was likely the day she was attacked.

"I can go," I said, unwilling to push her.

"I want to help," she said. "It's just…what if they recognize me?"

It would've been the same deputies who found her brutally attacked and mutilated. I'd read the report; I knew how unrecognizable she was when they found her.

"I don't blame you if you want to stay out here, but I promise you, none of them will know who you are. When they found you, there was swelling to your face and your hair was dyed a different color three years ago."

She took a tiny step closer. Without thinking, I held out my hand, and she looked at it for a moment before taking it.

Her skin was warm and her palm smooth.

I gave her a gentle, reassuring squeeze and held her hand as I pulled open the door and led her through.

She let go the moment she stepped inside.

That was all I got, a few seconds before she went back to putting up her walls.

I watched her shift uncomfortably, glancing around. I spotted a front desk with a woman behind it.

"Can I help you?" she quickly asked.

I pulled out the wallet I carried with my badge inside and flipped it open. I held it up to show her.

"I was hoping to speak to whoever was in charge of the Coastal Killer case three years ago."

11

—————

LENNY

I SHIFTED UNCOMFORTABLY, standing slightly behind Agent Beck. The woman at the front desk encouraged us to take a seat while she went to find if one of the deputies in charge was in.

We found two seats off to the side and sat down. Beck seemed quieter, more anxious than usual. Maybe I was projecting my own anxiety onto him.

The woman disappeared behind a locked metal door, the only one in and out of the rest of the building. While we waited, a few more people trailed in. I heard a couple murmuring about a car break in. I tried to focus on them instead of obsessively worrying about the chance someone could recognize me.

I tapped my foot, unable to stop myself.

"Agent Beck," the woman called out, reappearing from the door. "Come with me."

He stood and made his way towards the door while I remain seated. Beck froze and turned back to me.

"Are you coming?" he asked.

It hadn't crossed my mind I'd even be able to join. I quickly stood and trailed behind him, unwilling to wait alone in the lobby.

The backside of the station was far different. There were a few desks and cubicles spread across a middle space. Larger offices lined the space, and I read the plaques outside each door as we passed, realizing they were for deputies who worked their way up the chain.

The woman led us to a room with a single door and window. By the time I made it inside, I realized the window was one way glass, so we couldn't see back out of the room. She motioned for us to sit at the two chairs pulled up to the table.

Why did I suddenly feel like I was the one being interrogated? We came to find more information on the case, but I couldn't help that anxiety snaking its way through me, the voice telling me over and over that they know what I did. It was unforgivable; I barely could forgive myself for it.

I'd been weak, and I let someone else control me.

"You alright?" Beck asked softly, his eyes studying me.

I hated that he did that, knew everything about me with a single glance. At the same time, it made my cheeks warm.

"I'm fine," I said weakly.

Someone quickly knocked on the door and entered. An older gentleman with a round belly stepped inside. His face looked aged by the job.

"I'm Sheriff Graham," he said. "How can I help you?" His beady eyes glanced over us both and settled on Beck.

"Are you the one who was in charge of the Coastal Killer case?" Beck asked.

"I was one of them," he affirmed. "But that was a bit ago."

"I was hoping you tell a little more about the case," Beck pushed.

I sat quietly and folded my hands on the table. I was far too nervous to chime in.

"There's not much to tell beyond what's already in the case file, which the FBI should already have," he said. "Although, I wouldn't put it past you bureaucrats to have lost things."

I caught the scoff at the end of his sentence. His eyes remained fully on Beck, ignoring me.

Beck barely flinched at his words, but I caught the slight shift in his leg under the table. It moved ever so slightly closer toward me, like he was protecting me.

I was imagining it. I had to be. Had I really become that desperate for someone to give a shit about me?

"Yes, I've read the file, and I do think there are some holes in it. We're missing a statement from the local deputy in charge of the case, for instance," Beck started. "We also seem to be missing statements from those who work at the bar each victim visited before they were killed. It would seem the first team to look this case over completely missed that detail."

I could tell Beck was watching the way the sheriff reacted, gauging how much of a help he would be to us. Graham's brows furrowed, and he narrowed his eyes, his nose flaring.

"My deputies did not miss anything. If there were things overlooked, then that's on the FBI."

I caught the way Beck swallowed hard, like the accusation got under his skin. It still baffled me that not a single person put it together before. The High Tide Pub was clearly a hunting ground for whatever vile person killed all these women.

Beck cleared his throat. "That's why I'm here, to make sure the FBI doesn't miss anything this time."

"It's a cold case, so why bother?" Sheriff Graham said.

"Doesn't matter. The FBI needs a completed case file," he said, his voice steady with patience.

The sheriff's eyes flicked over to me. "Why is she here?" he asked, and I heard the disapproving tone.

I opened my mouth to answer but fell short of words.

"She," Beck started firmly, "is here as a supervisory agent. I expect you to treat her with the same respect." Beck leaned forward, his elbows on the table. Graham stood over us, trying to maintain some semblance of authority and power over us. I tried to keep my face neutral, his eyes bearing into me.

"Is something wrong?" Beck asked, raising a brow.

At this point, he was just pushing him to see how far he'd allow. I felt myself turning into pure heat, a mix of frustration and embarrassment filling me. I wanted as little attention as possible, and now, Beck made that impossible. No one had recognized me, but that didn't mean I was safe yet.

"My apologies," he muttered. "What do you need? I can grab whatever it is so you can be on your way."

I finally let myself breathe.

"What can you tell us about the case? You're the one who was in charge, correct?" Beck asked.

"I can tell you the case is a waste of time. There's no reason to waste more time and research looking for a killer who completely vanished," he grumbled.

My frustration and embarrassment slowly melted into

anger. This was the person in charge of protecting our town, and he was treating this case like it was nothing. If he wouldn't find justice for the victims, who would?

"I disagree," Beck stated, and I turned to listen. "There's still a serial killer out there. They're worth catching."

"You can keep wasting tax payor dollars," the sheriff groaned. "But this is my department, and I won't help. You can have whatever records you want to look at, that's all."

"Fine. We will take the final case file your station has," Beck said. "And then we will be on our way."

That was it? We'd gone through all this just to access a few records the FBI likely already had?

"I'll grab you the file," the sheriff said and turned away.

"And pull any files on other crimes that took place at the pub," I cut in before the sheriff could go.

"Excuse me?" he said, turning back.

I took a deep breath, pushing my shoulders back as I raised my chin. "If you missed the connection about the pub. I want to be sure we didn't miss anything else," I said as evenly as I could.

I watched the small movement from his nose and knew I'd struck a chord.

"Do you know how many calls we get from that place? Every little bar fight or unpaid tab," he hissed.

I shrugged. "I still would like to look at them all. Pull anything from the time the Coastal Killer was actively killing," I said. "Actually, make that a few months prior to the killing starting."

I gave him a sickly sweet smile, and the sheriff looked to Beck, but he refused to give him the satisfaction of undermining me.

"Fine; it's going to be a bit," he muttered and left the room.

As he walked out, I noticed the slight limp he had as he walked. I folded my arms and sat back, glaring at Beck.

"What?" he asked, raising his brows.

"Supervisory Agent?" I asked.

"I wasn't going to let him treat you like that," he muttered.

"I didn't want any attention on me," I pointed out.

"The way he was looking at you! The man was clearly stuck in the past with his outdated views," Beck grumbled, clearly flustered.

"It didn't give you the right to decide for me," I said.

He held my gaze, opening his mouth, but then closed it. "You're right," he said. "Sorry."

I half expected a fight. Jake never would've let something like this go. If I spoke my mind or opinions, they were wrong. Jake decided what was best for me.

That's not me anymore.

"Thank you," I said, surprising myself. I let my arms relax and leaned back in the chair, waiting for the sheriff to return. It was hard to let my guard down and accept help when I'd been doing everything on my own for three years.

A while passed without seeing the sheriff, and I was growing more and more anxious by the second. My leg bounced, and I couldn't help the way I found anything to fidget with. My hair, my skirt, the silver rings on my fingers—anything I could touch, I couldn't leave alone.

Something stopped my leg from bouncing, and I looked down to find Beck's hand on my thigh. Instantly, heat filled my body, and I lost every word in my head. His touch made me feel safe and alive all at once. The reality of that crashed into me like a wave.

I met his gaze as he lifted his eyes to meet mine.

"I'm sorry," he said. "I just know sometimes, it can snap you back from spiraling." He looked way and pulled his hand back. "At least it works for me. I figured it was worth trying..."

It was so matter of fact, like I was one of his cases to analyze. Maybe I was. My past was tangled in this, after all. Was that how he viewed me? Just another piece to the puzzle?

He had moved without hesitation, and with such careful calculation. It was nothing more, just Beck trying to stop my anxiety from giving myself away. I kept telling myself over and over it meant nothing.

I almost started to believe it when the sheriff finally came back.

"Here's what you asked for," he said after making us wait close to almost an hour. He tossed a folder on to the table, hundreds of printed sheets tucked inside. "That's everything we have and the FBI should already know, plus the incidents *she* asked for," he sneered.

Beck pulled the folder to him and opened it. I watched him quickly look through a few and close the folder again.

"Thank you for your help," he said and stood. "We will be back if we need anything else."

He moved around the table, and I followed. We brushed past the sheriff, leaving him with a dumbfounded frown on his face.

I hurried behind Beck back out into the scorching summer heat. He continued through the town without stopping for even a moment. I kept close, but my legs were tired, and my adrenaline was wearing off.

"Wait up," I huffed out.

He froze and turned, realizing he was leaving me in the dust. I caught up beside him, walking next to him.

"You know you could've been anything you wanted with a mind like yours, so why the museum?" he asked, and I was taken aback by the directness.

"I like the museum," I defended, my lips turning downward.

"I know. I just meant, what calls you there? From what I can tell, you aren't here just for family, and Francis treats you like nothing more than a helping hand. Why not see the world? Start your own research?"

I kept my eyes glued to the sidewalk. "I can't leave yet."

"Why not?" he pushed.

"Because I owe it to them," I sighed.

I found the pockets of my midi skirt and stuck my hands in them, ashamed. I knew I could start over anywhere I wanted, but I just couldn't convince myself to leave yet, not when there still was no justice. Not when I would spend every day looking over my own shoulder, terrified to be alive.

"To whom?" Beck asked softly.

I knew he already had the answer before even asking. His mind worked faster than anyone I knew.

"The other victims. The ones who weren't so lucky," I whispered.

I never spoke of myself as one of them. It was a piece of me I had shoved deep down for so long.

"I know the feeling," Beck said gently, and I glanced up.

His eyes were distant, filled with a deep sorrow, but I

didn't push. Instead, I walked beside him in silence the rest of the way to his place.

My phone started vibrating in the purse I carried, breaking the long, drawn out silence.

I pulled it out but didn't recognize the number on the screen. My worry got the better of me, and I answered, hoping it was not Francis searching for where I'd gone or retracting her agreement to let me help.

"This is Lenore," I answered in a polite tone I barely recognized.

The voice that came through the phone was muffled and robotic. "Stop searching, or you will regret it."

"Who is this?" I asked, my stomach sinking.

Agent Beck stopped in his tracks and watched me with careful precision. I saw the worry wash over his face, and he motioned for me to put it on speaker, which I quickly did.

"If you don't quit now, the killing will start again," the voiced answered, and the call cut short.

"Wait-"

It was too late. They'd already hung up.

My stomach sank, and I barely registered my hands slipping the phone back into my purse. It was the second threat, two days in a row. Reality started to wash over me, knowing the home I'd built and life I'd pieced together was no longer safe.

They were back, and I couldn't do anything about it.

"You're staying at my rental," Beck said firmly.

"No-" I started.

"Don't argue with me, Lenny," he said, cutting me off.

I'd never heard his voice turn so serious. I met his gaze and saw his worry.

"No one calls me Lenny," I answered in a low tone, holding his stare.

It was the only thing I could think to say. Realistically, trying to get him in and out of my apartment without Mal seeing would be near impossible. The couch was much smaller than the one at his rental, and all the work we'd begun was with him.

It's the logical choice.

I knew earlier, he'd only been obliging my hesitancy by being kind, but now, the threat seemed far too real, and his tone suggested there was not room for argument.

Beck knew better than anyone how quickly these threats could turn to reality. I had to trust him, to let someone in for once, to allow them to help.

"Birdie and Alonzo are coming too then," I said stubbornly.

If I'm abandoning my apartment, I'm doing it on my terms.

"I'm pretty sure my rental agreement said no pets allowed in the house," Beck noted.

"You actually read over that thing?" I asked, raising a brow.

I'd stayed in plenty of rental houses for trips, but never once did I actually read what I agreed to when I checked those tiny boxes.

"Read and memorized," he said without a second thought.

"Why am I not surprised?" I said, shaking my head with a soft laugh.

12

―――――

STONE

"Keys," I said, holding out my hand.

We'd taken an unexpected detour back to Len's apartment.

I tried not to show how much the call had shaken me. A trained FBI agent should have a better handle on his emotions, be able to put aside how he feels and act rationally in the face of a threat. Instead, my mind was racing, and I hadn't stopped replaying the call.

Len was packing to stay with me until I was able to say with certainty her apartment was safe again. I was not taking no for an answer.

Fine. Maybe I would have, because I wasn't going to kidnap her and keep her hostage.

But I would have fought with everything I had to convince her to change her mind. I was thankful when she'd barely argued. It was almost too easy, but I saw the way Len's face paled at the call. Whether she'd admit it or not, it'd gotten to her as well.

Len poked her head out of the room and tossed keys at me. I barely had time to register it and catch them.

She ushered her cats into little carriers she had for them. I picked up one and realized I was carrying Birdie. She meowed up at me, and I gave her a slight smile. No one could convince me cats weren't too smart for their own good.

It didn't take long before we were back at Len's car. This time, I had the keys and jumped into the driver's seat before she could protest. She safely placed both cats in the backseat and made sure they were secure. I heard her mutter something about my driving skills to the felines before she put her seat back up and join me in the front.

I drove through town, and it took us a bit longer to get to the rental, having to sit in the small town's tourist traffic. It was Saturday, which meant many tourists were leaving and just as many were coming into town.

Len kept tapping her fingers on the center console at every stop, the small sound pulling my attention away from the road. I tried to drown it out, but I couldn't ignore her growing anxiety.

It worked once before, which meant it could work again.

I reached out to place my right hand on hers. "We'll find them," I promised her.

"You can't possibly know that," she said.

"I have an IQ higher than anyone else in the FBI. I've won more awards than any other agent my age and have been on more cases. I memorize every fact I see and read. So listen to me when I promise you, we will find them. I won't leave until I do," I assured her.

Her fingers stopped fidgeting under my touch, and after a second, she pulled her hand away. I let her. It had only been to calm her down, an easy strategy used to bring someone back to reality, nothing more.

We sat in silence the rest of the ride until we made it to the rental house.

More colorful flowers bloomed in the front yard, and I watched Len stare out into the back as she got out of the car. I could hear the waves crashing against the cliffside.

"You coming?" I asked Len, her eyes distant as she stared out into the water.

"In a second," she said softly.

I followed her gaze and watched the waves as they rolled. Salty air reached us easily this close, its presence somehow calming. Off to the left, I spotted a tall, white lighthouse in my peripheral vision. I hadn't noticed it the first day, but I'd also been distracted when I arrived.

Len's movement snapped my attention back to her. She grabbed the cats out of the back of the convertible and made her way toward the house. I grabbed the large duffel bag she packed and carried it inside.

"You can take the room, and I'll stay in the living room," I offered.

She looked like she was about to argue but decided against it. Dark half circles sat under her eyes, and I noticed just how worn down she'd become. Len barely got any sleep the night before, and I dragged her around town. Beyond that, she must've been mentally exhausted. The Coastal Killer was back, and the killing would most likely start again.

My gut clenched, remembering just how gruesome and gory each kill had been the first time around. Most of the victims were left cut to bits, barely recognizable, and a ring shoved down their throat.

I'd seen some horrible things in the field, but this, by far, was one of the worst.

I carried Len's bag up to the room and quickly packed my stuff into my suitcase to bring back downstairs with me. Len walked into the room behind me.

"Why don't you rest?" I suggested. "You didn't sleep well."

"It's the middle of the day," she argued. "And I need to get Birdie and Alonzo set up."

She packed items for the two cats still in the trunk of the convertible.

"I'll grab everything and make sure they're all set," I assured her.

She sat down on the bed and looked as though she might fall asleep sitting up. "All right," she conceded. "I'll rest for an hour, and then I'll come back to help."

I closed the door on my way out, leaving her to relax. I wasn't worried about her helping for the rest of the day. There was plenty I could start on my own, and realistically, I didn't need a new partner.

There was just something about Len...

She was nothing like Blythe; the pair was almost complete opposites. Yet, somehow, I knew if my partner were still alive, she would've loved Len.

My heart twinged at the sharp pain of the memory. I found myself glancing down at my hands covered in red.

It wasn't real...

I shook my head, trying to push out the memory.

It didn't take long for me to get everything set up for the two cats, as well as for myself in the living room. Hours passed, and when Len didn't re-emerge, I started shifting through the papers the sheriff had given us, memorizing every little detail of the case and the reports Len had asked for.

Close to 9:00, Len appeared from the room.

"You let me sleep too long," she accused, rubbing her eyes.

"You needed rest," I pointed out.

She pursed her lips and walked to the kitchen. When she returned, she held a makeshift sandwich she managed to whip up with what little groceries I had. I realized I hadn't eaten at all and quickly hurried to the kitchen to find something for myself.

I should've made food for us both.

I settled on a basic salad and returned to the living room. Len sat in an armchair, her legs pulled in close. She'd already finished the sandwich, flipping through a book she found on the shelf beside the chair.

I could've watched her read all night long.

"I can feel you staring," she said without looking up from the book.

"I like that one," I said, recognizing the title and trying to find a valid excuse.

"I'm only three pages in," Len said. She closed the book and stood, eyes avoiding mine. "If there's nothing to help with tonight, I'm going to read this in bed."

"Do you need anything?" I asked gently.

I knew it was loaded question.

She shook her head. "Goodnight, Beck," she said quickly.

Before she passed the couch where I sat to head up the stairs, I reached out and caught her arm. "Stone," I said for the first time in months.

"What?"

"You don't have to call me Agent Beck," I said. "You can call me Stone."

"Shit!" Len yelled.

I came rushing into the kitchen to find her staring at her phone. It'd been a few days of Len staying in the rental with me, and I'd grown accustomed to her presence. The first day or two was hard; I wasn't used to sharing a space with someone else.

Blythe would've teased me about it.

Most nights, I stayed up as long as possible before falling asleep, afraid to subject Len to the nightmares. They were unpredictable, and I needed to get a handle on them.

"What's wrong?" I breathed out, realizing my panic was for nothing as she held up her phone.

"I have to have dinner with my family tonight," she grumbled.

"Your parents are in town," I recalled. She'd told me a few days prior—it was part of what had been bothering her that first meeting.

"Yes," she sighed.

"And you have to go to your brother's tonight?" I asked.

She nodded.

Not the crisis I expected to find. I could fix this. It couldn't be that hard, right?

"I could come with you," I offered.

What was I doing?

"No, you don't have to do that," she said, but I saw the

hopeful gleam in her eyes. How could I turn that down? It'd be cruel.

"I'm happy to," I said. "Parents love me."

"You've met lots?" she asked, raising a brow.

It was a test, an easy one. I aced every test I took, and this would be no different.

"No," I answered, watching as she physically relaxed. She tried to hide the cues, but she couldn't from me. "It's just what every man seems to say in this scenario, and a lot of studies show, manifesting success helps you achieve it."

She rolled her eyes. "My parents aren't some statistic you can so easily win over to your side."

"I know, but I'm willing to try. To win them over, that is," I answered.

She folded her arms and leaned back against the kitchen counter. "Fine. We need to get ready now then."

"What time are we meeting them?" I asked, noticing it was only 2:00 p.m.

"At 6:00, but I need to make sure there is nothing my mother can possibly comment on," she huffed and hurried out of the kitchen, going upstairs to the room she'd been using.

A couple hours later, Len emerged from her room; I'd been ready for a while. My suitcase didn't hold many options, but I managed to find a pair of slacks and a short sleeve button down I deemed fit for the occasion.

Len rounded the corner, and I nearly choked on the water I'd been sipping.

She'd pinned half of her hair out of her face, but her long, brown curls still fell over her shoulders, the thin straps of her black dress hidden under them.

The dress she wore hugged her torso, showing every curve of her body. It flowed only a little away from her at her hips. The deep v of the neck showed off a necklace she wore, a little charm on it with a letter. The longer I stared, I realized it was an M.

Not M for Jake. Perhaps for Mallory.

"What's wrong?" Len asked, looking concerned.

"Nothing," I said. "You look beautiful."

Her eyes avoided mine, and she clasped her hands in front of her. "You don't have to say that. I'm sure my mother will find something wrong with it all."

I closed the distance between us, standing inches away from her. I needed her to hear me. The only way I could possibly do that was to make sure I had her attention. It was as simple as that.

I tipped her chin to meet my gaze again. My fingers barely brushed against her skin, but I could feel how warm it was.

"Lenore Calder, hear me when I say, you are stunning, and nothing she says will change that." I dropped my hand and backed away.

Len bit the inside of her cheek, and I saw the way her eyes lingered on me, only to look away.

"We should go," I said quickly. "We don't want to be late."

I calculated exactly how long it would take to get to Calvin's house, leaving enough time to be on the earlier side. I knew how nervous Len was to see her parents and brother, and this was one tangible way I could help alleviate some of that.

She nodded and grabbed her purse from the kitchen counter. On our way out, I caught Lenore pausing in front of the mirror hanging next to the door. I studied her features, the way she intensely looked over her herself. It was like she was seeing herself for the first time—not in the way Jake had seen her, and not for all the flaws her mother pointed out.

"Thank you," she whispered, barely audible as she tore her eyes from the mirror.

I nodded and led her out to my rental car. I held the door open for her and then hurried to the driver's seat.

The drive took exactly the amount of time I'd calculated, and we arrived five minutes before Calvin had told Lenore to be there. We pulled up the narrow driveway to the small, yellow, colonial-style house.

I turned to Len and saw her swallow hard. Quickly, I got out of my car and made my way to the other side. I pulled open the door and saw Len hesitate.

I held out my hand to her. "Ready?"

She stared at it for a second before she grabbed it.

13

LENNY

Dinner was already chaos.

Eloise rushed to get everything finished in the kitchen while my brother entertained my parents. His eyes lit up when he saw me walk through the door, a new distraction for them to focus on. He frowned when he saw Stone following behind me.

Before I could introduce him, he brushed by me and held out a hand to my brother.

"Winston Beck," he said, shaking my brother's hand firmly.

I caught the confused look on my father's face and the raised brow from my mother.

It was going to be a long night.

"You didn't tell us you were bringing your..." my mother started. "Boyfriend?"

"He's not my boyfriend," I said quickly. "He's my-"

"Partner," Stone said, rescuing me.

"Same thing," my mother said, waving a hand at him and dismissing the comment. "Come in, come in. Calvin, stop making them just stand there," she scolded, and my brother hurried off to the kitchen, passing her attention to me.

"Winston, these are my parents, Zuri and Joseph."

Before he could move, my mother hurried toward me. I saw her glance over my outfit as she closed in for a hug. "You look smaller than the last I saw you," she said. "Overworking yourself again?"

"No," I muttered.

Already, I could feel her eyes raking me over, looking for every little flaw she could find. It was never enough for her. My mother demanded perfection, and I had yet to achieve that for her.

I felt Stone move closer, almost protectively.

Taking the protection thing a bit far?

The Coastal Killer, sure. Fine. I knew I needed his help with that. But my mother was a whole different issue, one I was well equipped to handle on my own.

"And your curls are falling flat," she said, brushing a hand over my hair.

"I don't have the same curls as you," I reminded her. Hers were tighter, more coiled compared to my own.

"If you just used the right product-"

"Stone, this is my father," I said, brushing past my mother and cutting her off. I sat Winston beside my father on Calvin's short couch in his living room. Before my mother could fawn over me anymore, I found my way to the kitchen to check on Eloise and find beverages.

"Sorry we didn't make it to visit yesterday," Eloise said the moment she saw me. "I wasn't feeling great after brunch."

"That's alright," I answered, having already forgot my call with my mother.

"Here," Calvin said as he handed me two beers. I caught the look on his face. The *you need this more than us* look.

"Thanks," I said and made my way back, afraid to leave Winston with my parents alone.

"Only five more minutes, I promise," Eloise called frantically after me.

I found Winston and my dad laughing together while my mom watched patiently from an armchair. My father had Winston deep in stories of when he was in the military, ones I heard a million times growing up.

I held out the beer to Winston.

"I'm all set," he said politely.

"Are you sure?" I asked, raising a brow.

"I actually don't drink," he said, his voice trailing off a bit.

"Oh," I said. "I didn't know."

My face warmed, and I took a nervous step back.

"I'll take it," my father offered as he grabbed the bottle from me quickly.

I'd been living with him for days. How had I not realized?

There was a bottle of scotch sitting right on his counter, but now that I thought about it, the bottle had definitely never been opened. The amber liquid filled the bottle to the brim.

It was probably one of Nelson's bottles, and I'd just assumed it belonged to Stone. I winced quietly, taking a seat in another armchair across from the couch.

"How did you two meet?" my mother asked, unable to contain her nosiness.

"Work," I said shortly. I didn't need to go down this path with them. If they knew what we were researching together, my mother would have a fit, and my father would take her side. It was the same as every argument I'd ever had with them.

"You work at the museum?" my mother pushed.

"No," I answered before Stone could. I cast him a quick glare to let him know I had this handled. His eyes looked pleading back, like he couldn't help himself from wanting to jump in, to protect me.

Seriously, Len, you're imagining it.

The longer I stayed with him, the more I thought the little touches and comments were becoming personal. I kept telling myself it was in my head. I was there for my safety, that was it. I'd help him solve the cold case and move on. He had to return to Virginia when the case was finished. There was no chance he thought of me beyond just another resource.

"Stone is here for research," I started. "I'm helping him."

His head turned back to me at the sound of his name. He tilted it, and I could feel his gaze pouring into me.

Shit, I needed dinner to be right now.

The way his eyes pushed through every wall I put up, I couldn't stand it much longer before I-

"Dinner!" Eloise called out, saving me.

I stood fast and hurried to the dining room. The others trailed behind me, and we all found seats around the table, Stone sitting beside me.

Dinner wasn't as painful as I expected. My father had both Stone and my brother chuckling through most of it, my mother keeping any comments to herself. I even made an effort to catch up with her, asking about work and her recent trips. It'd been awhile since I'd visited home.

I felt Stone glancing in my direction a few times, but I

tried hard not to glance up. Instead, I focused on eating the delicious pasta Eloise had worked so hard on.

"Dinner is fantastic, Eloise," Stone said.

I watched a smile grow, pride beaming from her, my brother's eyes falling on his wife with adoration. In the entire time they'd been together, there was never a second I doubted they were meant to be. They were one of those couples you just knew would get married.

Something I would never have.

I strived to find what they had. I thought I found it with Jake, but the more controlling he became, the faster I realized it was far different. Manipulation wasn't love.

"You alright?" Stone breathed the question so quiet, I barely caught it.

I nodded.

"Where'd you go?" he asked.

"Somewhere I never want to be again," I whispered back.

We finished through dinner with barely any leftovers to spare. No one was surprised; Eloise was a fantastic cook. If she hadn't found success in marketing, I was convinced she would've been a chef. Maybe in another life.

The polite and typical chatter continued, and I tried to join in where I could. It was hard when my mind kept wandering. Three years, I had distanced myself; did I really even know them anymore? It felt almost wrong to laugh at their new stories or pretend like I'd known what they had been dong the past few years.

I avoided seeing them in person as much as I could. I didn't want them to see how broken their daughter was. Calvin could spot a mile away how burnt out I was getting.

"Should we have dessert?" Eloise asked.

"I am so full, I don't know if I have the appetite," my dad chuckled.

"I think we should have dessert," Calvin pushed, and I heard the nerves there.

Strange.

I felt Stone shift beside me, and I knew he picked up on it too. My parents were oblivious to the change in the room. My brother hurried off behind his wife, helping her grab whatever they had planned.

"We will be coming back again for the clambake at the end of the month!" my mother exclaimed, cutting the tension.

"Will you still be here?" my dad asked Stone.

He looked shocked for only a moment before training his face back to its usual thoughtful disposition. "There is a good chance I will be," he admitted.

Part of me filled with relief.

Stop it.

I couldn't think like that. It had been only two weeks, and already, I was letting my judgement be clouded by Stone's protection. It had become a comfort. A comfort, nothing more.

You can't become reliant on him. He will leave. Everyone always leaves.

Jake left. My brother left when he had Eloise to take care of. Never once did I blame him for that, but I knew I'd far outstayed my welcome. My parents left. They never once noticed the signs, the desperate pleas for help at what my life had become.

My brother and his wife returned to the room carrying a cake. They walked side by side, Eloise with a large smile growing the closer she got.

My mom continued to go on about the logistics for the clambake; where they'd stay, all of us going together. I lost track of the noise as they got closer. My anxiety started to sink in.

I couldn't place it.

There was no occasion to celebrate. Perhaps being together for the first time in a while was a celebration, but I knew my brother well enough to know he wouldn't buy a cake for just that.

He placed the cake on the table, and I caught sight of writing on the top.

I had to lean forward in my seat to read it fully, my heart stopping as I gazed over the words. Those four small words should mean the world, four words that would change everything for the better.

Why did I feel so much sadness creeping in?

Stone finished reading the message at the same time as I did.

"Congratulations," he said with a sincere smile.

I tried to force the word out of my mouth, but it fell short.

My parents were still caught up in the details of their next visit and barely took notice of the cake. Calvin and Eloise stared nervously at them, waiting for them to see it. A few seconds passed before Calvin cleared his throat awkwardly.

My mother stopped mid-sentence and glanced to them. They still stood together at the head of the table, watching us all. Her eyes fell to the cake and lit up with delight as she finally saw the four words.

Baby Calder Coming Soon.

I read them again as she did and felt that sinking pit

inside of me grow. I should be happy, over the moon for them, but instead, all I felt was emptiness, a growing darkness threatening to consume me.

Stone gave me a worried glance, but I ignored it.

I should've known he'd see even the slightest change. He missed nothing. It was so annoyingly charming and inconvenient at the same time.

"This is wonderful news," my mother said, practically jumping from her seat.

"Congratulations," my father chimed in and stood to shake my brother's hand.

They'd be the perfect grandparents. I'd always known it. It pained my heart deeply that I could never be the one to give that to them, not after everything that happened.

I stood along with them and gave Eloise and Calvin quick hugs, feeling myself turn more and more numb to my surroundings. Sound was becoming a fuzzy haze, and my heartbeat started pounding louder in my ears.

Stone placed a gentle hand on my shoulder. "Are you okay?" he whispered, leaning in close enough for only us to hear.

"I just need to use the bathroom-" The words barely made it out before I started moving. "Excuse me," I added politely before leaving the room.

My parents and brother barely noticed, all caught in conversation about the newest member of the family.

I could barely breathe, my chest feeling tighter. I needed air. Any air.

The view of the front door was obscured from the dining room, and I headed straight for it instead of down the hall to the bathroom. I slipped outside, barely making a sound with the door. The cool summer night breeze hit me, and I finally was able to gasp in a breath.

My hand grasped at my chest and found my necklace. The tiny chain and charm brought me some comfort as I felt my heart pounding. I hadn't worn it in three years. It sat in my jewelry box, usually untouched, the memory too painful to tote around. But tonight had been different; I'd reached for it without hesitation.

My gut had known all along.

It shouldn't have been like this.

Three years. I should be over it.

"Lenny," Stone said, pulling me from my spiral in one jarring sweep.

The name stung my heart. I could hear the sincerity in his voice.

His steps closed in behind me, and I swallowed hard. My hand was still clenched around the charm of the necklace, my knees shaking, ready to buckle.

Stone caught me before they did. His arms wrapping tightly around me, and I was tempted to just sink into them. I kept my focus on the tattoos wrapping up one, trying to disappear from the world, and let every bit of darkness consume me once and for all. It'd all been shoved down deep inside, somewhere I never thought I'd have to face it.

Complete denial.

"What's wrong?" Stone asked, and I could hear the way not knowing drove him mad.

He always had it figured out. The two weeks I'd known him, I'd never once seen him rattled in the face of any problem.

"It's nothing," I managed.

My voice was hoarse and my throat stung, forcing the words out.

Stone spun me to face him, to get a look at my face and read over my expressions. There was no use in hiding. They were written all over my face, and there was nothing I could do about it.

"You're upset," he observed matter of fact.

Hearing it out loud hurt even more. What was wrong with me?

My brother was having a baby. I should be overjoyed. Every part of me wanted to be back inside, celebrating with them, making a toast to Eloise and obsessing over all the little details. But instead, I was outside, barely able to stand and feeling like my dinner might come right back up.

What the fuck was wrong with me?

My body was shaking, and I tried to cling tighter to the necklace as a source of stability.

Stone's hand cupped my cheek, still reading my every move and expression. I flinched at his touch, and he pulled away quickly.

Shit.

I had to push him away too. It was the easiest thing. Anytime someone got too close, I pushed them right back out. I couldn't have anyone knowing the full truth. They'd hate me.

Tears welled in my eyes, and I had to hold them back.

"Len," Stone said gently.

I watched his eyes trail down to the necklace I clung to and watched in horror as I knew he was putting each of the pieces together. I hadn't missed the way he glanced jealously at the initial on the chain earlier in the day, but now, I could see him unraveling the mistaken assumption he made.

"You can't tell them," I pleaded.

He stared blankly at me.

"Please, Stone," I begged.

"Support systems are important," he started.

"I don't need facts and analysis right now," I snapped. I hadn't meant to come out so harshly, but I watched him take each word like a bullet to the chest. I paused, barely able to catch my breath.

"Deep breath," he reminded me gently.

I tried to inhale deeply and let it out in one slow motion.

"What do you need, Len?"

And in that moment, I was certain he would've given me anything I wanted.

"I just need to go home," I sighed, already shoving every emotion I felt back into the box I kept them locked in.

He nodded and headed for the door to go back inside. I worried for a moment that he completely misunderstood what I was saying. My feet refused to move, and I waited while a few minutes passed.

Stone reappeared, carrying my purse I left inside. "I let them know your stomach wasn't feeling so well, and that I would be taking you home to rest."

I was still shaking. All I could manage was a curt nod. Stone wrapped an arm around me and led me back to the car.

The warmth of his body radiated with me tucked into his side. I imagined how comforting it would be to get used to it, a thought I barely allowed myself to even consider.

If he knew the truth, he would never touch me.

He'd stare at me with that same look I saw the day I told Jake.

All he'd done was protect me, stand up for me. It wasn't fair to make the assumption. I knew that; I knew it wasn't rational. Yet, every time I found myself wanting to give in, to see if I wasn't imagining every small touch or glance he gave, I found myself right back in that moment and remembered the pain. It wasn't a chance I was willing to take.

If Winston Beck broke my heart, I'd never recover.

14

STONE

I DROVE BACK to the rental, the drive completely silent. Len tucked her knees into her chest in the passenger seat and wrapped her arms around them. Her dress fell completely back, exposing more of her skin, but I kept my eyes glued to the road, knowing she didn't realize.

It wasn't hard to piece together what she had lost.

It was even easier to conclude that the man she was with before was an absolute despicable human. I saw the way he broke her, the utter sadness in her eyes when she realized her brother had the one thing she lost.

A new sense of rage built in me for what the Coastal Killer had done to her. I'd read the report, memorized every single wound inflicted on her. A stab to the lower abdomen. That was all it took. I didn't need to be a doctor to understand what the consequences of that single wound could have been.

I helped Len out of the car, taking her hand and leading her into the house. She mindlessly followed, and I wasn't certain she was even fully there.

We made our way inside, and she barely said anything before parting ways.

"Goodnight, Lenny," I called after her as she dragged her feet up the steps.

"Goodnight," her faint voice trailed back down to me.

I wandered into the kitchen, my mind far too awake now to sleep yet.

I found myself staring down the glass bottle that sat tauntingly on the counter in front of me. I brought it with me, and every second it sat there, I regretted it.

Beside the bottle, I noticed a new vase of flowers. Daisies sat in water, fully bloomed, a small touch of Len in the space.

The rage I felt at the Coastal Killer and the sadness I felt for everything Len lost was enough to trigger that horrible pit inside me trying to bury me in oblivion.

It was dragging up old memories I didn't want to face.

Too familiar with the consequences of loss, my heart ached for Len. It wasn't the same, but I knew that horrible feeling filling her, the same one that made me turn to alcohol and drugs when Blythe died in my arms.

I wanted to tell her that, to be there for her, but I saw the way she flinched at my touch.

She needed space, and I respected that, but as long as she kept showing up and letting me, I would continue to protect her, to keep her safe. And now, I vowed to myself as I turned away from the bottle glaring at me, I would make sure Len never felt the same excruciating pain I'd seen haunting her eyes tonight ever again.

The next few days, we set to work sorting through all the papers the sheriff gave us. Len helped without complaint, but I could tell she was going through the motions. I needed something to drag her out of it, distract her mind.

I was failing miserably.

My eyes glanced over the list of calls the sheriff's office responded to at the pub in the months leading up to the killings. Bar scuffles, couple fighting after too many drinks, a few medical calls, but nothing close to standing out as significant.

"I'm finding a lot of discrepancies across each of these. Is that normal?" she asked, holding up the case reports I'd given her for half the victims.

"Like what?" I said, perking up.

I'd been sitting in the living room armchair for an hour, making notes in the margins of all the papers I had. She had taken to spreading things out on the floor. Birdie and Alonzo kept passing by her for occasional pets.

I swore I caught a glare from Alonzo on one of his laps.

"For example, this one says a witness saw her at the pub at 9:00 PM, but the final report and statement claim she was nowhere near there. Instead, it claims she must have been out for a run or walk," Len said, crinkling her nose.

I lean forward in the chair, taking in what she said. Someone messed with the report.

"This one says it was her first time visiting the bar, but I happen to know from my research, she was a regular there."

Someone was definitely messing with the reports. I started shifting through mine faster, trying to find similar mistakes. Although I didn't see as many glaring errors, the reports were certainly riddled with tiny ones, careless work.

"I don't get it," Len said. "Why would anyone falsify reports? How does that help them if it's obvious an officer did it?"

"I don't know," I admitted. "But it's somewhere to start."

"I don't think the sheriff will answer our questions so easily now," Len said.

"We aren't going to ask him," I said, rubbing at my chin. "We'll find another way. We don't have enough to say exactly who touched these."

She continued on the floor, barely making a sound. If not for me periodically glancing up to check on her, I wouldn't even know she was there. Every time her hand moved to her necklace, I caught the movement. Seeing her instinctively touch it hurt no less each time. She hadn't taken it off since the dinner. A lump formed in my throat, knowing what I had to ask her.

It wasn't fair, but we were running out of leads. She'd already been through so much pain, and I knew this would only drag up more.

I wouldn't ask if you weren't my only option.

I kept reminding myself over and over, working up the courage. It had been days since her brother's dinner, and I had to stop treating her like she was a ticking time bomb, give her more credit than that.

"Why are you giving me that look?" she asked.

"What?" I answered, taken aback.

She raised a brow and bit the inside of her cheek. "The one where you watch me like one of your puzzles to solve. It's hard to work when I feel you watching my every move."

Fair point.

"I think I know where to start."

Something lit up in her eyes for the first time in days. It was the first sign of emotion I'd seen, beyond just complete sadness consuming her. Maybe this wasn't such a bad idea.

"I think it's time I interview you," I suggested.

I saw the way her eyes widened, and she started to pull her limbs in, closing herself off from me without even realizing. The signs were all there.

"I already told you, I don't remember," she said softly.

I could see I was losing her. She was shrinking into herself. I slid out of the armchair onto the floor, only a foot from her, on her level.

"I wouldn't suggest it if I didn't think it was our only lead to start with," I said.

"But we have this," she said, motioning to the papers around her.

"We need more," I sighed. "The first lesson I teach trainees is that you can't look at things so narrow minded. You have to look at all the facts."

"I can't-" she started.

"I promise, I will not let anything hurt you," I said. "We need this."

We, because we were a team. As much as I hated to admit it, Len had become my partner in a matter of weeks. I swore I'd never work with someone again, let alone work in the field. Somehow, Len was slowly repairing the bullet-sized hole inside me.

"Do you trust me?" I asked.

A simple question, but there was more to it. I could see her unraveling the layers of my question, her lips pulling in how they did whenever she concentrated.

"I do," she whispered.

"What do you have for me, Mags?" I asked, answering the phone.

"Sorry it took so long, but I have the information about the bar you asked about."

"No worries. I appreciate you helping with this. I know you have a lot on your plate otherwise."

I could almost feel her smiling through the phone.

"It has minimal employees, fewer than twenty. It's owned by Bobby Evans, has been for fifteen years. I'm emailing you a list of the employees and more information about them all, including any records," she said.

"Thank you, Mags," I said.

"And Stone?" she added.

"Yes?"

"I also had a chance to look at that footage you sent."

My heart raced. I hadn't expected her to have news on that yet. "Were you able to make out the keychain?"

"Yes," she said. "I've sent you blown up screenshot that's been clarified too. It's a tag, a label for keys."

I pulled open my laptop as I paced back-and-forth in the dining room. Len was still upstairs, getting ready for the day. She'd finally accepted the inevitable fact that I had to interview her after I asked her only two days prior.

My email popped up right away, and I saw the attachment from Mags. I opened it before she said another word.

The tag was easy to read after Mags worked on it, and I could make out the three words.

High Tide Pub.

Len came down shortly after my call with Mags, and we

decided to walk the distance to the pub. I'd be trying to cover two leads in one visit. We originally planned to start at the pub during the day to walk through the night Len was attacked. It was the best way I could think of to compromise with her.

Len joined me in walking down the path into town. We walked down a lane of fully bloomed daisies. The daisies that had been sitting on my counter must have come from this small garden of them.

The walk down the path took approximately five minutes, and I had mapped out the rest of the way to the pub. It was located central in the town, an easy walking distance for both tourists and locals.

"Have you been back since?" I asked. I groaned internally, an obvious answer. Why was I so oblivious to other's feelings sometimes?

Len shook her head. "I haven't been able to step foot inside that place since that day."

I wasn't shocked. Most victims with PTSD avoided triggers. Going back to the place where it all started, there was no doubt in my mind that would resurface painful memories for her.

"Why is it you came alone? If we are asking questions here," she asked, "don't you have a partner or someone at the FBI looking for you?"

I hesitated. She'd find out at some point. "This isn't exactly a sanctioned FBI case."

"Excuse me?" She stopped walking.

"Didn't I tell you this," I asked, rubbing my hand behind my head.

I didn't. I'd been tip toeing around the truth. I never lied to

Len, but I wasn't exactly forthcoming in all the details of my trip. I never thought it'd get this far with her.

"No, you certainly left that portion out," she muttered.

"Well, no one is looking for me here, let's just say that," I offered, hoping she would drop the subject.

"But don't most agents have a partner, or even a team?" she asked instead.

"You've been watching far too many crime shows," I chuckled.

"You sound like Mal," she dismissed and gently nudged me with her shoulder.

"I used to have a partner," I started. Was I really going to go down this road? I never talked about Blythe to anyone— not Grey, nor the therapist he referred me to.

"You used to?" Len asked, picking up on the word choice as fast as I'd expected.

Clever girl. Her quick brilliance never failed.

"She died," I started. I wasn't sure if I could go further.

I took a deep breath, ready to try and share what I could, but I was interrupted.

"What's happening?" Len asked, and I followed her gaze to the giant crowd of people ahead.

I spotted the caution tape before she did and tucked her into my side instinctively. Crime rates were lower than most cities and towns in the entire country in Briarport. The worst this town had seen was petty theft or a bar fight until the Coastal Killer. That peace had returned the moment the serial killer disappeared.

I knew the pub wasn't far. This was the road it was on, so we'd have to pass whatever the commotion ahead was. I prepared myself for the worst, ready to protect Len.

We approached the crowd, and I could hear the whispers. Len's muscles tensed against my body as my arm remained firmly wrapped around her shoulders.

Two words were whispered over and over.

Coastal Killer.

I pushed her to the front, trying to get a look. It was hard to see through the massive amount of people, drawn in by the crowd. My arm dropped from around Len, but I managed to still guide her through.

I spotted the body bag before anything else. It was unzipped on the ground, a tarp covered mass beside it. I swallowed hard when I saw the manicured hand poking out from under it, covered in blood, dry and caked to the skin. I noticed the red nail polish underneath the blood. My mind tried to block out the image of what I assumed was underneath the tarp: a body brutally torn apart.

I noticed the sheriff nearby, and as his gaze caught mine, he came storming over to where we stood behind the caution tape.

"This is your fault," he hissed.

I felt Len trembling beside me at the sight of a covered body. I had to get her out of there. I knew they'd attempt to move the victim into the body bag to transport them to the morgue as fast as possible. I wouldn't let her see that. The growing crowd posed their only problem, but eventually they'd be forced to do it.

"Was there a ring?" I asked, ignoring the sheriff's outburst.

"What?" he stuttered.

"Was there a ring?" I repeated, slow and clear.

He paused for a moment and glanced back to where his deputies puttered around the scene. He turned back and nodded, careful not to answer out loud and draw attention. He'd only confirm what the people already whispered.

"They cut the ring finger clean off. We can't find it," he said quietly.

This was already growing out of my hands; the unsub had escalated. The killing turned it back into an active FBI case. The bureau would be alerted and arrive soon. I cursed under my breath, knowing what this meant.

My bargained time was over.

I smiled tightly. We had to get away from here.

"I suppose I'll be seeing you more," the sheriff scoffed.

"I look forward to working with you," I said through gritted teeth.

There was no escaping it: the FBI would be forced to work beside him—if Grey didn't throw me off the case the moment he realized what I did.

I turned away from the scene; there was nothing more we could do there. We had to get to the pub and figure out what Len remembered. That was the priority now.

I thought we were almost in the clear until I heard Len's name called out behind us.

"Len!" Mallory shouted, pushing through the crowd.

Great. I turned to find her friend following after her.

"Oh goodness, you're alright," she said and threw her arms around her. "They won't tell anyone who's under that tarp, and I haven't seen you at the apartment in a bit, so of course, I assumed the worst."

Not a single tear shed, I noted. I watched the way she feigned sadness and worry. That woman was truly incapable of caring about anyone other than herself.

"I'm alright," Len said with a shaky breath.

"Where have you been?" she asked.

"I-" Len started. "I've been staying with Stone."

Mallory's eyes fell on me, pure hatred in them. "Why don't you come stay with me?" Mallory asked.

"I'm just staying with him until things are safer. That threat really just got to my head. Besides, you live in the same building."

Mallory did not seem to like that answer. It felt like I was watching a cartoon, steam pouring out of her nostrils, anger seeping from her.

"We should really go," I said, and Len nodded firmly.

I glanced back to the scene and found the sheriff watching us intensely. Len's eyes followed mine, and I watched the way she stiffened again. Mal seem to pick up on it too.

"I don't know who put him in charge of anything," she scoffed.

Finally, something we agreed on.

"Do you know him?" I asked. He was my best leading suspect.

"I mean, he's sheriff, so most people in town do," she said. "Plus, he's also a piece of shit."

I held back a chuckle that almost escaped my lips. There was no way I was bonding with Len's narcissistic friend over this.

"His son is a total creep, and the sheriff covers for him," Mallory said. "Didn't your brother know him?" Mal looked to Len.

"Chris, right? I think he may have," Len answered slowly.

Another potential lead I noted in my head.

"Anyway, I have to go back to the shop. With all these

tourists pouring into the streets, they're bound to seek refuge from the heat eventually," she said, turning and bounding off down the road.

"Are you ready?" I asked, taking one last look at where the new victim was.

"Let's go," she said and started walking off in the direction of the pub.

15

LENNY

STONE NAVIGATED us to the High Tide Pub in minimal time. There was no doubt in my head the man was a genius, the only person I knew able to navigate these roads in record time. I would've found myself wandering up and down them until I happened upon the pub.

You've lived here three years. Get it together.

There were a few patrons inside when we arrived. My heart was already racing, and I recognized the interior of the place. Very little had changed in three years. There was the same smell of pub food and sticky alcohol, the dim lighting, the low music playing over the old speakers.

Stone led me to a high top table with two chairs. He pulled out mine before taking his own. I wasn't sure who looked more anxious—myself or him. He kept glancing over to the bar with bottles of liquor lined behind it.

Shit.

I kicked myself, remembering what he told me. Stone didn't drink. And now, because of me, we had to sit in the center of place revolved around drinking. I wasn't sure what the story was, but I got the sense he didn't stop drinking just because he chose to.

The waitress came over and asked if we wanted anything. Before I could answer to order just a water, Stone whispered, "What did you get that night?"

Instantly, I was transported back three years prior. I was pregnant, so I knew I didn't drink any of the alcohol behind the bar.

"Can I do a club soda with lime?" I asked. "And a side of fries."

She looked at Stone, waiting for his order, and he requested the same drink.

"Fries?" he said and eyed me.

"It was a pregnancy craving," I admitted, and I watched his face fall a little, only for a second, before smiling gently at me.

"I'm here every step of the way," he reminded me.

I took a deep breath while we waited quietly for the waitress to return. The pub wasn't busy, and it didn't take long before she carried over a basket of fries and our two drinks.

Stone scrolled through his phone while I nervously sipped. His eyes barely flicked up to me every few minutes.

"Now what?" I asked, finally breaking the silence.

"A colleague sent me information about this place," he answered. "I didn't have time to comb through it until now."

"Anything helpful?" I asked, raising a brow.

The conversation helped. It distracted me from focusing on my surroundings, the way the place made my skin crawl.

"Not exactly," Stone answered. "A few employees have prior records, but nothing that sticks out or fits the profile. It does help me at least whittle down who to consider, but I'm not fully eliminating anyone."

I nodded. Seeing Stone actively working on the case outside of the small bubble we had formed in his rental had my heart beating a little harder.

Stop it, Len.

There was no doubt in my mind that if anyone could find the person responsible for all this, it would be him, but I couldn't let the feelings growing inside me disrupt that.

"I should warn you, my colleague also found this," he said and held up his phone screen for me to see.

When he flipped it, my breath caught in my throat. On the screen, staring directly at me, was a blown up version of the footage I had sent him. The keychain I'd been adamant about was now readable. I didn't know what told me it was important, maybe it was instinct, but I knew there was a reason we had to read it. There were those three little words, staring right at me on the tag attached to a key inside whoever threatened me's pocket.

High Tide Pub.

The same pub we sat in now.

I glanced around the room, as if I was going to be able to spot the keys out in the open. Tourists walked in the front door, wearing hats with BP embroidered on them. Waitresses hustled around the place, taking orders and cleaning tables. The longer we sat, the busier it became.

If they were truly keys to the pub, anyone could have them. It wasn't exactly the damning evidence I hoped it was, but it did at least confirm we were starting in the right place.

"We should begin," Stone said gently.

"How?" I asked, unsure of what exactly it was he wanted me to do.

"Take a deep breath," he instructed. "And close your eyes."

I inhaled and let it out slowly, letting my eyelids flutter shut. I focused on what I could sense around me. The low hum of music and the distant conversations that carried through the air. The smell of food being brought out from the kitchen. Beneath me, I could feel the way the leather of the seat felt against my thighs.

I didn't need my eyes open to know exactly what the scene around me looked like.

"Where were you in the pub that night?" Stone asked.

Easy.

"I was over by the bar. It was Calvin's birthday."

"Good, keep that same focus," he instructed. "What do you remember about the atmosphere? Was it loud? Were there many others around you?"

We'd been singing happy birthday to Calvin, everyone holding their drinks in the air, giving a cheers to him. It was the first time I allowed myself happiness like that in a long time. Jake hovered close behind me, and I shuddered to remember the way he always had control. I recalled the way the bar was packed that night, a warm fall day with many out to enjoy it into the night.

"It was loud. I could barely hear Calvin and my friends over all the chatter," I said.

It was almost like a my mind placed me right back in the moment. Reality slipping away.

"Did you notice anyone? Someone around you who didn't fit or was taking notice of your group?"

I glanced around the room. I could see my friends, people I hadn't spoken to in years now. Calvin with his arm around Eloise. It was one of the first times I truly got to know her. Jake's hands were on the small of my back, but not in a comforting manner. It was in the type of way I knew, at any moment, he'd rip me from the joy.

I tried to look around, but I didn't notice anyone else.

"No," I said, feeling discouraged.

My heart raced, and I felt the sinking in my stomach.

"It's alright," Stone assured me. "You're doing great."

I knew it was the calm before the storm. I'd lived it out before. Any moment now, Jake would pick a fight and storm off, leaving me alone at the pub.

"What happens next, Lenny?" he pushed gently, and I ignored the flutter my stomach gave at the name.

My hands trembled in my lap the second I pushed forward in the timeline. I couldn't tell if it was real or just part of the memory.

Jake spun me around to let me quietly know it was time to go, but I hadn't wanted to leave. I wasn't ready. My brother's birthday was the first time I'd been able to celebrate with him, and I wanted to share my own news. I'd been waiting for the right moment to pull him aside and tell him, but I hadn't found my chance yet. All I wanted was to share one night with my friends and family, then go back to being the perfect fiancée Jake expected.

"He left," I said quietly.

"Who left?"

The moment I protested leaving, he'd been pissed. He pulled me off to the side of the bar and started laying into me as quietly as he could, but I could hear the anger behind every word he spat in my face.

Ungrateful, disobedient, bitch.

Just a few the choice words used to shame me. I remembered holding my stomach, praying it would end.

"Fine. If you want to throw everything away for this, I'm leaving," he hissed.

I watched him storm out before I had a chance to say anything. It was how all our arguments went. He was never willing to talk through or hear my side; he always stormed off, eventually forgiving me later when I begged for it.

This would be no different.

"Jake," I said.

"Did you follow after him?" Stone asked.

I shook my head. "No, I stayed a little longer."

The fight had left me feeling ill. Pregnancy didn't help. I was still in the first trimester, and morning sickness unfortunately wasn't just reserved for mornings.

I tried to go back to the group, but I felt like I was holding back everything in my stomach. I no longer felt present, could feel myself slowly slipping away. My mind always drifted after our arguments, trying to protect me, to hide the way it made my insides turn.

"What's wrong?" Calvin had asked.

"I think they made the drink a bit stronger than I realized." I had tried to force myself to laugh.

Wrapped up in the moment, Calvin barely noticed the way my smile didn't reach my eyes. He just laughed softly and wrapped an arm around my shoulders, hugging me.

"Where'd Jake go?" Calvin had asked, his tone hopeful, not a large fan of my fiancé.

I didn't want to ruin his night further, and I knew I was no longer in the headspace to be around friends and family. Jake had made sure of it.

"He's out grabbing the car," I had said. "Unfortunately, I think he's going to take me home."

My brother frowned, but only for a moment, as some of our friends came back carrying more drinks.

"Are you sure? You could stay with us tonight." He motioned to his fiancée.

"It's your birthday, Calvin," I remembered saying. "Enjoy it. I'm gonna go home, get some rest. And now I've learned my lesson about trusting this place to make my drinks."

He smiled and gave me a hug. "Don't be a stranger," he said. "Promise me you won't disappear for months again."

"I promise," I said gently, but I knew it was a lie.

Jake hated my family, hated whenever I wanted to see them. It had taken weeks of begging just to get him to let me come to Calvin's birthday.

"I'll see you soon," I said, turning to leave the place.

"Where'd you go?" Stone said, calling me a bit out of memory.

"I left," I said. "Calvin had been worried, but I convinced him Jake was grabbing the car, and I left. I needed space and air, so I decided to head for the beach."

The waves and salty air always cleared my mind, so I decided to head for my one place of comfort before calling a ride home.

"Did you make it to the beach?"

"No," I said and swallowed hard.

I knew what was coming next: the pain, the complete darkness.

My breathing picked up, and I placed my hands on the table to steady myself. Everything screamed at me to run in the other direction.

You're helping the other victims. Do it for them.

I had to remind myself of that over and over, forcing myself to continue.

I felt warmth over one of my hands and realized Stone had reached out to grab it. His touch made me feel a little safer.

I walked out of the bar and stood outside, trying to gain my bearings and figure out which way was the best way to reach the beach. Everything felt a bit hazy, and my mind started to feel cloudy, but I dismissed it as being distracted. The nausea didn't get any better. I could barely focus long enough to look at my phone and find directions. The music had still been playing in the background, and I remembered taking a small step forward.

"I hadn't felt well," I said to Stone. "I remember it being hard to focus, and it taking me a while to even figure out which way to head to the beach."

"Was it the pregnancy?" he asked.

I never thought about it at the time, but now, I was certain.

"No, I don't think it was," I said firmly. "I always assumed that's why I started not to feel well, but no matter what I do, that night is a blur. I can barely remember anything, besides the fact that my head felt fuzzy, and then it's just black."

"You were drugged," Stone guessed.

Reality hit me like a ton of bricks. Never once had I considered it. I didn't stick around long enough at the hospital to know if they ever tested me.

I walked without another thought. I was confident I was heading toward the beach, but the cloudier my head became, the harder it was to keep track of my surroundings.

Something hard and blunt hit my head, my legs giving out. I remembered the feeling of my knees hitting the ground, the stinging pain of the pavement against them. I definitely did not make it to the beach.

I tried to look up, but my head felt heavy, another hit forcing me to the ground completely.

A mind-splitting headache spread across my skull.

My breathing picked up, and I felt Stone squeeze my hand tighter. I couldn't do this. There was nothing further to remember, everything just black from there on.

"Len," Stone said slowly. "You can do this."

I was tempted to open my eyes, to find his gentle brown eyes watching me, protecting me every step of the way. If I did, this would all end.

The pain, the torture, the burden of remembering.

"I can't breathe," I gasped, my other hand grasping at my chest.

My mind wouldn't push on.

"What do you hear?" Stone pushed.

"I can't-"

"You can, Len," he pushed. "I am right here."

Hear? I tried to listen, the sound of footsteps falling next to my head.

Leaves.

The footsteps fell on leaves.

What else? There had to be something, any bit of information to help Stone. There was a cool breeze against my skin, a consistent pounding in my head. The music, though distant, rang through my mind.

Music?

That should be impossible. I walked away from the pub.

"Music," I rasped through broken breaths.

"Music?" Stone repeated back to me.

The music was so low, I barely could hear it. One voice, a low tune reached my ears, a sound that would haunt me the rest of my life. One single voice raked against my memory like claws dragging along my skin.

"No," I said, even more confused.

"Take a breathe, Len," Stone reminded me. "What exactly do you hear?"

I put myself back into the memory. The voice was distant yet close all at once. I tried to focus on it, but I couldn't grasp it. It wasn't something I could hold on to. It was low, unrecognizable. There were no instruments or words to it.

"Humming," I said, and realized it was the killer.

My heart raced and my chest ached. I couldn't continue like this. I needed air, to get out of the pub.

"Len, I'm here. It's okay," Stone said, and I heard the worry growing in his voice.

"I need to get out," I said, standing and finally opening my eyes.

The entire memory fell away, the darkness retreating right back to where I kept it locked up. I hurried past Stone, whose wide eyes were on me. I couldn't stay; I had to get air.

I barely made it outside before I collapsed, my back against the side of the building as I slid to the ground, my vision darkening. My hearing was fuzzy, and I let my head fall into my hands.

Strong arms wrapped around me, and before I knew what was happening, Stone was holding me. He guided my head to his chest, and I listened to the steady beat of his heart.

"I've got you," he said. "I'm here, Len."

"No one was there," I said, tears falling down my face. "I

was alone. He should have been there. Someone should have been there."

"I know," he said.

"No one stopped them. How did no one stop them?" I cried into his chest.

"I will never let them harm you again," he promised, and I almost believed the words.

"You can't promise that," I whispered, trying to wipe the tears trickling down my cheeks.

"I am promising that," Stone said.

We sat for a few minutes before I heard footsteps.

"You can't loiter here," a male voice said from above us, and I glanced up to find someone sneering down at us.

The man wore a hoodie with High Tide Pub written across it, his hands shoved into the front pocket. I tilted my head, something about his face familiar.

"We were just leaving," Stone snapped.

He stood, only inches from the man, towering over him. I slid myself up the wall, still using it for balance, not ready to trust myself.

The man scowled up at Stone, and I realized immediately where I knew him from.

When I glanced around the room at Calvin and our friends, there had been one person. Behind them, cleaning off the counter and carrying the empty glasses away, it was the same man, the same scowl plastered to his face.

16

STONE

"I'm sorry you got nothing from my memory of the night," Len said, sitting on the couch.

I'd waited until she was stable enough to walk and then helped her back to my rental. She was still shaking by the time I helped her to the couch, and my stomach sank knowing I was the reason why. I never should've pushed her.

"That's not true," I said.

"It is. I panicked, and I cut us short. I should've pushed harder."

"That would have done neither of us any good, Lenny," I assured her. I needed to diffuse the situation, fast. I'd learned basics of diffusing a bomb, talking down a gunman from pulling the trigger, working through hostage negotiations, but no book or instruction manual ever told me how to solve this.

"Len, you gave us more information than we had. No one knew the Coastal Killer was using drugs to subdue their victims."

"Wouldn't the morgue have found that in their assess-ments?" Len said, glancing up with her big brown eyes.

God, I loved the way she looked at me. So intuitive; she really would make a great agent. Maybe I wasn't entirely messing things up.

"Exactly, which tells us..." I pushed.

"That it was a substance not detectable in the normal toxicology screen?" she asked, catching on quickly.

"Yes, which gives us more information than the FBI or sheriff had three years ago. That is not nothing," I promised.

Her entire body still trembled, adrenaline and painful memories still rushing through her. I sat down beside her, hoping to find a way to stop it. This wasn't like my field assignments; I couldn't apply any of that knowledge to this.

I had to improvise.

The last time I improvised, someone was killed.

This wasn't that, not even close. I took a deep breath. What calmed me when I felt like losing control? For a while, that was alcohol and drugs to numb the pain, but eventually, I'd stopped. I turned to books. When I felt the world crumbling around me, life no longer making sense, I threw myself into books and learned everything I possibly could.

I picked up my most recent read off the side table and opened it—tales of Greek mythology, some of my favorites, all under one cover.

The story of Perseus and Medusa was the first I opened to. Len was twiddling with rings on her fingers but stopped the moment she heard my voice.

I started reading, all too aware of her keen focus on me. Usually, I read in private, enjoying my time alone with the stories and information I consumed, but I didn't mind sharing this with Len.

My arm outstretched without thinking to pull her closer. Without looking up, I knew she was watching me, rather than the book in my hands, taking in every word from my mouth.

"I love this story," I murmured, pausing as I turned the page.

"Why?" Len asked. Her head fell to my shoulder, and I felt the warmth of her skin against my exposed arm.

"Because Perseus never choose to be a hero out of ambition or chasing glory. He was trapped into an impossible situation. No matter what, though, he persevered. He fought against the impossible and came out on top. He's a lot like you," I finished.

She laughed. "I'm a coward," she scoffed. "I'm no hero out of Greek mythology."

"I'm serious. I know you didn't choose this," I started. "But everything you have done has brought us one step closer to finding justice for those victims. That to me, Lenny Calder, is bravery."

I could feel her shaking subsiding the longer she leaned in to me. My own heart rate slowed, the anxiety of not knowing how to fix the situation slowly fading.

I did the one thing I knew best.

Reading.

Books were always a welcomed distraction. It didn't matter what it was—I would read it. The classics were my comfort, but I would never turn down the opportunity to learn more. It was like an addiction, but one I could at least justify.

And Lenny absorbed every single word of the story. We

sat like that for what felt like forever, me reading as her body melted further against me. Eventually, I found her trying to adjust to get more comfortable.

"Lay down," I instructed.

"What?" she asked, her cheeks warming and her eyes avoiding mine.

"Rest," I instructed. "It's been a long day."

Nothing more. Just rest.

She slowly sank into the couch, kicking her feet up and laying down. My lap became her pillow, and her warm brown curls spilled over my legs. I held the book with one hand and let my other fall to her head, stroking her hair gently, careful not to mess up each curl.

Each page I turned, I glimpsed down to check on her. Minutes turned to an hour, and soon, her eyes were fluttering shut. I kept going with multiple stories of heroes and goddesses, all with a new lesson learned.

Alonzo and Birdie joined us on the couch, curling around their owner.

"Sneaky felines," I whispered at them.

Alonzo moved himself closer to me, snuggling right up against my leg.

"You win this time," I said, and I swore, Len smiled.

I couldn't help it; my body reacted before I could even think it through. My free hand moved to grab her hand, pulling it up to my lips. I pressed a light kiss to the back of her hand, thankful she was here and safe.

"I heard them," she whispered. "I can't exactly remember, but I know I heard them," she murmured as she drifted off in my lap.

"Try not to think about that," I whispered as I went back to stroking her hair.

I continued my reading as she fell asleep. I knew the moment she was no longer awake, recognizing the deeper breaths she took and the way her head felt heavier in my lap. The cats eventually left us, but I refused to leave the couch.

I refused to take my eyes off Len until I knew she was alright. I'd pushed her to her limit, and everything in me hated me for it. The pale look on her face when I'd pulled her into my arms outside the pub would haunt me forever.

No matter how many times I told myself I was only doing this to solve the case for the FBI, it was a lie, one that was growing out of hand. I stayed for her. I continued to let her help me and piece together this case because my mind couldn't stand the thought of sending her away.

I was breaking every possible rule. The system I believed in and followed religiously was completely disregarded.

I couldn't face the facts.

Instead, I did the singular thing I could think of: I threw myself back into the book and pushed all those feelings back down where I wouldn't be able to find them.

17

LENNY

I woke with a jolt and sat up, slamming into a hard surface. My hands flew to my nose, pain spreading across it, a warm, sticky liquid now dripping down my face.

"Are you okay?" Stone said, mildly panicked. "You're bleeding!"

I pulled my hands away from my face just long enough to see the red covering them. The blood dripped down onto the white shirt I wore. I jumped up and realized Stone held a hardcover book I must've hit my face on when I woke so suddenly.

He followed my line of sight. "I'm so sorry," he said, rushing to the kitchen and coming back with a rag.

The rag replaced my hands, and I clung to it, hoping the bleeding would eventually stop. I couldn't even recall the last time I'd given myself a bloody nose. A small laugh escaped my lips, and Stone looked even more concerned.

"Are you alright?" he asked as I nodded. "Are you laughing?" He tilted his head to read my face, but the rag kept it mostly covered.

"It's just so absurd," I laughed. "My whole life has been falling apart for years. I can barely remember when anything was simple enough that my worries were small, like nose bleeds or which book to read next." My words came out nasally, my nose blocked by the rag.

Stone chuckled. "I know what you mean," he said, sitting back down.

I noticed the way he nervously clasped his hands together, his arms tensing and the vines that wrapped up one arm more noticeable than ever.

"I don't remember the last time I could just go to the bar and have a drink with colleagues. I don't remember the days when I used to call my mom and sister to make sure they were doing okay without worrying they would know I'm not. And red—I can't remember the last time I could see red and not be reminded of the death I caused."

Death he caused...

That had to be a mistake. He was an agent, responsible for protecting people, myself included. There was no possible way...

"I don't deserve that kindness," he said at my confused look. "My partner is dead because of me."

A pit formed in my stomach. He'd rarely mentioned his partner. I knew she died, but he never said more than that. The look of pain on his face was enough to make a wave of nausea wash over me, the blood still pouring from my nose not helping.

"Stone..." I tried.

"You asked why no one was looking for me," Stone said, the pain in his eyes making my heart split in two. "A little under a year ago, my partner died in the field. We were supposed to be waiting for back up, but the unsub had taken a young girl hostage. Blythe wanted to go in. I knew the protocol, I knew our orders, but still, I considered it." His face fell.

"Stone, you can't blame yourself if you followed orders and didn't follow her," I said.

"I didn't. I knew what the risk was, calculated everything that could go wrong, and I still followed her into that building," he answered.

I reached for his hand.

You're comforting him. He would do the same for you.

"You tried to protect her," I said slowly.

He shook his head. "Tried and failed. We got inside, and the place was a maze. We were running out of time; the little girl had no time left. We had to find her. So, I made a choice, one I will live with for the rest of my life. I suggested we split up. It was a calculated risk. The probability of us finding her alive increased, we both had our guns, and were both trained agents."

I listened in horror, pulling the rag away and realizing my nose bleed had finally ceased. The rag landed on the side table as I tossed it aside.

"You couldn't have known," I said.

"But I did. I knew from the start what the risk was. I knew the statistics of waiting for back up. The statistics of agents killed and assaulted in the field are much higher for those who do not wait."

"Stone," I tried, squeezing his hand even tighter. "What happened is not your fault."

"The chance of fatality is two times higher when an agent does not wait. Two times! I never should have been okay with that number. I never should have let her go into that building. And now, I live with the consequences every single day."

"It's not your fault," I repeated.

"I found her still alive," he said. "When I arrived, it was too late. The unsub had stabbed her. I shot them, but it was far too late. She'd just fallen to the ground, limp. I'll live with the picture of that for the rest of my life. If I had gotten there seconds earlier, maybe it would be different. The little girl lived, but Blythe didn't. Those first few months after were brutal. I tortured myself, thinking about what I could have done differently. I drank myself into oblivion and took a leave of absence from the FBI. It wasn't until Agent Grey found me and dragged me back to Quantico that I got sober. I knew Blythe would hate what I became, and somehow, that was far worse than hiding from the memory of what happened."

I had no words. Nothing I could say would make this better. I wanted to pull him close, for Stone to know someone cared. I was there and listening, and I would never run from this. There may not be anyone in the world who understood this type of pain better than me.

I tortured myself with the thought of what if I never ran from the hospital. What if I had stayed and helped the police? Maybe they would have already found the killer by now.

"I'm here," I said, the one thing I could think of that might bring him some comfort.

"I'm here, and I'm not leaving. You did everything right; you can't keep torturing yourself like this. I didn't know Blythe, but I can guarantee she wouldn't want this. You don't know if that little girl would have lived if you didn't go in there when you did. You saved her, gave her a chance at living life. That is not nothing; it's not something to keep tearing yourself apart over. Nothing I say can bring back Blythe or make the memory of her hurt any less, but if you are going to play that memory over and over in your mind, you need to remember what she sacrificed herself for. You saved a life, a little girl with no one else to protect her. That to me makes you both heroes."

Stone nodded slowly, averting his gaze from mine. He stared down at my hand that he now held with both of his.

"You are covered in blood," Stone said suddenly, as if just noticing the red on my hands.

"Let me help," he said and jumped up from the couch.

His suitcase sat across the room, and he sifted through it, pulling out a band tee I'd never seen him wear. He handed it to me. "I'll wash the one you're wearing for you," he offered.

He just shared his deepest trauma, and now he's offering to rinse the blood from my own shirt?

Men like this didn't exist. Stone couldn't be real. Three years ago, I would've done everything to hide the stain so I wouldn't be yelled at for it.

I stood and pulled my white shirt over my head without thinking. My bralette kept me covered, but Stone's eyes trailed down my torso the second it was exposed. The moment his eyes halted, I knew what he saw: the grotesque scars still prominent across my skin. His gaze settled on the one I hated most.

The reminder of everything I lost that night.

"Sorry," I muttered, trying to scramble to untangle my arms from the white shirt.

"Don't apologize," he said firmly, moving closer to me. His hand reached out, but he paused before touching my skin.

"It's okay," I told him.

His fingers brushed gently against my skin, running along the jagged scar, the stitches rushed because of how many wounds I had when I arrived.

"It's a miracle you survived with only scars," Stone said in awe.

"Involuntary hysterectomy," I whispered. "Thats the price I paid. I can't ever become pregnant again."

My eyes dropped to the floor. The reason Jake threw me out, the thing that continued to haunt me from that night. It was why I could barely bring myself to face my brother after his announcement, why the thought of being around a baby in the family pained me, my heart breaking.

Stone's strong hands immediately grasped my hips and pulled me in. He held me in his arms, hugging me to him. I wanted to cry, but nothing came out. Instead, I let my head fall to his chest and stood there in silence.

"We will find them," Stone said. "We will find the Coastal Killer, and I will make sure they pay for everything they have done."

I dug through Stone's fridge the next morning, trying to find anything I could eat. Stone made a pot of coffee behind me, and I could feel his eyes on me every few seconds. He hadn't stopped checking on me since the pub. I could feel his need to protect me growing by the second.

He's worse than you two. The pair of cats at my feet just glanced up at me, waiting for breakfast.

I found a few breakfast sausages and read the ingredients

on a few breakfast pastries I found, passing on each of them. By the time I scraped together a meal, we ended up with sausage, fruit, and yogurt.

Stone didn't complain when I placed his breakfast in front of him.

My cellphone kept lighting up on the counter, but I ignored it.

Probably just Calvin or my mother.

"I think we should go back to the pub," I said, breaking the silence we'd been sitting in for a few minutes.

"What?" Stone choked on the sausage in his mouth.

I waited for him to stop coughing before continuing. "That man from outside yesterday was there that night. I didn't know it until I saw his face, but he was working the night I was attacked. Maybe he knows something.".

'Len," Stone warned. "You really want to go back?"

I knew he would never tell me not to, but I heard the hesitation. He was looking out for me, but who would look out for the victims it was too late for? I was their only chance at justice.

"Yes," I answered firmly.

The phone lit up again, but I ignored it, too focused on convincing Stone. My mind was made up, and no one would talk me out of it. I was ready to go back; this time, I could face it. I had to.

He sighed as he carried his plate to the sink. The water turned on, and he scrubbed the plate before collecting mine. When the water finally stopped, he turned back to me.

"Alright," he agreed. "We go back today to chase down the last of our leads. But if you want to leave at any moment, just say the word."

I nodded.

"I'm serious, Lenny," he said. "One word, and we can leave."

My phone lit up yet again, and I finally gave in, checking the screen. I had ten unread messages from an unknown phone number. I opened it and immediately dropped the phone. The screen landed with a smack on the tile floor, and I prayed it didn't crack.

Stone was up and across the kitchen before I could pick it up. He bent down to grab it, looking at the still-open screen. His brows furrowed, and eyes narrowed on the photo I knew he saw. There, on my phone, was a picture of the most recent victim of the Coastal Killer.

It was a dark photo, taken before the sun rose. I could just make out the shape of the body on the ground.

I ran to the trash can and emptied the contents of my stomach.

Stone was immediately behind me, rubbing my back.

"Sorry," I murmured.

"I threw up all over my partner the first time I saw a body in the field," he admitted.

I straightened and gave him a weak smile, but it didn't last. The other messages remained unread; I hadn't seen them before the photo that first popped up.

"What else does it say?" I asked.

"*I did this for you*," Stone read aloud.

"What?" I asked. "They killed them because of me?"

I knew this was coming. The killer had warned me to stop, but I didn't listen. Neither of us did. Instead, we kept pushing on, leaving no stone unturned.

"This isn't your fault. Stop thinking that," Stone scolded.

"They would have become emboldened eventually. If not now, maybe two years from now. There is no way to know for sure. At least now, we have more evidence to follow and can put a stop to all of this."

"I should've listened. That woman is dead because of me," I said, my stomach still turning.

"No, that woman is dead because of a serial killer," Stone said firmly.

I grabbed a cup from the cupboard and filled it with water at the sink. My head hurt and my throat burned. The water was refreshing but not enough to fix it all.

"Do you still want to go back?" Stone asked.

"I have to," I answered. "Let's go."

18

STONE

I SHOULD'VE KNOWN I wouldn't be so lucky to find myself alone with Len. Instead, Mal bounced next to her friend, trailing along with us. We'd walked halfway to the pub before bumping into her.

The streets were packed with tourists, and we pushed through the crowds on the sidewalk. There were too many people surrounding us for comfort, but there was not much I could do to change it.

The texts she received told me the unsub was becoming bolder. They were fixated on her, as their victim who got away, and that fact alone had me on edge. I knew how dangerous an obsession like that could become.

"Why are you going to High Tide?" Mal asked.

"For drinks," Len answered quickly, keeping her answer short and simple.

That was my girl. A natural.

Thoughts like that were dangerous. I had limited time left, especially with the case becoming active once more. I'd be leaving for Quantico before I knew it.

"I thought you loved this place," Len said to her friend.

"I do, but it doesn't seem like your scene. You always refuse to come with me," Mallory said, casting me a look of pure hatred and jealousy.

"Well, I changed my mind." Len shrugged. "I heard they have great margaritas, so I told Stone we had to come check it out while he was still in town. It felt like a tourist staple he couldn't miss."

"It is always packed with tourists," Mallory agreed. "We could come back for your birthday!"

"Birthday?" I cut in.

"In a few days," Mallory answered, rolling her eyes. "You know nothing about her, do you?"

So blunt. I held back the frustrated grumble threatening to tumble out. Mallory was insufferable no matter how much I tried to like her for Len's sake.

"On Saturday," Len interrupted, diffusing the situation.

It bothered me that I didn't know when Len's birthday was, though I never thought to ask. I didn't think I'd be sticking around long enough to celebrate it. Mallory had a look of victory on her face that she knew something I didn't, like she was slowly winning her best friend back. It wasn't a contest, but somehow, I found myself in the middle of a competition.

I needed to find a gift and put something together for Len. My mind was distracted, brainstorming ideas; I didn't even realize we made it to the pub. We walked inside, and immediately, Len froze.

Gently, I took her hand and led her further toward a table so she could sit and I could find her a water. Mal caught sight of the movement and scowled in my direction. She linked her arm through Len's other one and dragged her off to a booth away from me.

As she passed the bar, she said, "two margaritas," then continued toward the open seats.

The woman behind it tilted her head at me, as if she expected me to bark an order at her as well. Instead, I opened my wallet, grabbed a few bills, and placed them on the counter.

"That's for theirs, and I'll just take a water, please," I said with a smile.

Her features softened, and she smiled back. "I'll bring them over to the table."

I met Lenny and Mal at the booth and sat across from them. I knew we wouldn't be able to talk freely about the case, not with Len's best friend joining us.

I needed to ask for the owner, find out if they still had the footage from the night Len was attacked. With the new knowledge that she remembered the bus boy and the fact that we knew she was drugged, there had to be something in that footage. Whoever drugged her most likely was whoever tried to kill her. It was our best lead.

"I really think you should move home," Mal said to Len, breaking the silence.

"I don't think that's a good idea," she said sheepishly.

"Why not? Stay with me, safety in numbers. Besides, it was probably a prank."

"Some small prank doesn't involve threats being left at her door before a body is found in the middle of town," I grumbled under my breath.

"I never asked you," Mal said.

The waitress brought over our drinks, and Mallory forced

Len to cheers before downing her margarita faster than I'd ever seen someone drink one. I was mildly impressed.

Tequila was never my choice of alcohol those long days I drank myself into oblivion, but I could appreciate a good margarita.

"What are you drinking?" Mal asked, scowling at my cup of water.

"Just water for me," I said.

"No fun," Mal pouted immediately.

"Someone has to stay sober to make the decisions around here," I said with a shrug.

Mallory did not like that. Instead, she turned her body completely sideways, trying to block me out of the conversation. They caught up on life, and Mallory droned on and on about the tourists. I'd never met someone so judgmental in my life.

It wasn't long before I found myself rolling my eyes, barely able to take her repetitive stories all about herself. It could keep her busy enough not to notice where I went. A perfect distraction.

"Excuse me. I am going to use the bathroom," I said.

I headed for the sign to the restroom right past the bar. I paused at the counter, trying to catch the waitress behind it. She saw me and hurried right over.

I pulled out my wallet again and showed her my badge. In a low tone, I asked, "Is the owner here?"

She nodded, understanding I was trying not to cause a scene, likely not wanting that for the bar either.

"He lives above it, so he's practically always in," she whispered. "I'll go grab him."

I waited for a few minutes and realized I was just out of

sight of the booth Len and Mal sat in, so she wouldn't see me talking to the owner.

I didn't trust Len's friend, and I certainly didn't trust her all-too-eager mouth not to gossip about what we were looking into.

The woman reappeared, this time with a man beside her. He hurried over and reached out a hand to shake to mine.

"Bob," he introduced.

"Agent Beck," I said. "I just had a quick question for you. Given the recent killing nearby, the FBI is looking into an old case."

"The Coastal Killer," Bob guessed.

I nodded. "I was hoping you could help me."

"Of course. Whatever you need."

His willingness to help and most of his demeanor and nature did not fit the profile we'd been building. He was not clear completely, but I did eliminate him from the list of my most considered suspects. Being the owner of the bar had landed him on the list, but he was being helpful. He didn't seem to have any distaste toward law enforcement. In fact, he was more respectful than most people I interviewed on the job.

"I was hoping you might still have footage from three years ago. We have new reason to suspect Jane Doe, who survived, visited here the night she was attacked."

"Did you find Jane Doe? Did she come forward?"

I'm sure it was the question most people in town had three years ago when Jane Doe disappeared. With the return of the unsub, people around Briarport would be praying for any speck of hope.

"No," I said. "It's just a potential lead we're tracking down.

We don't have concrete evidence. That's why I came to you for the footage. I'm hoping that maybe, we can recognize her on it."

"I wish I could help," Bob said. "But I turned over all that footage to the FBI three years ago, and unfortunately, my system doesn't save things beyond a year."

I sighed. It wasn't unexpected. A place like this, I couldn't imagine it having a complex security system, but it was worth asking.

"Thank you," I said. "I'll let you know if we have any further questions."

Before I turned, I noticed the same bus boy watching us all too interested from the other end of the bar.

"Actually," I said, catching Bob before he walked away, "has he worked here long?" I asked, nodding at the bus boy.

"Ethan? He's is one of my longest employees."

I swallowed hard. He would've been there three years ago, like Len said, and worked through every single one of the killings. He was quickly rising in my list of suspects.

"Have you ever had any problems with him?" I asked.

"No, Ethan keeps his head down and does his job cleaning up the dishes and transporting items here from our warehouse. Sure, we've had a few complaints. Not everybody appreciates his direct tone, but he keeps mainly to himself," Bob explained.

"What type of complaints?" I asked.

"You can't think-" Bob started.

"What type of complaints?" I repeated, keeping my voice low.

Bob looked back to where Ethan was, but he'd already disappeared back to the kitchen. "Men complained they didn't like how he spoke to their girlfriends. A woman here and there was upset when he cut them off or asked them to leave."

"Is that part of his job?"

"No, but it does help me from time to time. He knows when someone's had too much, and we usually cut them off or kick them out before they cause trouble. Nobody likes to be told they've had one too many, and even worse—no man wants to see someone correcting the woman they came with. He means well; he just comes off wrong," Bob tried to explain.

He sought more control than he had, found a way to get himself more power at the job.

"Does he do it to men?"

"I'm sure he has," Bob answered.

"But have you seen it? Can you definitely tell me he does it to men as well?" I pushed.

Bob paused and shook his head.

A clear dislike toward women mixed with seeking out that type of power—he was starting to find himself at the top of my list. A narcissist who thought himself more important than others. A dislike for women. The pieces were starting to fit. I just didn't have them all figured out, certainly not enough to bring to the FBI and make an arrest.

I knew what I had to do next. We needed to confirm it was Ethan who snuck those drugs in Len's drink.

"Thank you," I told Bob. "Truly."

He nodded and left while I went back to the booth with Len and Mal.

"That was the longest bathroom break ever," Mallory said dramatically.

Len used her elbow to nudge her friend. "Don't be rude," she scolded.

The two let out a giggle. I'd been gone no more than fifteen minutes, and already, I found them on their second margaritas.

"Miranda?" the waitress said and held out another drink.

"It's Mallory," Len's friend snapped, annoyed.

"Sorry, I got mixed up, but you ordered another margarita, correct?" she asked.

"Yes, that's mine," she said and snatched the glass from the woman.

"Thank you," Len said to the waitress, who turned red.

"Let me know if you need anything else," she answered and turned, hurrying off.

I smiled at Len, trying not to give anything away while we continued our drinks at the pub.

Hours passed and Len stared at the wall where we'd updated our information. It'd been like this since we returned from the pub. Eventually, she and Mallory tired of the place and parted ways, much to my satisfaction.

Len continued to look at the two pictures we'd hung of our most likely suspects. Visualizing it all helped me build the pieces of the case and see things from a bigger picture, even if it was cliché.

The sheriff and Ethan's photos hung side by side, the best leads we had.

I knew what I had to do next, but I dreaded it. The moment the FBI arrived, I'd have to turn over what I'd found so they could look over that security footage. Asking Mags now was too risky. It was an active case, and if she found anything, it would raise too many questions that could reflect on her reputation. I wasn't willing to do that to her.

Instead, I'd wait.

"I don't see it," Len said suddenly.

"That sounds like the margarita talking," I teased, but Lenny scowled back at me.

"I only had two. Mal was the one who left tipsy."

"For that, we are lucky, or she may have never agreed to let you come back with me," I answered.

Len chuckled. "Thank you. For letting her come along. It was nice to feel normal, even if just for an hour."

I pulled a chair from the dining room table to sit next to her. "What are you trying to see?"

"How it all connects. How do you know it could be them?" she asked.

"I'm building the profile piece by piece. That's what all of this is," I said, motioning to the wall.

"How?" she repeated.

"I'll show you," I said, taking her hand and helping her up.

I walked her over to the start of the wall, where we hung the photos of the victims.

"What are the two things investigators found to be common amongst them?" I asked.

I sound like such a teacher. Maybe the academy had become a bigger part of me than I thought.

"The pub," Len guessed.

"And?"

She stared at the photos of each victim before shaking her head.

"There's nothing else connecting them," she said.

"Are you sure?"

She glanced back to the board, following my line of thought, noticing the purposeful way I'd arranged everything.

"The rings," she answered, glancing to me for approval.

I nodded. "Those two connections give us a lot more information than it may seem. The pub tells us the unsub has a hunting ground, a place where they feel comfortable enough to stalk their victims and pick them out. It will be someone who frequents the pub; it also tells us the likelihood of it being a tourist is much lower."

"So it's someone who lives here year round and is familiar with the town," Len said, nodding along.

"Exactly, although that still leaves a whole pool of people, so we need more," I said. "That's where the ring comes in. It's their MO, a piece of every single killing. The ring tells us about the demographic of the victims but also about the unsub."

"How?" Lenny asked.

"The ring symbolizes commitment, a relationship. This tells us the unsub is targeting women they've identified as in relationships. It helps us build victimology which is a key piece to the profile. The aggressive and hateful nature of taking the ring off the victim and shoving it down their throat tells us the unsub feels some type of resentment toward those in happy relationships," I explained.

"So they were probably hurt at some point in a relationship?" Len asked.

I had her full attention.

"It's highly likely a woman left them or broke their heart. I would be willing to guess the unsub was engaged or in a serious relationship with a woman that ended poorly," I answered.

There were other possibilities, but this was the one that fit the case the best. I always considered all my options, though.

"Of course, there is also the chance something else triggered them. They could have grown up in a household with an unhealthy relationship. Maybe they witnessed their mother being unfaithful. This is why we don't rely solely on the profile to make an arrest."

"I think I get it now," Len said.

I moved down the wall to other pieces of evidence we'd hung. "You confirmed the theory that the unsub targets those in relationships. You were with Jake that night, you were engaged, the unsub likely saw the pair of you at the bar," I explained and pointed to the question mark we'd hung to represent Jane Doe, or Len.

"And now, you also know about the drugging," Len pointed out.

I could see the excitement on her face. She moved along the wall with me, her mind starting to piece together exactly what I saw.

"Which tells us the unsub needs the victims weakened. It could be because they hunt in such a populated area, but it could also mean they're impaired in some capacity. It also tells us they like the rush of power. I wouldn't be surprised if they carried this over to their work, put themselves in positions of power in their daily life."

"I think I'm starting to see what you mean," Len said,

leaning against me as I stopped moving down the wall. "Each of these is like a puzzle piece. We just need to figure out how it all fits, right?"

I nodded. "The sheriff and Ethan from the pub fit the profile we've built so far the best, but we don't want to blind ourselves from other options, since we don't have all the pieces yet. That's why we are considering multiple people," I said, waving at where I'd hung them.

"So you're pretty much saying we have everything and nothing all at once," she sighed.

"I'm saying we have a hell of a start, and with you by my side, there is no doubt in my mind we will figure this all out."

Blood pooled on the floor around me, the same scene every single time. I held Blythe in my arms and watched the life drain from her. There was nothing I could do but watch in horror as she took her last breath. The red around us grew until it was the only thing that filled my vision.

Red.

The floor around me was a pool of it. My hands and arms were covered. My breathing became shaky at the sight.

"Please," I begged.

I was trapped in my own horrible nightmare. I couldn't escape the mistakes of my past.

Red continued to grow.

The little girl I saved stood close behind me, her tiny hand on my shoulder.

"Go find help," I instructed her, just as I had every single time I lived this nightmare.

The moment she sprinted off, I called out, hoping anyone would find us before it was too late. In my heart, I knew she was beyond help, but I continued to scream.

Arms pulled me into someone's grasp. I fought against it until I heard her voice.

"Stone," Len said frantically. "Stone, wake up! It's a dream. Wake up."

The desperation in her words snapped me out of it. I sat up and opened my eyes, finding her watching me. Her brows furrowed, her hands shaking on my shoulders. She pulled them back quickly.

I caught a glance at the clock hanging on the wall—10:00pm, which meant I hadn't been asleep long. We'd spent the rest of the day looking over the case details until our eyes were heavy with sleep.

"I'm sorry. I heard you yelling. I thought something was wrong..." She slid back from the couch, ready to return to her room.

"Sorry, I didn't mean to wake you," I apologized.

"What were you dreaming of?" she asked gently.

I took a deep breath. She already knew everything, the whole story. What harm would telling her this do?

"I have nightmares about Blythe and everything that happened," I admitted.

She didn't look shocked, nor did her features slip into judgment. Instead, I found understanding.

"I have them too," she said softly. "About my attack."

"I'm sorry," I said, knowing the pain and horror of the nightmares that plagued me nightly.

She shook her head. "You shouldn't be alone down here," she said, her brows bunching. "Being alone is the worst part. I've spent three years plagued by the nightmares, trust me. Just come up to bed with me. It's yours anyway," Len finished quietly.

I hesitated, knowing that if I took this, everything would change. I'd be giving in to every emotion I was ignoring, the entire reason I'd allowed her to help me with this case in the first place. Something I'd never experienced before her.

"Okay," I said gently.

A smile spread across her face, and she stood, heading for the stairs.

It was just the nightmares. This was to help them, a purely selfish reason. Nothing beyond that. I couldn't let myself feel more than that, could I? How could I keep Len safe if I let myself feel too much?

I walked up the stairs behind her, my head racing. No matter how much I wanted to run back down them, I couldn't my mind needed this.

I needed this.

I needed just one night of sound sleep, no nightmares plaguing me. That was all.

I found myself back in the room I had given up earlier for Len. Her stuff was sprawled in the corner, but otherwise, it remained as I left it.

She climbed back under the covers and left enough room for me to join. Slowly, I followed behind her, hesitant to cross any boundaries.

You're already well past boundaries.

Grey would not see this as acceptable if he found out.

Merely inches from each other, I could feel the warmth of her body. I held my breath, afraid to even move. Already, I could feel the tension leaving me, forgetting about the nightmares that consumed me. Len's presence was comforting, and somehow, I felt safer around her.

You still barely know her.

Yet, it felt like I'd known her a lifetime.

Enough to make me question everything enough to drive any man to insanity. Maybe that was what this was: my mind finally turning on me, driving me slowly to madness. I knew everything about this was wrong, to be involved with someone so wrapped up in the case. It broke just about every rule, but I couldn't help it.

"Hold me," she said so softly, I thought I misheard.

"What?"

"Can you hold me? It helps knowing you're there."

I knew what she meant, just like my body craved her and knew it needed her to feel safe.

I moved closer, my arms wrapping around her, pulling her against my body. Everything in me should hate this, should know that this was wrong; instead, I felt peace from the nightmares. She relaxed in my arms, and her breathing became heavier. With each deep breath I took, I found myself inhaling the scent of sea salt and sage.

Not once did the nightmares come back for me.

My phone buzzed the next morning, Mags' name flashing on the screen

"Hello?" I sleepily answered, crawling out of the bed before Len could wake.

"Stone?" she answered.

"What's wrong, Mags?" I asked, getting worried. I hurried into the hall, away from Len.

"They're on their way," she warned.

"What? Who?" I asked.

"Agent Grey and the rest of the team. They got the call about the latest Coastal Killer victim and are heading there today," Mags said, her voice steady. "Grey wanted me to call you."

"Does he know I'm here?" I asked quickly, my heart dropping.

If he was on his way, the second he realized I'd been here, Grey would send me back to Quantico. He told me to leave this case alone, and I didn't listen.

"No," Mags said. "That's part of why I 'm calling. He wanted me to inform you they were heading to Briarport..." Her voice trailed off at the end.

"What is it, Mags?"

"He wants you to join them. He thinks it's time you finally got back into the field," she answered.

Oh, I was in so much more trouble than I originally calculated.

19

LENNY

STONE WAS GONE by early morning, and I woke up to no one in the house. At first, I thought I was dreaming, hearing a noise downstairs, but then, another knock came to the door.

I knew Nelson fairly well. He visited the museum often, an old friend of Francis. If he was stopping by, the least I could do was answer. Stone clearly wasn't around to do it.

I hurried downstairs, still in my pink fuzzy bathrobe, and opened the door. Instead of Nelson, I found Calvin grinning like a complete idiot in the doorway.

"Happy Birthday," he said and pushed by me into the house.

I had no time to register what he was doing. He moved into the living room and plopped down on the couch, setting a tray of something he'd carried in aside.

"How did you know where to find me?" I asked.

"Stone," he said.

"When did Stone tell you?" I pushed, crossing my arms and standing in front of him.

"When he came to tell me you were leaving with a stomach ache from dinner," Calvin explained.

Duh, Len.

I kicked myself for almost forgetting about the dinner I bailed on.

"I'm sorry. I hope the rest of the night went well," I said and sincerely meant it. "I'm really happy for you two."

My heart still stung at the thought, but I was genuinely excited for my brother. Even if I couldn't become pregnant again, that didn't mean he didn't deserve to have kids of his own. No matter what tragedy I faced, the world kept moving, and eventually, I had to face that.

"Do you know what you're having?" I dared to ask.

"A girl," he answered with a warm smile.

My heart swelled. Picturing my brother as a girl dad made me incredibly happy. I sat down beside him and threw my arms around him. He grunted but wrapped a hesitant arm around me.

"You really will be great parents," I said.

"I don't know about that," Calvin said, pulling his arm back and rubbing his head.

"You guys practically took care of me for a year when Jake left me, and look how I turned out," I teased.

"I don't know-" Calvin started. "You're still a little strange."

He smiled wickedly at me, but the usual older brother teasing rolled right off my back.

"Seriously, though. You guys will do great."

"Thank you," he said.

He grabbed the tray he'd placed aside and handed it to me. "Eloise sent birthday cookies."

"Tell her thank you for me," I answered, noticing she'd made my favorite: double chocolate.

"Will you be spending today with Stone?" Calvin asked.

I heard the real question hidden under it. Nosey brother, trying to figure out what exactly me and Stone were.

"Doubt it," I shrugged. "He's not here, and I honestly have no idea where he went."

"Then Mallory?" he asked, and I saw the slight frown growing.

"Yes," I lied, not wanting to worry him.

"Good. I have to run into work today. Otherwise, I'd offer," Calvin said.

"Work on Saturday?"

"I'm working overtime to prepare for this baby," he answered with a smile.

"Now who's the workaholic?"

He threw his hands up. "I suppose it's me now," he laughed.

I hated that he had to go. I didn't want to return to sitting in this empty house, the lie of seeing Mallory causing more disappointment. Her name reminded me of something I needed to ask my brother.

"Hey, you used to be friends with the sheriff's son, Chris, right?" I asked.

"I did," Calvin said, his brows furrowing.

"But you aren't anymore?" I asked.

"Not since that trip I helped him and his father with three years ago."

"Trip?"

"Remember the one I borrowed your camping gear for?" he said.

The Briarport Wilderness Trip—Id completely forgotten about the annual trip sponsored by the sheriff's office meant to teach elementary students wilderness skills.

"I do now," I said with a nod.

"Well, when we were on the trip, I just realized what an asshole the guy is," he said.

"That seems to be the sentiment around town," I murmured.

"When news reached the sheriff of another killing, Chris thought it'd be hilarious to scare the kids on the trip. Half of them wanted to leave early, thinking the Coastal Killer would be coming for our trip next," Calvin said as he shook his head. "Made me realize that wasn't someone I wanted to be friends with."

A killing while they were on the trip meant...

"Mallory doesn't like him either," I added.

"Good. You both should stay far away from him."

It was rare I saw Calvin's overprotective side, but his words came out firm, with no room for argument. I appreciated the sentiment.

"I have to get to work, but I hope you have a good birthday, Len," he said, standing and heading toward the door. "I'll see you at the clambake, right?"

"I'd never leave you to fend for yourself with our parents," I joked.

"Good, because you owe me for leaving me alone with them before dinner was over," he teased back.

I watched him head out the door and back to his car before returning to the kitchen to start my breakfast and coffee.

I sat alone in the rental for hours before deciding to go for a walk to the beach. Stone had been gone all day, and I was starting to think he'd entirely forgotten my birthday.

Impossible; that man remembered everything.

Maybe he just didn't care. Maybe birthdays were just another day to him.

He didn't owe me anything, but I would be lying if I said my heart didn't ache a bit at his absence. When I woke, he'd already left the house—without me.

The past few weeks, we'd become inseparable. Everywhere he went to investigate the case, he'd taken me with him. There was the possibility he just needed time to himself, but why'd it have to be today?

I'd spent so many birthdays alone, I just thought this one would be-

Don't finish the thought.

It will only hurt more.

I kept walking down the path until it turned to sidewalk. I continued until I found an outlet that led to the water. The sand was warm against my feet as I slipped my sandals off and carried them.

There wasn't anything I enjoyed more than this view, the waves crashing against the shore and the sun shining down on the water's surface.

The tourists were well down the beach, and the portion I sat on was practically empty. I tucked my knees in, holding them to my chest. I could spend hours just watching the way the waves moved, listening to their lulling sound.

I sat for what felt like hours without moving, just sitting with my thoughts.

Maybe I'd misread everything. Maybe I really just was Stone's partner.

I'd slept wrapped in his arms, free from nightmares for the first time in years. That couldn't be nothing. I needed it to be something.

I continued to watch the sun move across the sky and the ocean. Birds flew overheard, and a few locals walked by every now and then. I barely moved. There was not a single piece of me motivated to return to the empty rental.

If I did, I would just curl up in bed with a book and hide until Stone finally came back. Could I just pretend like this meant nothing to me? Maybe I could go back to sleep and wake up to forget everything?

I could just go back to cuddle with Alonzo and Birdie.

And that was when I realized I had become completely pathetic. Spending my birthday with my cats as company? I didn't expect to reach this point until at least sixty, not my late-twenties.

A shadow grew over me, and I forced myself to turn to see who had blocked my sun. I squinted as I glanced up, still partially blinded by the sun.

Towering over me, staring down at me with his curious brown eyes, Stone held out a hand.

20

STONE

I HAD JUST one day of freedom left before I knew I had to face my Supervisory Agent. I'd made the call and agreed to meet him in Briarport. What he didn't realize was, I was already there. It bought me a few days, but Sunday, I had to finally meet him.

For now, I had one last day.

It was Len's birthday, and instead of spending it with her, I was running around town to find everything I needed to make it perfect.

This was what unprepared felt like?

Not a feeling I was familiar with.

When I got back to the house, finally, Len wasn't anywhere to be found. I was slightly thankful, since I would have the opportunity to finish what I started.

Everything I planned was almost completed. There was just one last thing to do.

What I hadn't expected was for it to take me another few hours to finish. By the time I was done, it was already well into the afternoon. Len still hadn't turned up at the house, and I had a sneaking suspicion I knew exactly where she was.

I packed everything I prepared into a picnic basket and closed the lid. The basket had been laying around in the house, perfect for the rest of the day I planned for her.

The door shut behind me as I walked out of the rental and made my way through the garden. I could hear the ocean and knew if I just followed it down the path, I'd find Len.

I took the first outlet I saw to the private beach, free from tourists but a perfect spot for locals. I spotted her long, curly hair straight ahead of me, sitting in the sand, her favorite place.

"There you are," I said, reaching out a hand as I approached her.

She was already turning around, tipped off by my shadow. There was a gloom in her eyes that made my heart sink.

She took my hand and stood without a word.

"Come on. I'm taking you somewhere new," I said, trying to be upbeat.

You're imagining it. It's her birthday; she can't possibly be this upset, right?

She barely reacted.

Wrong. Time to work double time to fix it.

It didn't take us long to walk back to the rental and to my car. I opened the door for her like I always did and shut it behind her. The drive would only be fifteen minutes, from everything I calculated. The chance I was taking was starting to feel like a bit of a miscalculation. Maybe I'd been wrong to think this was what she'd want...

The car shifted to park as we arrived just on the outskirts of town. Before I could get out, Len had already opened her door and hopped out. I hurried after her, grabbing the basket and a blanket I'd placed in the back seat.

"A picnic," I said. "Follow me."

She walked behind me as I headed for the path. I knew exactly the spot. I'd spent hours researching online to find it. It was only a quick walk, and from what I could tell, it was a lesser known location. Most tourists didn't bother coming out here when they had the beach.

The spot was empty, a small hill leading to it. I paused and waited for Len, holding out a hand, which she hesitantly took.

We climbed the small hill to the cliffside. The grass was plush in this area, and the view was beyond what I'd expected, the sky a pink and orange mix as the sun started to set.

Sunrises over the ocean and sunsets over a view like this? I was starting to see why so many chose to remain in Briarport.

Len let go of my hand, her grasp already reluctant before releasing me. I spread the black gingham blanket I packed on the ground, plopping the wicker basket on top of it. We both sat, and already, I could sense her reluctance.

"What's wrong, Len?" I asked, searching her rich brown eyes for answers I couldn't quite grasp myself.

"It's nothing," she muttered.

"It isn't nothing," I pushed. She was holding back. I didn't want her to hide things from me, to close herself off.

She'd done enough of that for the last three years; there was no need for her to carry that pain alone. I knew something was wrong. I could see it in the way her eyes focused on a single spot on the blanket, and her brows furrowed ever so slightly. Her gaze was distant, like she was barely there in the moment.

"It's just-" she started. "It's seriously nothing."

"Lenny," I pushed, the name grabbing her attention.

"You're the only one who calls me that," she pointed out, avoiding my prodding.

"I'm the only one who noticed the way your lips slightly pull up into a smile at the sound of it, or the way you sometimes blush when you hear it."

That brought a familiar pink to her cheeks.

"You can tell me," I added. "I won't judge you."

"The past three years, I have had no one. No one to celebrate with, no one who wanted to do anything for my birthday. Sure, I get the yearly birthday call from my parents, or the occasional visit from my brother, but they have been far too busy to make a day of it. I've never really cared much for my birthday, but it would be nice just once to spend a day forgetting about the rest of the world. I thought this might be that year, but-"

She cut off, averting her gaze again.

"I didn't show," I guessed, finishing her thought.

My heart sunk. She'd been waiting all day for me to show, and I let her down. Why had I been so insistent on getting the details right? I should have been there; maybe putting together this entire afternoon had been a mistake.

"You barely know me," she whispered, her eyes settling on a bunched up portion of the blanket. "You weren't obligated to spend my birthday with me."

A twinge of guilt shot through me. I'd assumed Mallory or Calvin would have spent the day with her while I was out. I never wished for her to sit alone at the beach on her birthday, but gathering everything I needed had taken all day before I could make it to her.

Communication and feelings were never my strengths, and I was already drowning trying to show Lenny today mattered.

"I do know you," I said quietly.

Her rich, dark eyes glanced up to find mine, and I pulled the basket I'd brought closer, slipping a hand inside. "I know that every few days, you change out the flowers in the vase on the counter, but they are always the same," I said, pulling out a bouquet of daisies and handing them to her.

Her eyes widened, taking in what I'd calculated to be her favorite flower. Each time I'd seen the vase, daisies sat inside, but as days passed, I noticed they were changed out for new ones.

I pulled out a small gift wrapped in simple brown parchment paper and handed it to her.

"What's this?" she asked softly.

"My gift to you."

Her fingers fiddled with it until she finally unveiled the gift hidden inside. She pulled out the book, flipping it in her hands. The edges were a shining gold, and the cover was embossed with a floral design. I'd found the special edition in a tiny bookshop in town.

"Little Women?" she asked. "Like the classic?"

"Yes. I know you mainly read romances, but I wanted to share one of my favorite classics with you. One I thought you too may enjoy, based on the books I found on your shelf."

Her cheeks turned pink at the mention of me browsing through her own collection.

"Thank you," she answered, struggling to find more

words. "I-" She turned it in her hands again and flipped through the pages. Her eyes widened, and my own smile grew.

"You annotated it?" she asked, looking quickly to me." When did you have time?"

"I did," I said. "I've been adding the notes the past few days when I could. I wanted you to have my own thoughts and comments as you read through as well. "

I didn't add the part I'd been avoiding.

In case I was back in Virginia by then.

Her face started to fall reading between the lines. My clever girl, too smart for even my distractions.

"I know you spend time reading every single food label you pick up. Some probably assume you're just checking the calories or sugar, but I've seen the way your eyes read over every ingredient."

I continued trying to avoid the topic of when I leave all together.

I saw her eyes water a little. She grasped her bouquet of flowers, and I could see her taking in every word I said. Her attention was entirely mine, and I wanted to savor every second of it.

"I also know you don't keeps eggs in your fridge and avoid the ones in mine because you're allergic. It's why you check every single label. Eggs, a staple and key ingredient in most birthday cakes. It took me a little longer to find you today, because after quickly realizing not a single grocery store or bake shop in this little town makes eggless cakes, I decided to give it a try myself. Admittedly, even though baking is a science I am familiar with, I seem to lack that magic touch bakers have." I laughed and opened the lid of the basket fully.

I pulled out the small plate with the makeshift cover, revealing the small cake I had made. It was crumbly and the frosting was lumpy, but it was chocolate cake and frosting with strawberries on top. Again, her favorite.

"Why?" she asked.

"Because I do know you, Lenny," I stated. "And I wasn't going to let you spend another birthday alone. I'm sorry I wasn't there sooner. I should have found you this morning instead of this." I nodded to the cake.

"No." She stopped me, placing a hand on my chest. "It's perfect."

"You deserve nothing less," I said, watching her flip through the book still.

She set it down and reached out for one of the strawberries on top of the cake, taking a bite and giggling in delight. "You didn't have to do all of this, really. I'm sorry I let my emotions get to me today."

"Do not ever apologize for feeling," I quickly said. "That is what makes you so perfect in my eyes. You never once hide what you feel. You care, and that is what matters. You care enough to find justice for victims many forgot about. You care enough to put yourself in danger just to protect this town."

"I can't help it. Someone needs to care for them," she said.

"I am glad I met you, Lenny," I admitted, and she glanced up from the book.

She sucked in her lower lip trying to hide the growing smile, her cheeks warming.

"You are my aftermath," I continued. "After every horrible

thing we've been through, this is the future we deserve. I promise you, we will get justice for the victims, and you will never have to live in fear again."

Before I could say another word, Len leaned in and crashed her lips into mine, taking me by surprise.

They were light and delicate, gentle. Shock overcame me for only a moment before I returned the kiss just as passionately. Each second that passed I wanted to savor forever. It was everything I imagined, sweet but desperate. There was nothing that could take this moment from me.

Not the thoughts I kept trying to shove away, not Agent Grey and the rest of the FBI, and certainly not the Coastal Killer.

Len's hands draped over my shoulders and clasped behind my neck as she settled in to the kiss. I pulled back for only a second, our noses practically touching. The warm flecks in the brown of her eyes were even more noticeable up close.

I wanted everything she had to offer. Those were dangerous thoughts, but in the moment, I couldn't help myself. All logic went out the window.

"Are you sure?" I asked Len.

Never once did I want her to feel she had to take this risk.

"I have never once been more sure in my life," she whispered.

If I don't kiss her again, I might lose my mind.

There was nothing that could hold me back anymore. I kissed her again with even more intensity. My lips pressed to hers, and I let my hand drift up to cup her cheek. I was gentle, but I let myself hold her with a certain level of desperation.

Len was everything.

Every logical thought in me told me to pull back, that the FBI would find out and throw me off the case the moment they arrived. That this would only incite the killer further, their obsession with Len growing by the day.

Her fingers dug into the back of my neck, like she was clinging to me, afraid to let go. The cool summer breeze up on the cliffside blew her curls forward, tickling my skin. An eternity passed before I even considered pulling back.

Her lips tasted like strawberries, the fruit still fresh on her tongue. I bit gently at her lip and felt her fingers curl in response. If this was all I ever got, then that was enough. As much as I wanted to give myself fully to Len, I knew it wasn't that simple for her.

Len had a life in Briarport. Even if we found the Coastal Killer, I would be leaving for Quantico after. It wasn't fair to promise her something I couldn't give her here.

She continued to kiss me, each second more passionately than the last. We were in our own little bubble of peace and blissful ignorance to the problems we left behind in the coastal town.

A sound off to the side had Len pulling back. She giggled, catching sight of two squirrels chasing each other across the grass.

The sky over the cliff was already growing dark, and I didn't want to keep Len out in the park when it finally grew pitch black.

"We should head back," I said, each word paining me.

The wince that escaped her lips hurt me even more. At least I hadn't imagined her wanting this as much as I had.

"I don't think we want to find out what it's like here after the sun sets," I pointed out.

"Stop being so reasonable," she said and shoved my arm.

"Unfortunately, there's no off switch," I laughed.

She rolled her eyes. That was the Lenny I knew.

"Let's go," I said, cleaning up the picnic. "If we hurry, we can get back with enough time for you to read at least two chapters of that thing before you fall asleep."

Len's smile grew even more, something I didn't think possible.

"We need to stop somewhere on the way back," she said.

"What are you looking for?" I asked.

Len still had a key to the museum and had used it to let us in. No one else was around, and she dragged me to the back, to the filing system. "I need to find an old article."

Folders sat a mile high on top of the cabinets as she pulled them out and disregarded them.

"Can I help?" I offered.

"No," she stated, pulling another folder out and setting it aside. "I organized this. I know it's in here somewhere."

The stacks only grew, and eventually, I took a seat in an office chair to watch. I wanted to give her the space to search without me hovering over her every move.

With each folder that came out, I tried to catch a glimpse. I saw dates labeled on some and event titles on others. Most were from three years ago, and I tried not get too far ahead of myself, assuming Len had something to help our case.

My phone buzzed from where it sat on the desk I had commandeered. My mother's name flashed on the screen.

"Hello?" I answered.

"Winston?" my mother said through the phone.

I noticed the way Len slowed her search, listening while she worked.

"Is everything alright?" I asked.

"It's been a bit since we've heard from you. I know you're on an assignment in the field, according to your sister, and I just wanted to make sure everything was going well."

Even in my late twenties, the worrying never stopped.

I appreciated the concern. More than anything, my mother cared about Lyla and me.

"The case is moving along," I said, careful not to share much detail. "I believe it will be wrapping up soon."

Len froze at those words. The way her body tensed made me immediately regret them.

"That's perfect!" she said, her voice growing more excited. "That means you may just be able to make it home for the holidays this year after all."

Ah, there it was.

I knew it was coming eventually. It'd been far too long since I last visited, and I was longing for a trip anyway.

"As long as nothing else comes up, I will be there," I promised her. "But we have a few months still to plan the details."

"I know, but you're hard to nail down with how busy the FBI keeps you. I wanted to make sure I brought it up early."

"I appreciate it," I said. "I do have to get back to work right now, but I promise, we can discuss more the moment this case ends."

Guilt washed over me for rushing her off the phone, but I knew I should get back to supporting Len with whatever she'd dragged us to the museum for.

"I love you, Winston," she said.

"I love you too," I answered before hanging up the phone.

Len glanced back over her shoulder, as if she was just realizing I had been on the phone. I knew better than that.

"Sorry," I said and slid my hand through my hair. "It's been awhile since I've seen my mother and sister, so they have been a bit more antsy to get me on the phone lately."

"I don't mind," Len answered with a shrug.

She turned back to flipping through the files. I watched her for a few more minutes, waiting for her to give some hint of what she was looking for.

"Here!" she shouted.

The folder was thin, and she pulled a single sheet of paper from it. I walked over to get a better look at it. *The Briarport Chronicle* header was on the top, an article and photo printed on the sheet.

"The sheriff?" I asked, immediately recognizing the man.

"Look at the date," she insisted.

My eyes wandered to the top to find it dated three years prior. June 10th, to be exact. The date immediately stood out in my mind. I'd memorized every detail of the case, and my stomach sank, knowing what this meant.

It couldn't be him.

"The last victim before you," I said.

She nodded. "My brother went on this trip. He reminded me today when he stopped by this morning, and I asked about Chris. It's when he stopped being friends with the sheriff's son, but it also means the sheriff wasn't here to commit one of the murders. That trip takes place an hour away. They bus the kids and chaperones out there. It'd be almost impossible."

"That takes him off of our suspect list," I confirmed.

"That just leaves us with Ethan, then?" she asked, a disappointed look on her face.

"You don't think it's him?" I asked.

"It's just-" she started. "It's nothing."

She put the article away in the folder, returning everything to where she'd found it. I grabbed folders to help her and passed each to her as she started asking for specific ones.

"It's not nothing," I urged. "If you know something more, it could help us."

"It's just a feeling," she answered. "When I saw Ethan, I barely remembered him from that night. I just don't feel like he's the one who attacked me."

It only took a few minutes for us to return all the folders to their spots.

"I told you it was nothing," she said pointedly.

"That isn't nothing. You should trust your instincts. We don't have enough evidence to point to Ethan either. We will keep investigating and keep our options open," I assured her.

Ethan fit the profile, but I also trusted Len's instincts. There wasn't enough to convict him, but I would keep going until I had enough to make an arrest. Whether that was Ethan or someone else we'd missed was yet to be decided.

"Thank you," Len said.

"This took no time at all. You don't have to thank me," I assured her.

"Not for this," she answered. "For believing me."

My heart swelled, and I took Len's hand as we left the museum. There was nothing that could take this night away from us.

Our last night of normalcy.

There was a package sitting on the steps when we returned.

The automatic lantern lights were turned on, hanging on the porch. It was hard to see in the growing darkness, but the package was placed right by the door.

A perfectly tied red ribbon sat on top of the white box. I froze to examine it, but Len kept walking toward the package. The gift had a tag that became visible the second Len picked it up.

"For me," she beamed.

Calvin already stopped by, and Mallory didn't strike me as the type to be thoughtful enough to drop off a gift...

Someone else whose attention was on Len.

The way my heart sped up had me rushing toward Len, but she pulled the lid off before I could stop her.

The way her face blanched, I knew something was wrong. She almost dropped the package before I managed to grab it from her hands. The lid fell to the ground, but the package itself remained in my hands.

Inside sat two items, perfectly placed on top of white tissue paper partially stained red.

A note, scrawled in red writing, the words *the first of many gifts* written on it. The red was still sticky, like paint that had yet to dry.

In the center of the box, placed perfectly, sat a ring finger. The cut was clean, the nails perfectly polished. Red.

"Len, come inside," I instructed.

I guided her inside and placed the box on the table, not touching anything. There could be fingerprints or other pieces of evidence inside. The more intact the box remained, the way we found it, the better for the FBI techs.

"Was that blood?" Len asked, her eyes distant.

"What?" I asked gently, guiding her to a chair.

"The note—was it written in blood?" Her eyes widened as they met mine.

"No," I assured her. "It looks like paint."

She nodded. "And the finger, it belongs to the victim from the other day, right? I saw her hand, the nails..."

"Yes," I answered.

I wouldn't lie to her, no matter how hard the truth was.

"This is all my fault," she muttered, her eyes filling with tears.

"No, Len. You can't think like that." I knelt next to the chair. Her gaze was set on her lap, but she moved to find me staring at her.

"This is not your fault. The sadistic things this unsub does are not your fault. They are toying with you," I explained.

"What do we do?" she said, her voice barely a whisper.

"I don't have the technology needed to examine this, and it's technically evidence in an active investigation. Hiding this would-"

Her face melted in both understanding and devastation.

"We have to turn it over?" she asked, but I knew she had the answer.

"Len, I would never suggest this if I didn't think it was the only option, but this unsub is escalating quickly. I need back up," I said.

Her hand found mine, and she held it in her lap. I needed back up; I couldn't do this myself. The last time I'd tried, someone died. That couldn't be Len. I wouldn't repeat my mistakes.

"I need to correct the past. I ran last time; I won't do that again, no matter the consequences," Len said, a determined look on her face.

A tear slipped down her cheek, and I reached up to brush it away.

"I'll be here every step of the way."

21

———

STONE

I SENT Grey and the rest of the team the location of the rental, and they arrived promptly at 7:00 the next morning.

The second Grey walked inside, I showed him the box, and he had another agent, Corson, tag it for evidence. The sheriff's office showed up shortly after to mark the rental a crime scene.

For Len's sake, I lied and said I found the box early in the morning, right before they all arrived.

Another agent, Alexir, asked Len a few questions while I stood close by and listened.

She stuck to everything I told her to say, which bought me time to explain everything to Grey.

"Stone," Grey called out, motioning for me to follow him into the dining room.

I knew what was coming—time had finally run out, and I needed to come clean. I'd run over the possibilities in my head a million times. The only one that made logical sense was telling him everything. We needed his resources, and I couldn't make an arrest without the FBI. Even if it meant sharing Len's secret, I knew it was the best choice. I still made sure she was alright with it the second we woke in the morning. If it wasn't what she wanted, I'd never force her into it. It was not my secret to share.

She agreed, even though I saw the fear that came with it, but she knew in the end, it was the only way to keep the town safe.

"What is this?" he asked and motioned to the wall I'd been building the case on.

I swallowed hard before sharing everything with him.

It'd been fifteen minutes of Grey laying into me. I'd fully expected it, but hearing him as livid as I knew he'd be was a horrible feeling. I swallowed hard as he sucked in a breath, ready to continue with every reason I'd messed up.

"You involved a civilian on an investigation I specifically told you to leave alone?" Grey shouted.

The house was not very large, and there weren't many rooms Len could be in where she wouldn't hear the scolding. A twang of guilt rushed through me, wishing I'd sent her somewhere else for this.

"We can do good here," I said. "I was useless at Quantico. Here, I'm actually helping, finding a killer we couldn't find the first time."

Grey crossed his arms, and his lips remained thin. "You weren't cleared to be in the field. I gave you orders. I risked my own badge to vouch for you. Your talent shouldn't be wasted, but I can't have you in the field if you are going to continue to be this reckless."

I nodded. He was right. Ever since that one decision that cost Blythe her life, I barely recognized myself.

I used to follow every rule. I'd memorized them, made

sure to implement every protocol the FBI had. They were there for a reason. It was how we saved lives.

Now, I'd become impulsive. Len clouded my judgement, and it was hard to stay impartial, to follow those same rules when it came to her.

"You directly disobeyed my order. This was reckless. You could've gotten her hurt. Not only that, but your presence emboldened the Coastal Killer to start again."

"They would've eventually killed more, and we both know it. Something set them off, and if it wasn't me, it could've been anything. It was bound to happen, and I'm glad I was here to step in when it did."

I felt his eyes boring into me. My decision may have been reckless, but it was right. If we had a chance to finally bring this town peace, there was no reason we shouldn't have taken it.

"It doesn't matter now. We're here because of you, regard-less of how asinine your actions may have been. I want you to brief me on everything you have."

Everything I had…

I knew I had to tell him, but everything in me dreaded it. I gestured toward the wall behind him. "This is everything I've gathered so far. We eliminated a few initial suspects, but Ethan, the bus boy at the High Tide Pub, seems most likely. I have a way to confirm it, but I need to pull footage from the tapes we took into evidence three years ago from the pub."

"What are we looking for?" Grey asked. Though I could tell he was still livid with me, he put that aside for the sake of the case. That's what made him a great supervisory agent: he was able to put aside his emotions to get the job done at the end of the day.

I knew this wouldn't excuse me, and I'd still face disciplinary action when I returned to Quantico, but I didn't care. If it kept Len safe, it was worth it.

"The night Jane Doe was attacked. We need to go back through the footage for that night."

"We've tried. There are far too many woman in that tape to identify who she is. She was mutilated when we found her. We could barely recognize her or match her with anyone from that footage. Her face was far too swollen when she arrived to the hospital and then vanished."

"But I know who she is now," I admitted.

Grey stared at me for a moment, taking in every word I'd said. His eyes seemed to shift beyond me to the doorway, and I knew he'd already pieced it together.

"No," Grey said. "Stone, I know you are not this oblivious."

"It was the only way," I said. "She had information. She's been working on this the last three years and gave me more than I had before. I was able to walk her through that night, and I have a way for us to confirm who attacked her."

"How?" Grey gritted through his teeth.

"Someone drugged her with something that wouldn't have shown up on a toxicology report. Something that went quickly through her system and wasn't initially tested for. If we watch that footage to see who drugged her drink, we'd know who attacked her. I'm willing to bet it was Ethan."

Grey stared at me for a moment, fury building in his eyes. I knew this would cost me my badge, but I didn't care.

"I'll call Mags to pull the footage. We'll deal with this after we make an arrest. I need your mind still on this."

I nodded.

Grey started to walk out of the room, but he turned one last time. "I hope she's worth this Stone."

I never felt more confident of an answer.

"She is," I whispered under my breath.

Grey returned shortly after, letting me know Mags was already diving into the footage. Len hadn't reappeared, but I imagined she was doing her best to avoid the agents and deputies swarming the house.

My stomach twisted with guilt, knowing this was her worst nightmare. Everything she'd run from had just showed up on the front porch.

It only took an hour before Grey's phone rang. He answered and turned on the speaker, Mag's voice immediately coming through the phone.

"You were right," she said. Her voice sounded shaken. "I went through all the footage from that night, focusing on Len. Approximately fifteen minutes before she leaves, Ethan very clearly slips something into her drink. I'm sending it to you now."

I opened my laptop on the dining room table and found the video clip already waiting for me. Grey moved to watch beside me. The second I clicked play, I spotted Ethan hovering near where the drink sat on the bar. It was ever so slight, hard to miss. His hand slipped over her drink, dropping something in, and then he hurried away to clear empty glasses from the counter.

My stomach turned at the sight. Knowing what came next made it all the more horrifying to watch and confirm.

Len had been right. She was drugged before she was attacked.

"Thank you, Mags," Agent Grey said. "I'll let you know if we need anything else."

He hung up and turned to me. "I need everything you have on him," he ordered. "If he is the Coastal Killer, I don't want him slipping through our fingers this time."

I hurried over to the wall, pulling down everything linking Ethan to the killings. I turned over all of it to Grey. "He fits the working profile." I showed him the blown up picture of a man about the same stature as Ethan wearing the hoodie with keys to the pub hanging out of their pocket. "Whoever left a threat at Len's door is linked to the pub."

"This is all circumstantial at best," Grey said.

"But now we have the footage," I pointed out. "Len also received threats via text and a call. I'll forward Mags the number and see what she can get from it."

"What about the latest victim?" Grey asked. "Do you have anything linking him to her?"

"I don't have any of the information on her yet, but if you give me everything you have, I will find something."

He typed something into his phone and gathered the papers I'd given them before walking toward the door. "Mags is forwarding you everything we know. Call me the second you have something."

I saw that Mags was already sending over information. A report with the woman's name popped up—like all the others, she was engaged.

One of the cats jumped into my lap, and I looked down to find Alonzo curling up. I'd given up on keeping them away in any capacity. They were starting to grow on me, honestly.

"It's Ethan?" Len said, standing in the kitchen doorway, startling me.

I cast a sympathetic look toward her. "How long have you been there?"

"Long enough."

"You know you're not supposed to be tangled up in this anymore," I said. "It's for your own protection."

"You didn't tell me any of this. I heard it myself," she noted. "Grey can't be angry when I heard it from his own mouth." She crossed her arms.

A warm chuckle escaped my mouth. Clever as always.

Seriously, was I going to let this girl go?

The memory of her birthday ran through my mind, the way it felt to kiss her finally.

I pushed it away. I couldn't lose focus. I needed to do whatever it took to keep her safe.

"Seriously, Len," I said.

"I know," she sighed. "I just still can't shake the feeling he's not the one who attacked me."

I knew I shouldn't, but I couldn't help it. I pulled out the chair next to me for her to join. The same video I watched played when she sat down. Her eyes widened, watching the screen as she saw the same thing I did: Ethan dropping something in her drink.

"I know it's hard to watch, but we need this to arrest him. He was definitely there that night. It's likely the side effects from whatever he used that left your memory hazy," I explained gently.

I did believe her, but the video itself couldn't lie. Ethan was involved in this.

She nodded and stood. As she did, she pressed a gentle kiss to my cheek, and I felt my skin warm at the contact.

"I'm going to go up and read for a little, since it's getting late," she said.

"I'll be up soon," I promised.

I hadn't missed a single night in the bed with her since that first time. We slept inches from each other, our presence enough to keep each other safe from the nightmares. She left the room, and I turned back to the laptop. I was desperate to find anything to connect Ethan to the most recent victim. I wouldn't stop looking until I did.

<hr>

I climbed in to bed with Len after a few hours of still finding nothing. She was turned away, reading the book I gave her. I tried not to disrupt her, but she closed the book and turned around, her brown eyes meeting mine.

"My family will be back in town soon," she said.

"For the clambake?" I inferred.

She nodded her head. "It will be the first I've seen them since leaving the dinner, besides Calvin stopping by on my birthday."

There was a hint of uncertainty there. If I could take away everything she was feeling to reassure her, I would, but there was no manual on how to do so. Everything with Len was a learning process. I was way out of my depth.

When it came to piecing together cases or evidence, analyzing what was in front of me, that was simple, an easy task. Trying to navigate what was happening between Len and I was impossible.

"They are your family," I said. "I don't think they'll hold it against you."

"It wasn't just one dinner," she said, and my eyebrows pulled together.

"What do you mean?"

"I haven't seen them in forever, not truly. Jake kept me away from them as much as he could, isolated me from anyone who might notice how controlling he was. I've been blowing them off for years. After him, I avoided them, afraid the damage I'd done was irreversible."

"That's not true," I said. "I avoided my family after everything with Blythe. I still haven't seen them in person. But after everything, when Grey pulled me back from the very bottom, I tried to make amends with my mistakes. The second I called my mother for the first time in months, the relief in her voice was enough to make me realize her love was not something so easily taken away. I saw how excited your family was to see you that night. Just let them in and give them a chance. You never know."

She gave me slight smile. "You really are always a voice of reason, aren't you?"

I pulled her in closer so we were only an inch apart. My lips pressed to her forehead as I leaned in and kissed her.

"I'm always here to be what you need," I said. "Goodnight, Lenny."

She rolled over, smiling as her eyes fluttered shut. It wasn't long before we both slipped into a deep sleep, easier than either of us ever had before.

22

STONE

I SPENT every waking hour trying to find the connection we needed to arrest Ethan. It'd been over a week, but still, nothing. We had enough to bring him in for questioning based on the footage we found of him drugging Len, but that was it.

Mags had combed back through all the footage the FBI had collected and found a few more clips showing him doing the same to the other victims. I forced myself to watch each one, fueling my motivation even more.

Part of me wanted to hurry and bring him in so he couldn't hurt anyone else, but I knew the second we showed our hand, he would retreat. There was a chance we'd lose him again. This time, he might move on to another town and evade us until he decided to kill again. If he waited three years this time, I could only imagine how long he could hold out the next time.

"You're killing yourself working on that," Len scolded from behind me.

"I can't stop until I figure out what I'm missing," I groaned.

"What about for a break to grab coffee?" she asked, batting her long eyelashes at me.

How could I deny that? "I suppose just an hour to clear my head could help."

She grinned and hurried off to find her purse. I shut my laptop and met her by the front door, ready to walk down into town.

By the time we made it to the café, Len had already tried to get more details of the investigation at least five times. It physically pained me to keep it from her.

"Two iced vanilla lattes," she told the barista when we made it to the counter.

"How'd you know that's what I want?"

"Lucky guess," she said with a wink. "I will say, I wouldn't have guessed you were an iced coffee person before I knew you, though."

"Lattes are gentler on my stomach, and they have less caffeine, so I can have more than one in a day," I explained.

"I should have known there'd be a practical reason," she laughed.

We grabbed the cups as they appeared at the end of the counter. Our walk back was mild, the weather not as scorching hot as when I first arrived in Briarport.

"I don't know if I could deal with such drastic changes of seasons living up here. This summer has been brutally hot, and yet you all deal with obscene amounts of snow come winter."

"I don't think I'll stay here forever," she answered. "I like the snow, but the winters are long. I think I want to experience a change in scenery eventually."

My ice rattled in my cup as I swirled the latte around,

trying to mix in the vanilla syrup that collected at the bottom.

"Virginia is perfectly mild. We still experience summer and winter, but it's a perfect balance between the two."

"Maybe that will be my first stop when I finally get out of here," she teased.

My heart jumped. I didn't mean to let my hopes rise, but the promise of seeing Len again, even when this was over, was far too great to ignore. If I could hold on to that possibility, it would make the painful reality feel dulled.

"Then I'll have to show you around," I answered, trying to keep the desire from my voice.

For a moment, there was a pause in which she stared back at me, her eyes full of longing. Before Len could answer, her phone began to ring inside her purse. She grumbled at the noise and ignored it.

"You should really check that," I said. "What if it's your parents or Calvin with news on their visit?"

"Fine," she sighed.

Her eyes widened the second they saw the screen, and I caught a glance over her shoulder at the number scrolling across it. I'd memorized it the last time they called. My hands scrambled for my phone and dialed Mags.

"Mags, I need you to trace a call on Len's phone," I said when she answered after barely a single ring.

Len answered her phone, and I knew Mags would already be well into trying to trace the caller. She'd need only a minute to find the exact location.

"Hello?" Len said, her voice hesitant.

"Keep them talking," I tried to mouth as softly as I could.

"Did you like your gift?" a robotic voice came through the speaker, muffled.

Len looked to me for guidance. The killer was seeking her praise, almost like they relied on it. She was the key to this all; we just didn't know how yet.

I nodded slowly.

"Yes," she said, and I could tell the word physically pained her. "It was thoughtful for you to think of me on my birthday."

Perfect answer.

It kept the Coastal Killer satisfied with her praise without mentioning the severed finger or victim at all. Len was doing great, and I reached out for her hand to give her reassurance. Her face flushed a little, and I felt her hand shaking.

"You've got this," I whispered.

"Another thirty seconds or so," Mags said into my ear.

"There will be more," the voice said through the speaker again.

"Please don't," Len said before I could cue her not to engage. Her voice trembled, and I knew the killer would hear it too.

"This is what happens when you don't listen," the voice scolded.

The phone call clicked off, and I knew the unsub was gone. Len handed the phone to me, like the killer might come right through the screen.

"For evidence," she said as she shoved it at me.

"It's alright. You can hold on to it," I said, trying to give it back, but she shook her head.

"Not right now," she answered softly.

I pocketed the phone so she no longer had to look at it.

"Please tell me you know where they are," I said into my own phone.

"Not exactly," Mags answered. "But we have a pretty small area narrowed down."

"Send the perimeter to my phone," I said. "And call Grey, let him know where to meet me."

The warehouses we pulled up to were clustered in a large lot near the water. The ocean abutted the business park, and there were a couple ships docked nearby.

Len and I hoped out of my car and glanced around. We made it back to the house in no time to grab my car and were given orders to wait until Grey arrived.

The rest of the team pulled up minutes later, Grey scowling as he stepped out of his own vehicle.

"I told you to stop involving her," he grumbled at me.

Len flinched at the statement.

"She was with me when the call came through. I wasn't wasting time arguing with her to stay at the rental rather than coming straight here," I argued.

"Fine," Grey snapped. "But she stays here. I won't have a civilian wandering around."

I nodded and glanced over at Len. Her eyes narrowed on me, and I knew I deserved it. I was complicit in Grey's orders and wasted no time removing Len from the case. This was her work the past three years, and as simple as that, she had been cut off from it.

Everything inside me hated that.

My mind was meant to follow rules and orders, but when

it came to Len, none of that applied. There wasn't a single rule that could convince me to let her go.

I was pushing every boundary I could while making sure I saw the case through for her.

I walked over and opened the passenger door of my car. "Stay here."

Len barely acknowledged my words, sitting with her arms crossed as I shut the door. When had this become so complicated? My loyalties to the FBI warred with everything I owed to Len.

I followed Grey, pulling out my gun and holding it in front of me. We didn't know exactly what we were searching for, but I kept my eye out for anyone I recognized from town. There weren't many workers in the area, and the ones who milled around saw us and steered clear.

Mags had narrowed it to a single warehouse, divided to house about five businesses. The team split up, half taking two and Grey and I taking the other three.

The first space we entered was small, and we found piles of pet supplies.

"Clear," Grey called out, and I echoed the same back to him.

We moved on to the second one and found an entirely empty space, abandoned by whatever business used it before.

We gave each other a wary look and pushed on to the third.

When I entered, I kept my gun raised and split off to the right. The warehouse space was small, filled with restaurant supplies. Boxes of beer and liquor were stacked high. I made my way down the row of them, finding nothing.

"Clear," Grey shouted across the space.

I made my way back to him, checking the last row of mine.

"Clear," I said, rounding the corner to find him waiting.

He pulled out his phone and dialed. "Did the others check in?" he spoke into it. "Alright." He hung up and turned to me. "Mags says the rest is clear as well."

I let out a groan as I holstered my weapon.

"Did you really think they'd still be here?" Grey asked.

"No, but I hoped something would." What was I even expecting?

Grey holstered his weapon and led me back to the door. A bunch of paperwork hung in a folder next to it and caught my eye. Receipts and order confirmations for everything inside the warehouse spilled over the edge, disorganized. Grey held open the door, but before I stepped through, I noticed a slip on the ground.

I froze, reading the name of the business written on it.

High Tide Pub.

I pulled out my phone and dialed.

"I just let Grey know everyone checked in," Mags answered cheerily.

"The warehouse we're in, does High Tide Pub rent a space?" I asked.

Grey's eyes bore into me, taking note of every word. I heard her fingers typing on the keyboard frantically, and another minute passed before she answered.

"Yes, it looks like one of the businesses they rent a space to is High Tide Pub."

"Thanks," I said before I hung up. "That's the connection," I said to Grey.

"We'll have to get a warrant for the security footage of the area. It's going to take a bit," he said, already typing out a message to Mags.

A weight lifted from my chest, knowing this was what we were looking for. The needle in the haystack of the case. We need something to tie everything to Ethan, and this was enough to do so. If we could prove he was here when the call was made, we could start tying everything back to him.

Grey and I walked back to the cars together, and a sinking feeling grew in my stomach the moment I spotted mine. Len was no longer the passenger seat. I glanced around, not seeing her anywhere nearby, and panic set in.

"Where did she go?" I asked.

Grey looked up from his phone and saw what I meant. He turned in a circle, not spotting her. I was already walking off, hurrying to find her. Was there a chance we missed something? Could the unsub have still been in the area, waiting for us to leave her alone?

My heart raced, and I found it hard to force myself to swallow.

I rounded the corner of a small building closer to the water and saw her standing with her back to me. Relief washed over me. I wasn't surprised to find her watching the waves.

"Len," I called out, but she didn't move. "Len, we're done here. There's nothing more. Let's go."

She still didn't budge.

I walked toward her and placed a gentle hand on her shoulder, trying not to startle her. She flinched and jumped away from me, her hand clutching the necklace she'd worn since dinner with her family.

"What's wrong?" I asked, seeing the look on her face.

She looked back out toward the water and pointed. I followed her finger and finally saw what had held her attention.

Propped against a wooden pole, right next to the water, was a body. The woman looked no older than Len, her head hung, lifeless.

I left Len and rushed over, immediately checking her pulse. The body was barely cold, but I couldn't find one. She couldn't have been sitting there longer than an hour. Blood seeped through her shirt, and I saw the wound that ended her life: one stab straight to the chest.

I rushed back to Len, my hands stained red. I was careful not to touch her, instead leading her back to where I knew the rest of the team stood.

The second Grey spotted us rounding the corner, he hurried over.

"There's a body," I said in a low tone.

He signaled to the other two agents to follow while I walked Len back to the car. I drove her straight back to the house and waited for Grey to come with an update. It wasn't until the sun set and I had Len sitting on the couch with a cup of tea that he finally came.

He knocked on the door before letting himself in. He went straight to the kitchen, away from Len. I followed, double checking she was alright before I did.

She'd barely spoken since we got back, still in shock.

"Another victim," Grey confirmed. "We found a ring shoved into her mouth like all the others."

"Do we know who she is or if she has any connections to the other suspects?" I asked.

"The sheriff's office ID-ed her, but we haven't found any

connections yet," Grey answered and shook his head. "Our best option is going to be the footage. We checked, and where she was left is a blind spot without cameras on it. We will have to canvas all of the others in the area."

I wasn't shocked. The unsub had been careful and calculated thus far. I doubted they'd leave a body in the open if they thought it would get them caught. No, their motivation was solely to leave it for Len. The killer kept us on the phone long enough for us to find that group of warehouses. They knew we'd be there.

"How is she?" Grey asked, and I was taken by surprise at his question.

"As good as she can be."

"Keep her close," Grey said. "Make sure she's alright. I doubt this unsub is done with her."

I knew he was right. The killer only seemed to escalate when it came to her.

"Let me know the second you have something from the footage," I said. "I'll be here, watching over her."

Grey nodded before he left, and I returned to Len. She sat with her legs pulled up on the couch, both of her cats beside her.

I sat on the other side, careful not to disrupt the felines.

"How are you?" I asked, a simple question, yet also impossible.

I knew it was more than just a one word answer. The entire case revolved around her; I couldn't imagine what that felt like.

"I just can't stop thinking about how that could've been me," she admitted. "All of this is happening because of me.

The unsub isn't going to stop killing. It's my fault. I said the wrong thing on the phone."

"No, Len," I stopped her. "That woman would've already been dead before you said that. The unsub is taunting you, trying to get a reaction. I know it's hard, but you have to try to ignore what they're attempting to wring out of you."

"I just can't stop blaming myself," she sniffled.

I knew nothing I said to comfort her would help, but I wanted to try anyway. "You are not to blame for the Coastal Killer's actions. You're as much a victim as any of the others. They're taunting you because they couldn't get to you. They know you're stronger than they are. Don't let them take that away from you."

She set aside her tea and moved closer, cuddling into my side. I wrapped an arm around her, holding her until she fell asleep after only a few minutes, exhausted from everything. Shock was mentally draining on a person.

After a bit, I scooped her up bridal-style and carried her up the stairs. I was still wearing my slacks and button down, but I didn't want to risk putting her down and waking her if I left her alone. I knew she needed me more than ever tonight.

I placed her gently down in bed and pulled the covers up over her before climbing in next to her. My arm wrapped around her waist and held her tight, hoping I could chase away the nightmares I knew would come.

The next morning, Len was up before I was. It was just before sunrise, and I could smell bacon filling the air in the house.

The scent of fresh brewed coffee hit me about halfway down the stairs.

When I made it to the kitchen, I found an entire plate and cup of coffee ready for me. The door to the sun room was open, and I walked in, carrying my breakfast, to find Len watching the sun rise over the water beneath the cliffside.

"Couldn't sleep?" I asked.

She shook her head, not looking away from the water.

"Can I join you?" I asked before I stepped up to her chair.

"Sure," she murmured, but she was barely present. Her mind was wandering.

I sat in a chair across from her at the small glass table set in the center of the room. With the sun rising, it was starting to warm already, the cool morning breeze disappearing. I'd miss views like this when I had to go back to Quantico.

The closest beaches were still far, and the view was nothing like what I found here. New England would forever leave its mark on me.

Len continued to sip at her own cup, gaze never faltering from the window. I watched the way her mind spun, the few times her lips parted like she wanted to say something. It was thirty minutes before I couldn't take the silence any longer.

"It's okay to not be alright," I said, hoping I could get through to her.

She turned toward me, her eyes locking with mine, as if trying to decide whether this was something she was ready to admit.

"It's also alright to be frustrated with me. I deserve it," I said.

"It's not that," she said immediately.

I couldn't help but feel a bit of relief hearing that.

"It's just-" she started and paused.

"This is your work," I guessed. "And now, in the blink of an eye, it has been taken from you. On top of that, you've already been through an ordeal."

She nodded.

"I'm not used to this. I worked hard to climb my way up at the museum. For the last three years, I have done nothing but throw myself into work, into research. To lose all of that in seconds? I'm just not sure how to process it yet," she admitted. "But at the same time, I never imagined things would escalate to this."

I was happy to see the incident from the prior day hadn't shaken her too badly. For all the trauma she'd been through, she was in better shape than most I had seen in the field.

"You haven't lost it all," I said. "Everything you have done is the reason the FBI is even here. Grey may be keeping you away from the case, but it's only for your own safety. You got us closer than we ever were before to making an arrest. That is all because of you. This town may finally get closure because of you, Lenny," I insisted.

"And you," she breathed.

"Don't give up on things yet," I said. "Even removed from the case, there is still plenty to be done. This town is going to need someone when this case ends, someone who knows it inside and out to assure them we arrested the right person. Someone to make sure every last victim is remembered."

She nodded along, and I saw the slight smile growing on her face.

"This town needs you, just as much as I needed you," I finally said.

Just as much as I still need you.

Her eyes searched mine before she stood from her seat. Her hands gripped either side of my chair as she leaned in.

"As much as I need you," she whispered before she kissed me.

It wasn't until later that day when I realized some of Len's distance was anxiety about her parents coming to town. They'd be arriving soon for the upcoming clambake, which I promised to attend.

We still hadn't heard from the FBI or Mags on how the warrant was going, or about combing through the footage from the warehouse area.

It would be a grueling process, which I knew could take days, weeks even.

The next few days passed, and Len only grew more anxious. There was little I could say to help, my own anxiety starting to take over, worried we'd find nothing tying Ethan to the warehouses.

Trust the process.

I repeated the mantra over and over to myself. If I could control my own fears and nerves, I could help Len as well.

We spent time exploring town, grabbing lattes, and reading through the books in the rental. Len was already on her re-read of the book I gifted her, and I caught her adding little notes of her own to it.

My heart swelled at that.

It wasn't until the night before the clambake that I finally saw Grey again. Len had gone to her apartment to swap out her clothing and visit Mallory. She insisted on going alone, given Mallory's distaste for me. The only way she'd forced me into agreeing was that she promised to be less than an hour and would text me every ten minutes. Excessive, but effective.

I had the rental to myself for a while, but quickly, a knock to the front door changed that.

The second I pulled the door open, I knew something was different. Grey's face looked almost excited.

"What's happened?" I asked, trying to contain the thoughts running through my mind and manage my expectations.

"The warrant came through, and they finished going through the footage," he said.

My heart stopped for a second before I forced myself to push forward.

"They found something?" I asked.

A grin spread across his face.

"We got him."

23

LENNY

MY PARENTS, Calvin, and Eloise all sat at a table I spotted as I walked up. The smell of the clambake filled the air, mixing with the salt of the nearby sea. My stomach growled just thinking about it.

A flash stunned me for a second, and I blinked away the brightness from my eyes, realizing a Briarport Chronicle journalist was snapping photos of everyone entering the event.

I gave a smile to the journalist, and they nodded back.

Where was Stone?

We agreed to meet at the festival, but I didn't see him anywhere. He promised to come, which meant he'd be there. There wasn't a single doubt in my mind.

I walked over to join my family—the last time we'd been together was the dinner I'd run off from.

"Lenore," my mother called. "Eloise was just telling us some of the names they're considering for the baby."

My sister-in-law smiled warmly at me, one of her hands resting on her tiny bump.

259

A tiny sting of sadness brushed against my heart, the feeling of having that same bump only a distant memory, but I was also overjoyed for her.

"Lenore is on that list, right?" I joked.

Laugh through the pain.

It was the only way I would survive. Push through, make the best of the situation. I didn't deserve to continue to live in misery.

My brother laughed while Eloise punched him lovingly in the arm before giving me a gentle smile.

"I think Lenore would make a fantastic middle name," she said and raised her brows toward my brother.

He scowled back at first, but eventually, her gave her a smile, which I knew meant she'd won that battle.

We talked and caught up on the past few weeks as people filtered in. Volunteers cooked, and some came by with bowls of melted butter to prepare for the clambake itself.

A movement caught my eye, and I spotted Stone walking nearby. I raised my hand and waved to him, catching his eye.

He reciprocated the wave and walked over quickly. By the time he made it over, I knew something was off.

"What's wrong?" I asked, catching his nervous glances.

His gaze was avoidant, but no one else seemed to notice.

"It's nothing," he said, but I could tell it was a lot more than nothing.

I knew my family was within hearing range, so I dropped it. Grey had already made it abundantly clear he was not to include me in any more of the investigation, but to share and risk my family overhearing was even worse.

I gave him a smile, trying to signal I understood, that we

could talk later. He grabbed my hand under the table in response.

For a while, my mother went on with baby questions, needing to know every last detail. I felt a bit bad for Eloise by the fourth or fifth round of interrogations. That was no small feat, getting through them all.

"I just don't know where I'm supposed to learn this stuff," Calvin complained. "There is far too much to remember."

"You'll get the hang of it faster than you'd think," Stone said.

My head turned quickly toward him, surprised by the comment. I didn't know he had any interest in babies, and my stomach started to turn, overthinking the comment.

Seeing the confused looks from the others, Stone chuckled warmly. "I have a younger sister," he said to my parents. "I've been helping since she was a baby, so I guess I know a little bit about what it's like to raise a newborn."

I let out a sigh of relief, squashing the thoughts cruelly forming in my mind and only making me anxious.

"Then I'll be coming to you with a million questions," Calvin teased.

A smile grew across my face, and my heart warmed watching them. He fit right in with the rest of us.

"Does your sister live in Quantico?" my mother asked Stone.

His face fell, but only for a second. "No, she lives in California with my mom," he said. "I'm hoping to go out there soon to visit."

I knew by his voice how much he missed them. He told me he hadn't seen them since before everything happened to Blythe. My heart ached for him.

"Len has never been to California," my mom pointed out.

I wanted to melt on the spot, completely and utterly embarrassed by her words. I knew she was playing matchmaker.

"I suppose I'll just have to take her with me," Stone said confidently, and my entire body just about caught on fire.

I glanced to him, and he gave me a genuine smile.

So he meant it?

I didn't have time to sort through all the feelings there. Nothing more had happened since my birthday, and I was starting to believe I may have dreamt it all along. Sitting here, I genuinely believed he meant every last word.

I tried to shake the feeling, knowing all it could bring was heartache. Stone had to return to Quantico to his job.

Volunteers carried out trays of food, setting everything on the tables. Clams, lobster, and corn, which my family dug straight into, and I gave Stone a quick grin before grabbing some for myself. It was his first time at the festival, and his first clambake, for that matter. I felt almost honored for it to be with me.

Everything was delicious, and it wasn't long before we'd ate our way through most of the food on the table.

"I've truly been missing out," Stone groaned after a bite of lobster.

Everyone around us chatted and enjoyed second help-ings. My parents had found us drinks, including soda for Stone. It warmed my heart that they'd even taken the time to remember he didn't drink.

It wasn't long before I felt the shift in the air, the way people started nervously glancing around, how the joyous chatter turned to whispers. I realized many were staring at

Stone and exchanging hushed words. I swallowed hard as my parents continued their conversation, blissfully unaware, and my brother helped Eloise pick apart her lobster.

"What happened?" I whispered under my breath.

"There's been a development in the case," he answered, noticing the unwanted attention.

"What happened?" I asked.

"We found Ethan on the footage at the warehouse, tying him there during the phone call and when we estimate the body was dropped."

My stomach turned, and I felt nauseous. This was the moment I'd imagined for years: the Coastal Killer finally seeing justice, so why did it feel so horrid?

"Did you arrest him?"

He nodded.

"That's why you were late," I stated pointedly.

"Yes," he admitted. "I wanted to tell you, but I didn't want to ruin this for you."

"You didn't think I'd find out?" I asked. "The whole town knew before I did."

"I'm sorry. I should've said something sooner. I just wanted you to have this one bit of peace with your family," he said.

I knew he meant it, that he had the best of intentions, but part of me still felt a little hurt that he didn't tell me sooner.

"The news is spreading. I'm sure the sheriff's office has already put out a statement," Stone said.

People stood from the tables, hurrying from the festival, and I knew they were heading to the sheriff's office. An arrest like this would draw a crowd.

My heart pounded, realizing what this news also meant. "When?" I asked.

Stone looked at me with pain in his eyes. I knew he felt it too. Whatever had grown between us was beyond just this case. I relied on him.

The way he chased away my nightmares, how he knew what I needed before I even said it, was a privilege I never knew I'd have to learn to miss.

"Three days," he answered.

The pit in my stomach grew. Only three days before I had to say goodbye.

I nodded as my family stood, realizing the majority of the town was rapidly filing out.

"Where are they off to?" my mother asked.

"The sheriff's office," I answered.

My entire family turned toward me, and Stone waited patiently for me to take a breath before letting them know what happened.

"The Coastal Killer has been arrested," I said, the words not feeling real.

My brother and sister-in-law looked at each other, shock on their faces. My mother and father immediately went on about what great news this was for the town, how much news coverage this would attract to Briarport.

"Mallory!" my mother exclaimed, catching my friend as she walked by.

It'd been a few days since I'd seen her, and I gave her a friendly wave to join us.

"Are you heading to the sheriff's office too?" I asked.

"Of course," she scoffed. "This is the most interesting thing to happen to this town in years."

"I'm not sure what everyone thinks they'll see," Stone muttered. "He's already inside for processing."

"Doesn't matter," Mallory said. "Tourists will flock to whatever they think the newest entertainment is."

"You're not a tourist," Stone pointed out, and I watched her nostrils flare at the comment.

"I imagine you'll be leaving soon, then," Mallory said. "And Len can finally return to her apartment." I didn't miss the smug grin spreading across her face.

"We should go with you," my mother said, stepping up next to Mallory.

"You're welcome to join," she answered, smiling brightly at my parents.

I didn't have the stomach to tag along. Stone was right—it was unlikely they'd even catch a glimpse at Ethan. My mother more likely just wanted to be near the news cameras.

I, however, preferred to stay far away from that spotlight. I'd had enough of the Coastal Killer for a lifetime. With him in prison, the victims would know justice, and my job was finally complete. I could go back to living a peaceful, quiet life.

My parents started to wander away as Mallory led them off, giving me a quick wave goodbye. I nodded to her but stayed put with my brother and Stone.

"We're going to head home. You two heading back to your place?" Calvin asked Stone.

He nodded and grabbed my hand. "I think we've had enough excitement for the day," he admitted.

For a lifetime.

There was only one thought playing through my mind as Stone took my hand and led me back toward his rental.

The hard truth was one I needed to face: Stone was leaving Briarport.

24

LENNY

I ONLY HAD two days left with Stone before he left.

My parents were still in town at Calvin's place, and we decided to spend a day all together at the beach.

They met us at my favorite spot, a strip of the beach that fewer tourists knew about. Plus, it was only a short walk from my favorite smoothie shop.

We grabbed drinks on the way. I picked the strawberry delight and Stone went for one labeled banana blast. We picked up everyone else's orders as well, and I carried the tray while Stone carried a bag with towels.

It was odd seeing him do such a normal task, strange to picture him as anything but the FBI agent he was. I wondered when he last took a break.

He watched me as I set the towels on the ground, and when he dug through the bag of items he carried, I giggled when he pulled out a bottle of sunscreen. If anyone was going to remember it, it was definitely going to be Stone.

He pulled off his shirt, and I couldn't help but stare at his tattoos, at how toned he was. The muscles of his abdomen were perfectly carved. He wasn't a large or overly muscular man, but he was certainly in shape.

And not bad to look at.

Knock it off. I scolded internally, knowing I was only torturing myself further.

"What?" Stone asked, realizing I was staring.

My cheeks warmed a little. "I'm just not shocked you remembered to bring that," I covered, trying to save myself.

"Broad spectrum coverage," he said with a grin and held it up. "Protects against both harmful ultraviolet rays."

I laughed.

Behind us, I heard people calling out our names and turned to see my family approaching. Eloise was wearing a cute bikini that showed off her little bump. Already, seeing her again was getting easier. My parents carried a bag of snacks, and I traded my dad a smoothie in exchange for a tub of blueberries.

It felt nice, enjoying the last days of freedom and summer. I'd contacted Francis to let her know I'd be coming back to the museum. She was ecstatic to learn the project Stone was working on led to the arrest of the Coastal Killer. Somehow, he'd truly won her over.

I only hoped that level of enthusiasm carried over when I returned. It might be a good time to consider bringing up the memorial exhibit again.

"Come swim with me," Stone insisted as he stood.

He held out a hand to help me up. I still wore my cover-up dress. Normally, I didn't love taking it off in front of others. A lifetime of comments made me self-conscious enough, on top of my multiple scars.

"Are you coming?" Stone asked, staring back at me.

I pulled off the dress quickly and crossed my arms, feeling his eyes rake over me. It wasn't the first time he had seen me shirtless, but I felt more exposed now.

His eyes lingered on the scar on my lower abdomen. A devilish grin grew across his face, and I frowned, confused. My entire family broke out in laughter as Stone scooped me into his arms and ran off to the ocean.

The water was cold but refreshing as it splashed against us. Stone made his way past where the waves crashed, the tide calm and the waves docile enough to swim without fear of being knocked down. He carried us to where we could both stand.

"Are you going to put me down?" I asked.

His forehead pressed against mine, our noses barely brushing. "Do I have to?"

Again, my cheeks warmed, all too aware of my family on the beach watching us.

Stone sensed my hesitation and glanced to the sand where they sat.

"Don't worry," he said. "Your father and brother are tossing a football back-and-forth, and your mother has Eloise locked in conversation."

I risked my own glance and saw he was right. None of them were paying us any attention.

"Then I suppose not," I said and pressed a quick kiss to his lips.

He carried me for a few more minutes, walking through the water. After a little, I got antsy to swim around on my own. I threw myself out of his arms and found myself on my tiptoes to keep my head above water.

I let myself bounce, the small waves brushing by us. It was

lulling, the way they carried us for a moment, my feet leaving the sandy floor of the ocean.

Stone closed the space between us and stood chest to chest with me. A chill ran down my spine, his hands finding me under the water. They held my waist and kept me close, pinned against his body.

The urge to kiss him and never stop washed over me, but I knew we had too many watchful eyes. Instead, I felt his finger against the scar on my abdomen. He traced the line and lowered his head to mine.

"I'm sorry," he said.

"For what?" He caught the Coastal Killer like he promised and returned my sense of safety. On top of that, he helped me get justice for all the victims.

"For not getting here sooner," he said. "I wish I could have stopped this."

"It's not your fault," I said. "And besides, it only made me stronger." The words he said to me only days before echoed back at him.

"You are an extraordinary woman, Lenore Calder," he whispered.

I wrapped my arms around his neck, letting him steady me against the waves. Already on my tiptoes, I leaned in to place a gentle kiss on his lips. One of his hands came up from the water to cup to my face, kissing me back.

He pulled away, respecting my hesitation, knowing my family watched nearby. I was never a fan of PDA. With a quick glance back to the beach, I saw my mother smirking down at her book. Either she reached the romance in it, or she had been watching us in the water.

I wanted to duck beneath the waves and never come back up, realizing she'd seen everything.

"Stop worrying about it," Stone said. "I don't care who sees me kissing you."

"She's never going to leave me alone about it," I groaned.

"She will if you tell her you were kissing your boyfriend." His eyes locked on mine. I didn't expect the words from his mouth, and I scrambled to form of a response.

"Boyfriend?" was all I was able to repeat back to him.

"I mean, only if you want," he said. "I know Quantico is far, but there's a place for you if you want to come."

"I can't," I said before I could stop myself.

His face fell a bit, but he trained it back to neutral like the agent he was.

"I just got my life back here," I said. "I just...I can't right now."

I fought back tears stinging my eyes, terrified of hurting Stone and torn that I couldn't go with him.

"I understand," he said. There was barely any emotion on his face. He ducked in and kissed my cheek. "Truly, it's all right."

We stayed in the water a little bit longer before rejoining my family. I couldn't shake the awful feeling of turning Stone down.

"Mallory was telling us you haven't been at your apartment lately," my mother said, giving a knowing look to Stone.

"I fear that's my fault," Stone said, making her smile.

He left it at that, and I wanted to toss myself back in the ocean and disappear.

After his second of disappointment, Stone bounced right

back to his normal self. He chatted with my family and continued to be an absolute know it all in the best way.

It hurt me more than he knew to say no, to let this be the way our last day of normal was spent. I hated every second of it, but I slapped on a smile. If not for myself, then for Stone. He had done everything to give me my life back; he deserved my full attention, even if I couldn't give in to every last one of my desires.

Stone spent his very last day packing and cleaning the rental. He was leaving the next morning but staying with the rest of his team in a hotel for the night.

I packed my own items and threw them into my car. Alonzo and Birdie were at my feet all day, sensing a change.

I spotted Alonzo following Stone, the cat finally warming to him. It broke my heart knowing in less than a day, he'd be gone.

I could always visit Quantico, but would that be causing us more pain than good?

I kept trying to convince myself I'd move on. When Stone left, I'd go back to my apartment and spend my nights with Mallory, drinking wine and laughing at how terrible dating was.

Yet, there'd always be the pain of what could've been with Stone.

I pushed the thought out of my head, helping Stone wipe down the kitchen counters.

The bottle of scotch still sat untouched. He'd never once given in to the temptation of it.

"Don't forget to pack this," I reminded him, knowing Nelson didn't need such a nice bottle of alcohol.

Stone followed my gaze to the glass bottle, and I sucked in a breath as he picked it up and unscrewed the cap. My stomach sunk, and I almost reached out to snatch it from him. He'd made it this far—I wouldn't let him go back to that dark pit.

Instead, he turned to the sink and dumped the entire thing. My jaw fell open, and I stared in both horror and surprise. The first washed away quickly, realizing he wasn't going to drink it.

"I don't need this anymore," he said and tossed the bottle into the recycling bin.

I hurried forward and wrapped my arms around him. It took him by surprise, but he embraced me quickly.

Together, we'd grown. We'd fought our pasts and faced our mistakes head on. If anyone deserved this accomplishment, it was Stone.

My heart swelled for him.

"I'm proud of you," I said, pressed tightly to him.

"I'm proud of you too," he whispered back.

"I know it's not fair of me to ask, but are you sure you can't come to Quantico?" he asked, grabbing his bags and stacking them near the front door.

My chest ached as I tried to get a deep breath, holding back tears. Each time I tried to revisit the idea, I knew I couldn't. I had thought it over every day since the beach.

"Francis expects me back at the museum soon," I said,

trying to hold it together. "I just started working my way up there. I can't leave yet."

He nodded, understanding, but it still broke me inside. To see that hopeful glance disappear as fast as it came was like ripping my heart physically out of my chest.

I could see the same sadness I felt in his features, and it only made my heart hurt more.

"I wish Virginia wasn't so far away."

"You're welcome to visit anytime," he offered.

When I attempted to force Stone into letting me help with the case, I never expected our goodbye to be this painful. Everything in me wanted to go with him, to save what we found these past weeks, but I knew I couldn't.

I still had a life in Briarport.

My brother would become a father in only a few months, my job was waiting for me, and this was the first time I felt safety in my town.

Stone reached out, pulling me in quickly. I felt the tears escape my eyes, and as my face pressed to his chest, the little drops soaked into his white button down.

"Are you sure you have to go back?" I asked, trying to hide the shaking in my voice but failing miserably.

"I directly disobeyed orders. I have to go back and face whatever disciplinary action Grey has waiting for me," he said with a defeated breath.

One of his hands intertwined in my curls as he held my head gently against him. I could hear his heart beat, the steady rhythm helping me chase away the tears.

"You'll be okay," he promised. "This won't be goodbye forever."

25

STONE

"Let me cook you dinner," I offered Len after a few hours back at the rental house.

She'd brought in a new bouquet of daisies from outside and threw out the dying ones on the counter.

'You're just trying to bribe me to forget you didn't tell me you arrested Ethan," she said, pointing the new daisies at me accusingly before placing them in the vase.

"Is it working?" I dared to ask.

She narrowed her eyes dramatically enough that I knew she wasn't actually angry. "We'll see."

That wouldn't do.

I walked over to fridge, pulling out my recently purchased groceries.

I pulled out tomatoes and spinach. In the cabinet beside the fridge, I found olive oil and a box of pasta. If I had more time and ingredients, I would've made fresh pasta. I set to work, pulling out the other ingredients I needed and revisiting the fridge for some cheese and butter.

"What are you making?" Len asked, poking her head in from the dining room where she'd been relaxing.

I smiled. "My secret pasta recipe. No one can resist this, not even you."

"I thought you weren't good at cooking?"

"No, I said I'm not a *baker*. I didn't say anything about cooking."

A hint of a grin grew on her lips. I turned back to the stove, finding the water boiling, and grabbed a sauce pan. A bit passed by before Len came back to check on the food. She crossed her arms and stood next to me as I stirred the sauce.

"Where did you learn to make this?" she asked.

"I've always liked cooking, but all credit goes to my mother for this recipe. She taught me how to make it, and someday, I'll teach Lyla."

The water started to bubble, and I dumped in the box of pasta.

"You're close with them, right?" Len asked.

I wished I was closer. California was too far, and my job always got in the way, but they understood. "I am, but I wish I saw them more often," I admitted.

"I hope I can meet them someday," Len said.

It was the first time she had given any indication there could be a future for us. She denied my desire to be her boyfriend, but that didn't mean all hope was lost. I understood her reasoning, even agreed with it, but it didn't hurt any less.

"You will," I assured her. "Maybe I'll even bring them here to see the beaches."

She moved closer to me, and I grabbed her waist, shifting her in front of me while my arms wrapped around her. I placed the wooden spoon in her hand and guided her to stir the tomato sauce.

"The secret is in the spices," I admitted as I poured in some Italian seasoning, salt, and pepper. Len kept stirring, making sure it was distributed evenly.

"You're a natural," I teased.

She turned around to face me, and as she did so, she stood on her tiptoes to place a quick kiss to my lips.

Life was easy around Len. There was no thinking; everything just fell into place.

I leaned in to kiss her back, and as I did, sizzling broke out behind her. She moved away quickly, the water boiling over the pot holding the pasta.

I laughed and quickly turned down the temperature on the stove. I used the spoon to give it all a good stir and then focused my attention back on Len.

"I promise it'll be ready soon," I assured her.

That was enough for her. She made her way back into the dining room, and soon after, I followed her with two plates.

We spent the night eating and joking.

I'd never laughed so hard as I did when I was with Len. It was easy to pretend everything was going to be okay. In the back of my mind, though, the nagging feeling ate away at me that I only had so much time left with her. So, I spent every second soaking it in.

26

LENNY

I SOBBED the moment Stone pulled out of the driveway. I promised to lock up the house and did as I transported my two cats into my convertible.

Tears continued to cloud my eyes as I sat, unmoving, in the driver's seat.

My heart felt like it had crumbled. Why did something so wonderful have to hurt so excruciatingly bad?

Every moment with Stone was pure bliss.

The drive home was even worse. Each spot in town I passed reminded me of him. The coffee shop I took him to, the beach, and even the sheriff's office, all of which I had the misfortune of passing.

I parked my car in the small lot nearby and grabbed Alonzo and Birdie from the back seat. They made an obnoxious amount of noise on the walk to the apartment, enough to draw attention.

The pin pad at the side door clicked as it unlocked and let me inside. My feet felt heavy walking up each step. I dreaded being alone again.

There was always Mallory.

I passed her door, at least comforted in the fact my friend was close by. Wine night was no longer a want—it was becoming a need at this point. I'd text her and set up a night during the week. First, though, I needed to get organized for work. I had minimal time, and I knew for a fact I had no food and had been letting my laundry grow for a while.

All those things meant leaving Stone, and that was something I'd been unwilling to do the last few days.

Inside my own apartment, I found my laptop and pulled up a grocery delivery service. Depression caused by the one man I thought might be it for me leaving was reason enough to order food dropped at my door, right?

My laptop was opened to a file from the Coastal Killer case, and my finger hesitated before closing out of it. I picked out my food and ordered quickly, shoving the laptop across the kitchen island before I could be tempted to make myself even more sad looking through the case documents.

My cats sprinted through the apartment, chasing each other before stopping at the food bowl I filled for them. I continued working through my chores, returning to my life. It was surreal, coming home to complete such simple tasks.

For weeks, my life had been research and threats. I hadn't known silence like this in forever. The dreadful realization I would have to sleep alone washed over me.

It didn't take long before it grew dark outside my windows, and the noise from town died down. I could finally hear the waves in the distance. It wasn't as loud as it was at Stone's rental, which sent a new wave of disappointment through me.

Maybe when I saved up enough, I could buy a property closer to the water.

At least I still had the lulling sound to crawl into bed and fall asleep too.

I slipped into a pair of silk pajamas, and my cats followed me into the bed. They nestled up by my pillow, and I hopped in next to them, settling down.

The book Stone annotated for me sat on my bedside table. I opened it up and started flipping through it. There were other little notes I added, this being my second time reading through the story. He had been right—I absolutely loved it.

I started reading through all the little notes he left, and my chest felt heavy as I did. There wasn't a day that would go by when I wouldn't miss his presence. Every little smart comment he made and thoughtful thing he did for me—I'd remember each and every one.

The urge to hop on the first flight to Virginia hit me for the thousandth time, but I knew I risked reopening all the wounds of him leaving. I was lying to myself if I thought I could just let him go completely.

I checked my phone to see if he had texted me at all, but there was nothing. I wasn't surprised, knowing he was meeting the rest of his team and traveling early the next morning.

He would drive the rest of the team to the jet, return his rental car, and catch his own flight back. I'd offered to return it so he could travel with the rest of his team, but he insisted on it. Truthfully, I think he needed the time alone.

My eyes started to feel heavy the more I read through the book. I started to memorize every word Stone wrote. He may have memorized the book, but every last note he wrote me would be imprinted on my mind forever.

The one at the front caught my attention the most.

For my aftermath.

I wanted the word tattooed on my skin, to remind myself that, like Stone said, everything we'd gone through only made us stronger after.

The book slowly started to slip from my hands as my body gave in to exhaustion. I could finally rest, knowing I was safe, even if I still found it hard to accept the truth. This nightmare was over.

I tried to push that from my mind, telling myself eventually, it would go away. Instead, I put the book down and turned toward my cats, curling up beside them. It was the last thing I saw before the real nightmare began.

I couldn't breathe. Something covered my mouth, and I startled awake. I tried to thrash against it, but whoever stood over me held me down. Dizziness built in my head, and I felt my eyes start to flutter back to sleep.

My mouth opened to scream, but nothing came out. The rag over it was too much, and I knew instantly I was being drugged again.

If I didn't fight with everything in me, I knew this was it, but it was too late. Already, my body was going limp, and I couldn't stop my eyes from shutting any longer.

"Rest," a soft voice said from above me.

It was oddly chilling and calming all at once. I swore, I recognized it from somewhere.

Against my own will, my eyes betrayed me and closed one last time. My hearing went next, and before I knew it, my entire body became dead weight.

Stone had already left, but the killer wasn't done with me. The FBI arrested the wrong person. I knew in my gut it didn't end with Ethan. And now, I was paying the price.

27

STONE

I MADE it to the small hotel in town where the rest of the team was staying. Grey let me sleep in the spare double bed in his room. They were leaving early in the morning, and it was easier for me to already be there than to try to leave the rental that early. It also gave me more time to say a proper goodbye to Len.

My heart ached at that.

"Are you ready to go back?" Grey asked, looking me over as I piled my stuff in the corner of the room.

"Truthfully?" I asked. "Not entirely."

"You know it's breaking every single rule the FBI has by not letting her go?" Grey pointed out.

"I know every rule that exists, and somehow, I can't bring myself to accept them," I explained. "No matter how many times I tell myself it's wrong, I just can't do it. She's impossible to let go of."

Selfish.

I put her directly in harm's way, all because I couldn't separate my feelings and what needed to be done. It worked out in the end; Ethan was arrested and would be spending the rest of his life in prison, but there had still been too many close calls.

"Sometimes, not every rule is perfect," Grey said.

A concept my mind had trouble accepting. There'd always been a solution for every problem I faced.

I snapped my gaze to him. He kept his face even, but there was a glimpse of sympathy in his eyes.

"You're doing the right thing, going back," he said.

"What am I even going back to?" I asked. "Will I even have a job when I return?"

"It's not up to me entirely," he said. "The director will make the final call, but he will look to my recommendation."

"What is your recommendation?" I asked.

"You've been through a lot," he started as he stroked the stubble on his face. "I think you need to weigh how important this job is to you. Are you willing to do what's needed to get back in the field?"

I knew what he meant. My mind needed to be completely focused on my work. There could be no more slip ups with alcohol or drugs, I couldn't disappear for months when things got hard. I couldn't let Len become a distraction.

I shook my head, because I didn't have an answer to his question.

"Think on it," Grey said. "I don't need to give my recommendation until we're back, but I need to be sure you are fully on this team and can follow orders."

I climbed into the hotel bed, a sinking feeling in my chest growing as I realized this was the first night in a while Len was not beside me.

I prepared myself for the nightmares that would plague

me without her presence. Most agents had some sort of trauma, our job always putting us near death.

I only hoped I could contain it enough not to spark more worry.

I'd dropped the rest of the team off at the small airport nearby hosting the jet. It was only another thirty minute drive to my own airport, where I would drop off the rental car. The drive and flight alone gave me the space to clear my head.

It was only five minutes into the drive when my phone rang. Afraid Grey had forgotten something, I answered through the car's Bluetooth.

Mags' voice came through the speakers. "The lab results came back on the package left at your doorstep."

"Does it confirm Ethan left it?" I asked, barely phased.

"No, the fingerprints were inconclusive," she answered. "But there was something interesting. The letter inside was not written in paint like you originally suspected. The components came back consistent with lip gloss." '

Lip gloss?

That didn't make sense, nor did it fit Ethan's profile. He hated women, despised every part of them. Mimicking their behavior, and using a common makeup product wouldn't fit his profile at all.

My chest tightened, and the nagging feeling hit again, the one where I'd left Len still exposed to danger in Briarport. What if we didn't arrest the right person?

There was so much to point to Ethan being the Coastal Killer, but the more I thought back on it, there was a chance he didn't act alone. What if he had been helping someone else? Someone who had been pulling the strings the whole time?

I needed to get back to Len, fast.

"Mags, tell Grey to meet me back in Briarport," I said.

"What? Why?" she asked.

"I don't think this is over," I said.

"It will take them well over an hour to make it back.".

"I'm closer," I answered. "I can turn around and be back in under an hour. Tell him to meet me there. You have my location tracked, right?" I asked.

"Yes," she answered hesitantly. "But you should wait for Grey before doing anything."

"I can't," I answered. "Not when it comes to her."

I hung up and quickly dialed Len's number. Over and over, it went to voicemail.

"Come on, Len. Pick up the phone," I prayed.

Still nothing. Her voicemail message played each time I called, and my stomach started to sink further every time I heard it.

The car wasn't moving fast enough.

I needed to get back to Lenny. I tried not to let myself think about what her not answering meant. The killer had to have made a move the moment we left town, but that didn't mean Len was harmed.

I played every piece of evidence in my head.

The killer was obsessed with Len. Everything they'd done was to hold her attention. Someone saw a piece of themselves in her and spared her.

A sinking feeling grew inside me, a new unsub coming to mind.

The very first day I'd met her, she was applying the same red lip gloss I was willing to guess was used on the note.

I called Mags back, knowing Len wouldn't answer.

"I managed to get through to the team before they took off," Mags said. "But it will be at least twenty minutes before they get a car and can meet you. I sent the closest deputy to get them."

"What can you find about Len's landlord, Mallory?" I asked.

I heard Mags typing at the computer, and her voice came through the speaker again in seconds.

"Mallory Vice changed her name from Miranda Smith about five years ago. She has owned the building Len lives in for four. There's not much on her beyond that. She works in the shop under the building. She doesn't have family in the area and doesn't have much of a record."

"Much of a record?" I asked.

"Her name shows in one small report."

Miranda Smith. I knew that name sounded familiar.

"The couple fighting at the pub," I said

"Exactly. How did you know?"

"Len made the sheriff give us other small reports for the months before the killings started. Miranda Smith was escorted out of the pub alongside her former fiancé after their break up grew volatile."

"It's sad, really," Mags said. "It looks like he left her only weeks before their wedding."

The hate toward women and happy relationships... It wasn't a man who was left. No, she was targeting women like herself, women who had it all: the happy relationship, the bright future ahead of them. They were surrogates for her own self-hatred. She coveted what they had and couldn't stand to see others like that.

"Oh, God," Mags said through the phone. "You left Len back at her apartment with her."

My stomach sank, knowing Mallory had to be the reason she wasn't answering. I'd seen the way she cared for Len and couldn't imagine she would hurt her friend, but I didn't know what mental instability could do to change that.

"I need to figure out where Mallory would take Len if she is not there," I said.

"I'm on it," she said firmly. She hung up without a good-bye, and everything inside me hoped I was wrong.

My foot dropped heavy on the gas pedal as I sped through the back roads to Briarport. The car wasn't moving fast enough. Each second was one that Len may be in trouble.

It was easy to piece together the moment I came into town, Len's interest in me sparked Mallory to kill again. She was jealous of the attention Len gave me. She'd become codependent on her, and it was the only thing keeping this town safe, stopping the killings.

It could've turned bad any moment. Any fight, any new person in Len's life could've set it off. I was glad it was me. At least now, I had a chance to make things right, to get justice for all those victims.

I finally pulled up outside the apartment. The car was practically blocking the road, but I didn't care. I left it running and sprinted to the back door.

There was a code, but I didn't have time to call Mags to find it. Instead, I kicked in the door, and it flew open. My feet carried me up the stairs to Len's apartment. The door was cracked open, and I heard Alonzo and Birdie inside.

The cats sat by the food bowl, which was completely empty. Len never left without feeding them, which meant she'd been gone for a while. The chance was slim, but I still quickly walked through the apartment to make sure she wasn't injured somewhere.

Mallory had taken her, and I had no idea where.

As I realized everything I tried to avoid was happening all over again, I felt helpless. I'd been reckless, trying to work this case myself without back up. Now, Len was paying the price.

I would never forgive myself if something happened to her.

My phone buzzed in my pocket, and I quickly pulled it out to see Mag's name on the screen.

"Did you find her?" I asked.

"Not entirely, but I did track Mallory's phone to a location just outside of town, near the water.

"The warehouse," I guessed before Mags could say it, realizing it was the one place nearby with enough room for no one to notice if Mallory took her there.

"Should I send you the location again?" Mags asked.

"No I have it memorized," I said. "Call Grey and tell them where I'm heading."

I sprinted down the steps of the apartment and found my car still waiting outside.

My heart raced, and I could barely hear myself over the growing worry causing a rush in my head. My foot pressed down on the gas pedal, and the car lurched forward, flying through the streets. I avoided pedestrians and traffic while maintaining a speed far over the limits. Not a single thing could stop me from getting to Len.

My only worry was getting to her in time.

Mallory was obsessed with her. Even with that worry spreading, I knew there was a chance she wouldn't hurt her. It was more likely she was using her as bait. She needed control back, and that couldn't happen if I still existed. She wouldn't hurt Len unless I didn't give her what she wanted.

Me.

28

LENNY

Everything was black when I finally woke again. I tried to open my eyes, but they fluttered against something. When I tried to move my hands, I found them bound behind my back, my body upright and my hands touching a metal chair.

Finally, I heard someone speak and lifted my head, moving around to try to gain my bearings.

My body jumped as hands touched the back of my head. The fabric fell away, and it took a moment for my eyes to adjust to the light of the room. I tried to crane my neck to get a look at them.

I didn't need to. They walked around the chair to stand in front of me, and my breath caught in my throat.

No, this wasn't right.

Mallory hovered in front of me, red lips pursed and arms crossed. She scowled as I struggled to catch my breath again.

"Why did you have to do this?" she asked. "Everything is ruined."

"What do you mean?" I asked, still confused.

My mind raced with every possibility.

Mallory started to walk around my chair, examining me. Her hand brushed my shoulder, and she picked up my curls, slowly starting to hum.

The sound was eerie, almost haunting. I recognized it. My mind didn't want to admit it, but I'd heard that same exact sound before.

"It was you," I said. My throat burned as I got the words out.

"Obviously," Mallory said. "It was me who took care of you all these years."

"You tried to kill me," I choked. "You ruined my life."

"I saved you from him." Her hands tightened on my curls and yanked them. My neck snapped back, my head forced to look up at her. I found my eyes staring into hers, looking down at me.

"They all leave. I saved you from the pain of it. I saved all those women from the pain I had to endure."

"I don't understand. This isn't you, Mallory," I tried.

I knew I was lying to myself, but if there was a chance I could get out of here alive, I had to try.

She scoffed. "Do you know how I met Ethan?"

I shook my head, and she let go of my hair. I heard heels tapping against cement floor as she walked back around the chair. I tried to look at my surroundings, but I didn't recognize anything in the room.

"That's where he left me: The High Tide Pub. Ethan was working that night; he's the one who called the sheriff's office. We were supposed to get married only two weeks later, and he left me."

I'd never heard the story before. I knew Mallory hated men, but she never talked about any of the ones she'd been with. Never once had I heard her mention a fiancé. I always assumed she had bad luck with dating apps or some wild dates, but never this.

"I don't understand," I tried.

My throat was dry, a combination of whatever drug she used to get me here and the lack of water.

"They're all the same. He left me for some other woman and moved across the country, leaving me here. For months, I was forced to sit there and watch every happy couple who came to the pub. It was our spot, and he left me there."

She kept repeating it over and over.

"I'm sorry," I said, part of me meaning it.

Mallory was my friend, and it still hurt me to know she experienced such pain.

"I had to watch all those couples come to the pub and pretend like they were happy. I had to watch them get drunk and celebrate like everything was fine. It wasn't fine. Those men would have left them like he left me," she said, her eyes distant.

I could barely tell if she knew where she was. "I don't understand why Ethan would help you."

"He understood," she said. "I sat there for months at that bar. He cared. He knew what it was like to be left, to be overlooked. I saw the way that women at the pub stared at him and judged him. It wasn't fair," she said, shaking her head.

The perfect team. They found comfort in each other, a way to inflict pain on others who had something they never did.

"You used Ethan," I guessed. "You lied about the code needing to be changed that day, and you used him to deliver the threat."

She nodded. "I needed you to stop looking."

"You used him to place that last call?"

"It was easy enough to time the call with when I knew he made his weekly run to the warehouse for Bobby," she answered and shrugged.

"And the falsified police reports? That was you?" I asked, trying to buy myself time.

"I told you Chris was someone to stay away from. He has more secrets that should stay buried than myself. It was easy enough to find proof and blackmail the sheriff."

"I'm sorry, I really am, that your fiancé left you, but that isn't a reason to hurt others. They didn't deserve that," I tried, my mind reeling.

"They didn't deserve the pain. Don't you see?"

"See what?" I asked.

"I see them," she insisted. "I saved them. I gave them peace and made sure they never knew the pain I felt."

It was all coming together.

"I never wanted to be saved," I argued.

"You needed to be," she said firmly and shook her head.

"I would've left him eventually."

"He was only going to hurt you," Mallory insisted. "I saved you."

My stomach turned, and I held back the growing nausea. "Is that why you stopped?" I asked, my stomach thinking of every last victim who died at Mallory's hands.

"When I saw how free you were because of what I did to you, I knew I'd fulfilled my purpose," she said. "All this was meant to bring me to you. I know it was."

"You knew who I was," I guessed. "That day at the café when we first met. That wasn't an accident?"

"Of course not. I knew who you were. I had to know. When you survived, I had to make sure you didn't go back to him. When I met you, you were so sad. I knew you understood. I knew you felt the same pain as me. That's why the world brought us together."

The delusional thoughts only got worse the more I pushed. I tugged gently at the binds holding my hands, but they didn't budge.

"I believed you, all these years," I said, feeling the anger festering in my chest. Everything in me screamed at me to have some sense of self preservation, but I couldn't stop the words tumbling out.

"I trusted you! You were my friend."

"We still are friends! Can't you see? I did all of this for you," she cried.

"What do you mean?"

"I killed those two women for you to show you, to help you understand."

"No," I said. "That wasn't for me. I never wanted that."

Something seemed to snap inside of Mallory, and her entire face shifted, her scowl growing. I swallowed hard.

"Ungrateful," she spat into my face. "I did all of this for you. I sent you that gift, and you're going to sit here and pretend not to understand."

"I don't understand!" I shouted back.

I knew it was a mistake the second I said it. I was only adding fuel to the fire.

"You're only saying that because of him," Mallory accused. She paced back-and-forth in front of me. "He ruined it. He lied to you, made you hate me."

"What are you talking about?" I asked.

While she was distracted, I tried again to pull at the restraints holding my arms. There was no use; they were tied tight. I would have to break my thumbs to wiggle my way out of them, and I wasn't convinced I could do it without drawing her attention.

"That agent," she said. "The second he came to town, everything was ruined."

"Stone?" I asked.

"He took you from me. I warned you what men would do. I told you they all leave, that there's no point, that you don't want to end up like you did with Jake, but you didn't listen."

Her eyes burned with hatred. The drugs were wearing off, my head starting to feel a little less cloudy.

"I'm the one who invited him here," I said. "If you want to hate someone, hate me."

That was the final straw. She pulled out a knife and my entire body tensed, preparing for the pain it was so familiar with. The same knife that had taken all those lives pointed at me.

"He'll come back for you," she said quietly.

Before I could react, the knife was to my throat.

She forced me to stand, my arms sliding up and above the chair, still bound together.

The knife remained at my throat.

29

STONE

I PARKED near Mallory's car in the warehouse lot. Mags had called me on the drive over to confirm Grey and the rest of the team were on their way with the sheriff, and I'd asked for information on Mallory's vehicle, almost hoping I was wrong and wouldn't see it.

My heart dropped when I spotted the red car with the matching license plate sitting in front of me.

I pulled out my gun and made my way toward where I knew the High Tide Pub's warehouse space was.

There wasn't time to wait. I wouldn't risk Len's life waiting for the deputies to arrive as back up.

The last time I didn't wait, my partner ended up dead, but this wasn't that.

The decision was all mine this time. I was alone, and there was no one else at risk. Len was the victim, the one taken, and if I waited, and it was too late when we found her, I would never forgive myself. I would rather die than sit by and wait while she was in harm's away.

I slowly made my way across the lot, hoping I wouldn't

encounter anyone. I didn't want more roadblocks in the way of rescuing Len. My heart pounded each step I took.

My gun remained raised all the way until I made it to the building I had searched not long ago. There was only one door in and out; I knew that from the last time I was there to search for the Coastal Killer.

My next move wasn't really a decision at all.

With each passing second, the statistics for recovering Len unharmed worsened.

I checked the watch I wore on my wrist—only forty minutes had passed. I prayed they made it sooner rather than later.

My hand hovered over the handle of the door before I grabbed it and pushed it open. My weapon was raised once more, leading me into the warehouse.

The second I walked through that single door leading inside, I saw her. Len stood with a knife to her throat, her eyes pleading with me. I knew it was a trap, but there was nothing I could do.

I had to save Len.

"I knew you'd come," Mallory hissed.

Her voice vile, and the knife that had killed so many at the hands of the Coastal Killer remained pressed to Len's throat. I knew if we checked it against every last victim, it would match.

"Don't hurt her," I said, pointing my gun at Mallory.

I didn't have the shot. She was using Len like a human shield. There is no way for me to fire without potentially hitting Len.

"Let her go," I demanded, keeping my voice as even as possible.

I dealt with many hostage negotiations; I knew what to do, but it was hard to keep focused on the task with Len's life at stake. It was easier when I didn't know the victims.

"No," Mallory snapped. "You can't take her from me."

There it was: the fear, the idea I would take Len from her, that Len belonged to her.

"I won't do that. We both want her unharmed," I said, planting the idea in her head.

"You did this to her," Mallory snapped.

The knife moved a little, and I saw Len tense at the sharp edge touching her skin.

"It's me you want," I said.

"You tried to take her from me. I won't let you do it again," Mallory said.

"I'll do whatever; just let her go," I said, keeping my voice even.

I tried not to let the growing panic show on my face. Len needed me to remain focused. If I could reason with her, show her what she was doing would only harm Len, there was a chance.

There were only two endings to this all.

She would either Len go, her love and obsession enough to protect Len's life. Or, Mallory would kill her, her possessiveness enough to convince her if she couldn't have her, no one could.

I couldn't let the second happen.

"Put down your gun," Mallory demanded.

"How do I know you won't hurt her? How can I be sure you'll let her go?" I asked.

I knew it was a useless question. There was no way I would ever know for certain.

"You'll have to trust me," Mallory said.

Laughable.

"You put the gun down, I'll let her go. You take her place. If you care so much about her, you won't mind if it's you at the end of my knife instead."

I hadn't expected much else. The second I realized Mallory was the Coastal Killer, I knew her endgame.

With me out of the picture, Len would be all hers.

"I'm going to put my gun down slowly," I said.

My knees bent as I slowly lowered, one hand raised and my other hand placing the gun gently on the floor. I quickly stood back up, my hands raised.

It was by far the dumbest decision an agent could make. The second we lost our weapon, we lost all the power, all our control over the situation. Everything was at the hands of the unsub.

Yet, time and time again, we did it anyway. It was the only way to ensure the safety of those we took an oath to protect.

"Kick it over here," Mallory demanded.

I didn't argue. The gun skidded across the floor as I kicked it. I made sure to aim slightly off to the side so it was still out of her reach. If she took the gun, there was no leaving this warehouse alive.

"No!" Len called out.

"It's okay," I said directly to her. "You'll be okay."

"You for her. That's the deal," Mallory said.

I knew the second I took her place, Mallory would slit my throat. There would be no hesitation. If I wanted to protect Len and get her out of the warehouse alive, I needed to try to get closer to Mallory. If I could disarm her, she'd be useless.

I started to walk towards them, and Len writhed in her friend's grasp.

"Don't," she whimpered.

"Shut up," Mallory sneered.

"It's all right, Len." I needed her to stop struggling. Resistance would only anger Mallory further.

I knew what the profile said, and I needed Len to understand.

When I was only inches from them, Mallory turned Len away from me, the knife still pressed tightly to her throat. One small movement would end her life. She reached down to the belt holding her skirt up and unhooked a pair of handcuffs.

She handed them to me.

"Lock yourself to that," she said, nodding to a large metal shelving unit as high as the ceiling. There would be no escaping *that*.

"The second you do, I'll let her go."

I realized my mistake the second we took a few steps in the direction of the shelving. My gun sat feet away. I couldn't let her pick it up.

Len seemed to follow my gaze and understood. I met her eyes and saw the moment she made her decision.

"No," I said, catching Mallory's attention.

It was too late. She stomped her foot backward, landing right on top of Mallory's. Mallory stumbled in shock for a moment, and Len darted, heading for my gun. I tried to lunge for it, but I was the furthest.

Mallory recovered quickly, and with Len's arms tied, her movement was limited, and Mallory beat her to it. I was still moving toward the pair when the shot rang out, the piercing sound echoing through the warehouse.

For a moment, I thought Len was hit. Her eyes widened, and she stumbled away from Mallory. It wasn't until I felt the excruciating pain shoot through me a second later that I realized I was wrong.

My leg ached, the pain knocking me to one knee. Looking down, I noticed blood already dripping down the side of my leg.

"No," Len screamed.

I was lucky. It wasn't anything lethal, but the pain did limit me.

She raced over to me, and Mallory lifted the gun, aiming it at her.

"Stop," I called. "Don't hurt her."

Her eyes flickered between the two of us as she weighed the choice.

"Don't hurt her," I pleaded again. "You have what you want. I'm here. I'm not going anywhere."

I accepted my fate. One more bullet, that's all it would take. Tears streamed down Len's face.

Mallory stared at the pair of us. Movement to my right caught my eye at the doorway. It was slight, so slight that the other two didn't notice. The small reflection light flickered again, and I knew.

"Let me say goodbye," I said to Mallory.

"No," she said.

"Please," Len cried.

"It's not for me; it's for her," I assured Mallory. "Just let her say goodbye."

Mallory nodded and kept the gun pointed at us. Len

quickly melted to on the floor, wrapping her arms around my neck.

"Do something," she begged.

"Grey," I whispered in her ear.

It a one single word, but it was enough for me to feel the way her muscles relaxed for only a second.

She moved back, and her eyes held mine, searching.

I gave her a little nod, one Mallory would think was me encouraging her to go. Instead, I confirmed what she thought.

"I won't leave," Len said and stood to turn.

She put her body in front of me, placing herself between me and the gun.

"Move," Mallory demanded.

"No," she said. "If you want to kill him, you'll have to kill me first."

My chest ached at that. Len was playing with fire and I didn't like it, but there wasn't much more I could do. We needed to hold Mallory's attention.

"Move," Mallory demanded again.

"No," she said. "You'll have to make me."

Mallory started to stalk across the warehouse, gun still raised, pointed directly at Len's head. I tensed, praying my team would move fast.

With Mallory finally focused entirely on us, her back to the door, I saw the first person enter.

Mallory was inches from Len and held the gun straight to her head. I could see the way her finger twitched on the trigger and held my breath as Len closed her eyes.

Before she could pull the trigger, a shot rang out, and Mallory collapsed.

I forced myself toward her, the pain in my leg agonizing, but I was able to still limp.

Len rushed away from her, but I hurried toward her and knelt beside her to check her pulse. By the time my fingers met her neck she was completely gone .

I moved over to Len, who stood shaking and staring at her friend's lifeless body. I held her up.

"Are you okay? Are you hurt?" I asked.

"No, I'm all right," she said. Each word sounded unsure. Her friend kidnapped her and held her at knife point. That wasn't something you got over in a day.

I heard the sirens in the background, and Grey gave me a curt nod to head outside to meet them.

"Let me get you out of here," I said as I wrapped an arm around her, afraid her legs may give out any moment.

I walked outside, and immediately, an EMT met us with a blanket, wrapping it around Len as I slowly let go near the back of an ambulance. I let her go, knowing it was for the best.

Agent Grey was the first to exit the building behind me, meeting my gaze.

Deputies passed by me, heading inside with their guns raised; unbeknownst to them, they didn't need them anymore. I limped over to the rest of my team, near another ambulance. Some of the agents clapped me on the back while others gave me sad nods.

"You didn't wait for back up," Grey noted.

I pulled out my wallet and handed over my badge.

"What is this?" he asked.

"My badge. I didn't follow orders again. I know my time in the field is done," I admitted.

Grey stared at the badge, his hands turning it over. "You see that woman over there?" Grey motioned to Len. "If you had waited for us, I doubt she'd be alive. The moment the lab got those results back, you pieced it together, faster than anyone else could have. You built a profile all within moments and knew Len wasn't safe. You did what anyone else with the same profile would've done," he said.

"Len was a fixation for Mallory. With that attention taken away, she felt betrayed. When Len didn't appreciate the gifts she offered, she escalated to taking her. If she would've denied her what she wanted, Len would've been dead."

"I didn't wait for back up, the same as I didn't with Blythe," I answered.

"This is not the same," Grey said. "You made a decision based on a profile, a good one. You saved her life. This is not the same as last time." Grey placed a hand on my shoulder before he handed my badge back. "Once you complete your psych evaluation, you'll be cleared for the field. I've already submitted the recommendation."

"You can't be serious?" I asked.

"As long as you follow orders next time, you're still welcome on my team. Besides, where else will I find a brain like yours?" He chuckled.

"I'd be honored to come back," I admitted.

30

LENNY

My wrists ached as I rubbed at them, the blanket still wrapped around my shoulders. It was hard not to dissociate, not when every piece of me wanted to give in to the shock, to let myself slowly slip away into oblivion.

But that wasn't an option.

Pick yourself back up.

I kept repeating it, over and over. That was exactly what I planned to do: pick myself back up from the low I found myself in and push on, a newly forged person. This summer taught me one thing: I was stronger than I ever imagined.

I watched from the back of the ambulance as Stone talked to his supervisory agent at the other one. Everything felt numb. I'd watched my best friend die in front of me. The man I was beginning to love saved me. I knew she deserved it, but it still hurt.

"Your blood pressure is slightly high, but I think it's the adrenaline rush," the woman checking me over said. "You'll have to take care of those marks on your wrists from the restraints. Keep them clean and bandaged to stave off infection. If anything starts to hurt more or look worse, go to the hospital."

"Thanks," I murmured.

It was the first thing I could bring myself to really say.

Everything inside ached for Stone to come back. It was like piece of me was missing. My body felt on edge, and I tried to catch his eye.

After a few minutes of him speaking to the other agents, he turned and met my gaze.

His face softened, and he limped toward me.

I knew everything he'd done was to protect me, and I was forever grateful for that. There was nothing I could do or say to repay him for saving my life.

"Are you hurt at all?"

I noticed the way he didn't ask if I was alright. He knew the answer—I wasn't.

"No," I said. "Just elevated blood pressure."

"Just make sure to take it easy for a while," he said, looking like he didn't believe me.

I didn't know what he thought he would find. Was he expecting to see some wound everyone had missed?

"I promise, I'm not hurt," I assured him.

I knew this brought him back to everything with Blythe, and my heart ached to put him in that position. I wasn't her, and I hadn't been hurt, but I knew it was almost impossible for him to believe.

"What about you?" I asked, glancing at the fresh bandage on his leg.

"I'm lucky," he said. "Just a graze wound. Turns out, she had terrible aim."

He tried to laugh softly, but it barely came out.

The shakes were starting to subside, and I was able to stand finally.

My feet hit the ground, and Stone immediately held my arms to help steady me. He wrapped a firm arm around my waist, and I felt his muscles tighten slightly as he hugged me to his chest.

"I'm glad you're okay," he said.

"I'm alive because of you," I said.

"You had just as much a part in that as I did," he pointed out.

I shook my head. All I had done was distract Mallory enough for them to stop her. Another wave of nausea rushed over me, realizing I had a hand in her death.

Stone tensed, realizing his mistake. "None of this is your fault," he assured me. "I know no matter how many times I say that, it may not help, but you need to hear it."

I nodded, trying to convince myself but knowing I needed more time.

"Maybe someday," I whispered against him.

There were a few seconds of silence before I worked up the courage to ask my next question. The answer was going to crush me, but I forced myself to look Stone in the eyes and ask anyway.

"Are you leaving again?" I asked.

He nodded. "Grey says I still have a job if I want it."

Part of me had hoped when I saw him again, it meant he came back for good. I knew it was unfair to tie Stone to Briarport or me. There was so much I still wanted to see, and after everything that happened, deep down, I knew I couldn't stay in the small town either.

Stone saw it on my face and pulled me in, holding me to his chest.

"Where will you go?" he asked.

"I have a small bit of savings set aside," I answered. "I want to see the rest of the world. It's something Jake never let me do, and now that I'm finally free of the Coastal Killer, there's nothing stopping me."

"You deserve it," he said. "I'll be waiting the second you get back."

I choked on a sob, melting into Stone. I'd wanted to make things work at the museum, but this town was full of painful memories. I could always come back to visit Calvin, but staying would only hurt more. I needed to see the world, to figure out who I was.

"Lenny," Stone said, using a hand to tilt my chin up toward him. "Go live your life. There's nothing weighing on you here anymore."

I nodded, trying to hold back more tears.

The weight of everything hit me at once. Having to let go of Stone again. Mallory trying to kill me and killing herself. The truth that I wasn't strong enough to stay and face it all.

"I just can't be here," I said. "It's too much."

"Admitting that takes more strength than most people have," Stone said.

I nuzzled my head back into his chest as his strong hands gently stroked the back of my head.

"What if it's too late when I come back? What if you've moved on?" I dared to ask.

"It will never be too late," he started. "I would wait a million lifetimes for you."

EPILOGUE: STONE

I stood to the side of the stage, waiting for them to call my name. The award was not my first during my time with the FBI, but somehow, this one meant so much more.

This award was not just mine. It belonged to Blythe, who had pushed me to be the type of agent who didn't let up. It also belonged to the woman I still could not get out of my head.

She wanted to travel the world, to see beyond Briarport, and who was I to stop her?

After everything she'd gone through, the pain she'd suffered, I couldn't ask her to stay, to tie her down further.

Everything inside me had wanted to ask her to come to Virginia with me, to choose a quiet life, living in my trailer on the plot of land I'd bought, until some day, we could build a house together.

One Len designed herself to be everything she ever dreamed.

But that was my dream, not hers, and I had to let her go.

Maybe in another life, it would have worked, but not this one.

I almost didn't hear when they called my name, distracted by my thoughts.

I walked onto the stage, oblivious to the crowd cheering me on. There were several agents and their family members in the crowd, watching the FBI's most prestigious award ceremony.

I built myself back up from scratch, dragged myself from a pit of despair to solve a cold case, but my heart ached a bit knowing I couldn't have done it myself. Not only did Agent Grey, who stood before me now to present the award, help, but so did the kind hearted woman I left behind in Briarport. It had been months since I'd seen her.

We exchanged letters like a couple out of one of the romance classics, but that wasn't enough for my heart.

The last update I received was that Len was visiting the west coast. I'd sent her recommendations for places she had to try. I even made sure to mention Don's in there, in case she found herself in my hometown.

I forced myself to walk forward, holding out my hand to shake Grey's. He handed over the plaque and whispered his congratulations.

Grey pointed me toward a photographer right beneath the stage. We turned and stood side-by-side, smiling for the photo. Every single person who'd gone up before me had done the same.

A waving behind the camera caught my attention, and I saw my little sister frantically tossing her arms in the air.

My heart almost stopped in my chest when I saw the person sitting beside her. On her left was my mother, smiling ear-to-ear, proud of the son she raised. On her other side was a woman, her dark brown curls perfectly rippling over her shoulders, her warm, light brown skin complimenting the dark blue sundress she wore.

I felt myself grinning like a madman. I had to get off stage, fast.

I hurried through the photo op and quickly walked down the steps of the stage.

I looked at the seats but saw my family and Len missing from where they sat only moments before.

Before I could glance around, arms wrapped around me, almost knocking me over. I turned and quickly embraced whoever it was who had hugged me. I found Len's head already buried in my chest and rested my head on top of her curls.

"How did you know?" I asked, never once mentioning this in my letters.

"You really thought I'd visit your hometown and not stop at Don's?" Lenny said.

"How did you find my family?" I asked.

"I went to Don's on Tuesday like you said, and I spotted a girl who happened to look just like you. I was willing to take a bet."

"You told her?" I said to Lyla.

My sister giggled.

"I like her," Lyla whispered in a not-so-discreet fashion.

I spotted my mother beaming, watching us all. When Len pulled away, I walked over and gave her a hug.

"Thank you for being here," I said. "Thank you all for being here."

"We wouldn't miss it for the world," Len said, and before I could help myself, I grabbed her waist, pulling her close.

My lips were instantly on hers, soft and gentle, and the second they touched, she relaxed. I inhaled and was instantly transported back to Briarport. Somehow, she always smelt like sea salt and sage.

I heard some clapping behind me and broke away, only to see Agent Grey and the rest of my team cheering me on, but I didn't care. Let them watch.

"I think I'm ready for something new," Len said gently, her hands on my chest.

"What would that be?" I asked.

"I met Mags," Len stated, and my brows raised. "She told me she plans to retire soon, so there will be an opening for her spot. I thought maybe the FBI Academy sounded like the perfect new adventure."

"You mean move to Quantico?" I asked.

"Well, only if I get that teacher everyone talks about. He's incredibly handsome but a little bit of a hard ass with his expectations."

I chuckled. "I think I can put in a good word."

"I know I'm not meant to be a field agent, but you once said I could do so much more with my knowledge. Plus, analyzing and organizing is kind of my specialty."

"You'd be perfect," I assured her.

"Good, because I've already been accepted to start at the academy this fall."

"I guess I'm staying in Quantico," I said and placed a gentle kiss on her forehead.

ACKNOWLEDGMENTS

This was my first ever non-fantasy writing project and I cannot believe where it has brought me. When I spent six years of my life getting a bachelor's and master's degrees in national security, I never imagined it would lead me to writing an FBI romance. There are so many wonderful people I need to thank who made this possible.

To my partner in crime and husband, thank you for watching endless re-runs of *Criminal Minds* with me and never being terrified by the wild crime stories I tell you about. Your endless support means the world to me.

To my sister Rory and my mom, thank you for the endless girl's nights watching crime shows. I already know you will both love Stone and cannot wait to hear your thoughts on this new project.

To my sister Leah, thank you for not questioning me when I texted you asking for your nurse expertise on where someone could be stabbed and survive while resulting in an involuntary hysterectomy. I still don't know how I haven't ended up with the FBI at my doorstep with all of our texts.

To my dad, thank you for always showing up and being my number one fan. I wouldn't be where I am today without you.

To Biz, my cousin, best friend, and soon to be sister-in-law, I think our younger selves who dreamed of becoming forensic anthropologists would be proud to see this book. Thank you for always being my alpha reader.

To my PA Mikala, for always being believing in my work and cheering me on. Without your help, insight, and support I would be drowning in marketing.

To my editor Alexa, for being a great friend and editor. This past month before releasing this was a rocky one, and I am forever grateful for all of your kind words and being there for me when I needed someone.

To my writing and critique partner Allyn, thank you for all your help in brainstorming and shaping this story. Stone would be far less amazing without your input. Thank you for being my JJ.

To my readers, thank you for your endless love, support, and kindness. It will never stop amazing me the way you all always show up for me.

ABOUT THE AUTHOR

MK Ahearn grew up in Massachusetts as one of three sisters. She now lives in Maryland with her husband, son, and their four cats. She received her bachelor of arts in international relations and a master of professional studies in homeland security. When not writing or studying she can be found planning her next travel adventure.

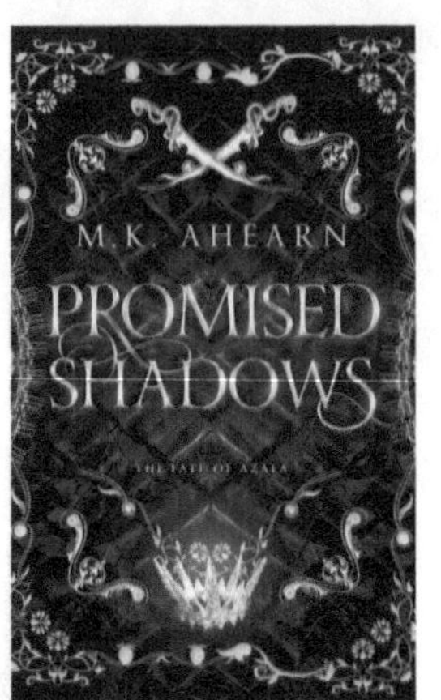

M.K. AHEARN
PROMISED SHADOWS
THE TALE OF AZALA

www.ingramcontent.com/pod-product-compliance
Lightning Source LLC
Chambersburg PA
CBHW021023310726
48969CB00006B/1524